THE
Call

MELISSA TEREZE

GPC
PUBLISHING

First Edition January 2020
Published by GPC Publishing
Copyright © 2020 Melissa Tereze
ISBN: 9781660631186

Cover Design: Melissa Tereze
Editor: Charlie Knight

Find out more at: www.melissaterezeauthor.com
Follow me on Twitter: @MelissaTereze
Follow me on Instagram: @melissatereze_author

All rights reserved. This book is for your personal enjoyment only. This book or any portion thereof may not be reproduced or used in any manner without the express permission of the author.

This is a work of fiction. All characters & happenings in this publication are fictitious and any resemblance to real persons (living or dead), locales or events is purely coincidental.

ACKNOWLEDGMENTS

This book wouldn't be staring back at you without the help and backing of some fabulous people.

Thank you to my beta readers. Without you, I would have scraped this book. I never realised how hard it would be to not only write a follow-up, but to actually let it go out into the world. Your encouragement and thumbs-up is the reason I continued.

To my editor, Charlie, you absolutely rock! They have shown me so much support and honesty throughout this journey. To my proofreader, Kira, I'm so happy you're still on this crazy road with me. I'm also happy about the final typos that you pointed out. You're a writer's best friend.

My biggest thanks has to go to my fiancée, Lee. Without her unconditional love and encouragement, I simply wouldn't write. She told me I could do this—cheered me on—and she was right. As she often is.

And finally, thank you to you, my readers. The response to the first book in this series truly blew me away. My only hope now is that this book fills your heart with as much love as it has mine. Your continued support does not go unnoticed. Thank you for letting me into your lives, your hearts, your kindles, and your palms.

I suppose my final words should go to the one and only Sam and Luciana. Please, for the love of God, get out of my head!

And don't forget to reach out to me. You guys keep me sane during the writing process. Here's to more beautiful characters in 2020.

Twitter: @MelissaTereze
Facebook: www.facebook.com/MelissaC.Author
Instagram: @melissatereze_author
Find out more at: www.melissaterezeauthor.com
Contact: info@melissaterezeauthor.com

ALSO BY MELISSA TEREZE

ANOTHER LOVE SERIES
THE ARRANGEMENT (BOOK ONE)

THE ASHFORTH SERIES
PLAYING FOR HER HEART (BOOK ONE)
HOLDING HER HEART (BOOK TWO)

OTHER NOVELS
ALWAYS ALLIE
MRS MIDDLETON
BREAKING ROUTINE
IN HER ARMS
BEFORE YOU GO
FOREVER YOURS
THE HEAT OF SUMMER
FORGET ME NOT
MORE THAN A FEELING
WHERE WE BELONG: LOVE RETURNS
NAKED

CO-WRITES
TEACH ME (WITH JOURDYN KELLY)

TITLES UNDER L.M CROFT (EROTICA)
PIECES OF ME

CHAPTER ONE

Luciana pushed through the bodies on the dancefloor, the bass throbbing through her feet and taking over her entire body. A mixture of alcohol and perfume wafted towards her, but she persevered, knowing that she would soon be home and in the arms of Sam. Luciana had been working overtime during the last month. Tonight, she should be letting her hair down, but she didn't care for it. She was meeting Shannon from the agency, and then she was leaving.

Sam had encouraged her to go out alone tonight, too much work and not enough time preventing her from joining Luciana. Sam had recently landed a huge project, and five weeks on, it was gathering momentum. That meant late nights at the office, or late nights at home while Luciana worked a night shift. It wasn't ideal, or what either of them wanted, but that was life. Something was always getting in the way.

Luciana was proud of Sam's success—even if she hadn't been around for most of it—but tonight she wanted her girlfriend here with her. Her body grinding, writhing against her own. She wanted Sam's intoxicating scent to swallow her up into *their* world, not that of the other customers, most too drunk to stand upright.

"Over here!" a familiar voice yelled in the direction of Luciana, catching her attention. As the crowd separated, she found Shannon waving at her.

"Hey!" Luciana pulled her ex-colleague into a hug before holding her at arm's length, examining her. "Looking good. Have you been back in the gym?"

Shannon offered Luciana a bottle of beer. "Actually, I have. A new client of mine really keeps me on my toes. I thought it would be a good idea to get in shape. I'll never keep up with her otherwise."

Luciana narrowed her eyes. "Interesting. I thought you were thinking about leaving the agency?"

"Couldn't do it." Shannon shrugged. "I love it too much."

"Whatever works for you."

"How's Sam?" Shannon smirked as Luciana's eyes lit up. "Good?"

"Fucking perfect." Luciana's heart fluttered, those butterflies settling deep inside her stomach. "Busy, but perfect."

"I was surprised you called to meet me."

"Why?" Luciana leaned back against the bar, surveying the club.

"Don't really see you much anymore."

"Just enjoying being at home."

Shannon nudged her shoulder. "I don't blame you. I saw the pictures you sent me. That place is gorgeous."

"You should come over one night for dinner. I know I've invited you before, but that invitation still stands."

"I don't like to intrude."

"You wouldn't be intruding." Luciana's forehead creased. "Why would you think that?"

Shannon laughed. "Oh, come on. I don't think Sam would

appreciate sharing dinner with an escort in her very expensive home."

"She's not like that." Luciana shook her head, surprised by Shannon's opinion of her girlfriend.

"I'm sure she wouldn't be rude, but that doesn't mean she would like me being there."

"Dinner. At our place. Make yourself available." Luciana looked pointedly at Shannon and added, "Seriously."

"I'll try my best."

"Please?"

Shannon sighed. "Fine.

"Don't sound too enthusiastic." Luciana rolled her eyes as she grabbed Shannon's wrist. "Come on. Let's get a table."

They weaved through the crowd, finding a table to the back of the club and away from the dancefloor. As Luciana took a seat, placing her beer bottle down on the table, her eyes scanned the room. Lindsay wasn't working tonight, but she still expected to see her here. She still liked to party hard, and after all, it was Saturday night.

Shannon gasped "Oh, my God! Is that who I think it is?"

"What? Who?" Luciana's eyes followed Shannon's. "Oh, shit!"

Standing at the bar, her hips swaying, Janet Mason smiled back at them both.

Luciana's mouth dried, her lips parting slightly as she tried to catch her breath. Janet was looking directly at her...almost into her soul. She hadn't seen her ex-client in quite some time, but as the seconds passed, she no longer felt fear. Instead, she felt an undeniable anger seeping through every pore. Giving Janet the once over, Luciana turned in her seat and focused on Shannon.

"You okay?"

Luciana's brows rose. "Me? Great."

"Are we going to ignore the fact that your old client is in the building? Where she shouldn't be?"

Though she didn't catch up with Shannon often, Luciana had kept her up to date with the Janet saga. She knew about the night when things officially ended between them, and about Luciana returning home black and blue. She also knew about the months that followed. They both chose not to mention it often, but that was hard to do when the woman in question was standing a few feet from them.

Shannon lowered her voice as much as the music would allow. "She's coming over. Do you want me to call the police?"

"No, it's fine. We were always going to bump into one another at some point."

"Alexis." Janet slipped into the seat beside Luciana. "How are you?"

"What do you want?" Luciana held back her anger, choosing to ignore the use of her escort name. "Correct me if I'm wrong, but you shouldn't be here. Not sitting next to me."

"I'm back in the city," Janet said. "I'm waiting for someone to arrive."

Luciana smiled sarcastically. "I can see that you're back in the city. Maybe you could drink in another club. Maybe even on another fucking planet."

"Less attitude would be great. I know we ended things on bad terms, but I'd like to reconcile."

"Oh, I don't think so." Luciana lifted her beer and sipped, just about done with this conversation. "Can you leave? You're ruining my night."

Janet sighed and stood. "You look great, by the way."

"Because you're no longer beating seven shades of shit out of me and calling it something that it wasn't."

Janet dropped her head on her shoulders, nodding slightly as she held up her hands. Though she appeared apologetic, Luciana wouldn't fall for it.

Luciana dipped her head. "Janet?" Janet's eyes brightened when they met hers. "Fuck off!"

Relaxing her body as Janet left the table, Luciana released a deep breath and cleared her throat. Shannon's hand had somehow found its way to hers, but she didn't need protecting. She could deal with Janet Mason on her own. There may have been a time when she didn't feel strong enough to do that, but being with Sam, she felt empowered every single day.

Shannon leaned in. "You good? We can go somewhere else if you want?"

"I'm only having another one or two and then I'm out of here."

"To another bar?"

"No. Home to Sam." Luciana offered Shannon a forced smile. "Let's just see how the night goes, okay?"

"You deserve a night out." Shannon gritted her teeth. "If that bitch thinks she's ruining it, she has another thing coming."

Two hours later, Luciana found herself standing outside the club and waiting for her call to connect with Sam. They'd texted each other once or twice, but Luciana knew how busy Sam was and she wouldn't interrupt her. Not if it meant she would get some time alone with her once her night in the city ended. When it went to voicemail, Luciana sighed and ended the call. Heading back towards the entrance, she glanced up to find Janet watching her. Just...staring.

Luciana steeled herself and demanded, "Can I help you?"

"Just getting some air." Janet smoothed the front of her dress before her eyes returned to Luciana's. "How are you, Alexis? I can't believe how long it's been."

Luciana shuddered. That name. It wasn't her. Not anymore. Janet knew that, but she still insisted on using a name that no longer meant anything to Luciana.

Luciana moved towards the entrance of the club, side-stepping Janet. "Shame it wasn't longer. If you don't mind, I have plans."

"Do you think perhaps we could get coffee together one afternoon? I'm going to be around a lot more."

"No, thanks."

"Alexis, please?" Janet gently gripped her wrist, her thumb stroking Luciana's skin. "I don't want to fight with you...or hurt you. I just want to make amends."

Luciana shrugged Janet's grip from her wrist. "I'm quite happy without your friendship, Janet."

"And I could never blame you for feeling that way. The way I treated you, how I acted, it was abhorrent."

"Yeah, it was," Luciana agreed readily. "But the thing is, I don't care how you *feel* about it. I don't care how sorry you are. All I want is an easy life. One that *doesn't* include you."

"You and Sam?"

Luciana's forehead creased. "What about us?"

"You're still together?" Janet asked. "Happily?"

"Like you couldn't begin to imagine. As for the apology, you really can shove it."

Luciana disappeared back inside the club, making a beeline for Shannon. One or two ex-clients had spotted her throughout the night, but she didn't make it a habit to feel as though it was an issue. That was her past life—one that she wasn't necessarily ashamed of, but she didn't need a reminder of the women she used to keep company. Whatever form that company came in. Sam was at home waiting for her; everything and everyone else in sight was simply a blur.

"You want another drink?" Shannon asked as she returned to their table. "One for the road?"

Luciana nodded. "Yeah, go on. I'll keep the seats." She returned to the screen of her phone and sent a message off to Sam.

L: Leaving soon, babe. I love you x

Relaxing back, Luciana watched the crowd grow in size and rowdiness. Girls younger than her flung themselves around the dancefloor or into the arms of anyone they could, while others bitched and argued amongst themselves. Rolling her eyes, she caught sight of Janet to the left of the dancefloor, the body of another woman grinding back into her lap. *At least she was being honest when she said she was waiting for someone.*

Luciana wanted to look away, but her heart plummeted when she recognised the woman Janet was dancing with. Soft, dark-blonde hair wisped around her face until the woman's profile came into view.

Oh, fuck! Lindsay?

Luciana bolted from the table, heading straight in the direction of Janet and Lindsay. She knew it meant nothing—Lindsay always flirted with the customers—but she didn't like it. Sam wouldn't like it either. Luciana would *not* be responsible for allowing Janet to build a friendship with her girlfriend's sister. Not in this lifetime. Hell would freeze over before Lindsay got friendly with a woman like Janet.

"Linds!" Luciana wrapped her arms around Lindsay, pulling her away from Janet. "So good to see you."

"Luciana, oh my God! Where's our Sam?"

"She's at home. Didn't think you'd be here tonight." Luciana danced with Lindsay, keeping one eye on Janet behind her.

"Oh, I didn't feel like sitting in."

"You should have come 'round to us." Taking Lindsay's hand, she twirled her. "Or called me. You could have come out with me."

"I thought you'd be home with Sam."

Luciana couldn't wait any longer. She needed answers. "So, who is your friend?"

"Oh, she's just a customer. She's really nice." Lindsay glanced back over her shoulder, gaining a full smile from Janet. "She's been here a lot lately."

"Yeah?"

"Actually, I was hoping I could speak to you and Sam tomorrow night when I come 'round..."

"Of course. Everything okay? Do you need help?" Luciana pulled Lindsay away from the crowd, a worry evident in her voice.

Lindsay laughed. "Help? No, but I need you to calm down."

"I am calm." Luciana relaxed her shoulders and let go of Lindsay. "So, you wanted to talk to us?"

"Tomorrow, yes."

"Right, okay." Luciana blew out a deep breath, aware that Lindsay had no idea about her worries. How could she? Luciana's past with Janet had been kept quiet. "I'll let you get back to your friend then." Was she worrying about nothing? Janet always hit the clubs when she was home. She couldn't interfere with something that was barely a friendship. Something that could actually be nothing at all.

Lindsay's eyes narrowed. "Yeah, thanks. Is everything okay with you?"

"Sure. Why wouldn't it be?" Luciana had to remain calm, but inside, everything about this moment felt wrong.

"You seem very on edge."

"No, just..." Luciana glanced over Lindsay's shoulder to find Janet still watching. If she didn't already know Lindsay was straight, she would assume they were together. "This friend of yours. How do you know her?"

"I told you. She's a customer."

"But is she *just* a customer? Do you go out together and meet up?"

"We have...a few times," Lindsay said. "She's more of a friend than a customer."

Luciana's heart sank. Was Lindsay trying to tell her something? Was that what she wanted to discuss tomorrow with Sam? No, surely not.

"Linds..."

"Mm?" Lindsay's smile grew when her eyes found Janet's.

"Is there something you need to tell me?"

"All will be revealed tomorrow." Lindsay kissed Luciana's

cheek and backed away. "Call me when you're both home tomorrow evening. I'll come over."

"Right, yeah." Luciana's entire world slowed. Nothing made any sense. Lindsay was dancing her way back to Janet, and Luciana felt like she was in another life. Another world. One that was completely messed up and wrong.

CHAPTER TWO

Luciana buried her head deeper into the pillow, covering her face with the duvet. Last night hadn't ended when she thought it would. Instead, Luciana and Shannon found their way inside a new gay bar in the city, taking shots with the drag queens on shift for the night. Luciana knew why she'd done it; she was avoiding coming home to Sam. When she did, when Sam opened her mouth to speak, Luciana would blurt out everything that had happened last night. Sam didn't need that right now. She didn't need Janet Mason on her mind when she had a shit tonne of work to get through.

Luciana swallowed, gagging as the smell of stale alcohol found its way to her nostrils. Throwing the cover back, she remained still for a moment, thankful that her girlfriend wasn't lying beside her. Sam would never call Luciana out on her drunken behaviour, she knew that, but it didn't make it right. She would joke about her hangover, offer to make a little breakfast, and then carry on with her busy schedule for the day. Yes, even Sundays had become a workday.

I miss having her to myself.

Luciana slowly climbed from the plush, super-king mattress,

her bare feet cooling against the hardwood flooring. She could hear Sam pottering about downstairs, but her stomach churned. Not from the alcohol, but because of the conversation she was about to have with Sam. *How am I supposed to tell her that Lindsay is friends with Janet?* Luciana rubbed her forehead, willing the headache approaching to disappear. Sunday was supposed to be for relaxing, but nothing about this day would come close to that.

She took the stairs slowly, catching sight of Sam out on the decking. Before she could think about this day, Luciana needed coffee. Grabbing a cup quietly, she poured a healthy measure from the cafetière and sipped slowly. Her eyes closed briefly, savouring the taste of the Costa Rican blend she'd recently purchased, before moving towards the open bi-folding doors.

"Hi, babe."

Sam glanced over her shoulder, black thick-rimmed glasses framing her eyes. Luciana was a vision every morning. "Morning, sleepy head. I didn't want to disturb you, so I came out here."

"You can disturb me any time you like." Luciana approached Sam, taking the seat facing her. "Busy day yesterday?"

"The busiest I've been in a while. What time did you get home last night?" Sam blew out a deep breath as she removed her glasses. As much as she wanted to pack away the paperwork strewn across her lap, she couldn't. It wouldn't take care of itself.

"Around two. I'm sorry."

Sam cocked her head, her deep brown eyes soft and enchanting. "Don't be. So long as you had a good night."

"Would have been better if I was here with you."

"I was in bed by ten," Sam said. "All that staring at a screen all day really wasn't good."

"Yet here you are, about to do it all over again."

"I'm taking a break soon. I have a flower arrangement to put on Lucia's grave and then I was hoping to take you to lunch or something." Sam would always appreciate the leeway Luciana gave her when it came to her late wife. Not everyone would be so accommodating or understanding.

"Sounds perfect." Luciana reached forward, taking Sam's hand. "You heard anything from Lindsay?"

"Was I supposed to?" Lindsay was due to come over tonight, but Luciana asking about it was unusual. Her sister often showed up without a word.

"No, I just...she's still coming over tonight?"

"As far as I'm aware, yes." Sam returned to the paperwork in her lap, only a pair of boy shorts covering her lower body. This work needed her attention. Then, Luciana was all hers. "Give me half an hour and I'm all yours."

"Whatever you want, babe. I'll take a quick shower." Luciana stood, leaning down and pressing a kiss to Sam's head.

She headed back inside, glancing over her shoulder at Sam as she went. She couldn't bring herself to talk about Janet, so she chose to forget about it for the time being. Sam would hit the roof when she eventually found out, but Luciana would deal with that when the time came.

The sun beamed down on the back of Luciana's neck as she stood back, giving Sam a moment to herself. Sunday mornings at Lucia's grave always gave Luciana the opportunity to think, but this morning she simply felt grateful. Heartbroken for Sam, of course, but grateful to have such a beautiful woman in her life. In all honesty, it was a routine neither of them wished to be a part of, but life would always have a cruel way of putting you in situations you never imagined in your wildest dreams.

Sam cleared her throat as she glanced back at Luciana. "Sorry, I'll just be another minute, I promise."

"I'm good here. No rush." Luciana stepped forward, squeezing her girlfriend's shoulder.

"Thank you." Placing a fresh arrangement down, Sam kissed the warming marble and climbed to her feet. "I do appreciate you coming here with me."

"I'll always be here with you, if that's what you want."

"It can't be easy for you." Sam stood beside Luciana. "Coming here to visit my wife's grave."

Luciana pressed a kiss to Sam's temple, her lips lingering. "I want to be here. Stop worrying about how I feel."

"How *do* you feel?"

"Like I'm where I should be." Luciana smiled as Sam's eyes softened. "With you. Completely in love with you. Unconditionally." *Yet you can't bring yourself to tell her about Janet.* Luciana felt a wave of guilt course through her.

"God." Sam wrapped an arm around her girlfriend's waist, resting her head on her shoulder. Luciana was the only woman Sam would *ever* consider bringing here. "I don't know what I did to deserve you."

"You gave me a chance." A year on, Luciana still couldn't believe her luck. It was one thing to be in love with Sam—that wasn't hard to do—but to wake beside her every morning, share dinner with her every night, build a life with her... Luciana couldn't comprehend it. Life, even with its issues, was incredibly fulfilling.

"I really don't want to get going with this project."

Luciana's forehead creased. "Of course you do. This one is huge, right?"

"Massive." Sam blew out a deep breath. "Potentially my biggest."

"Then you'll be doing what you love, babe."

"I know, but next weekend will be a working weekend. I have contractors to meet with, conference calls. You name it, I have it lined up."

"I know how much weekends together mean to us, but it's not the end of the world." Luciana would be lying if she said she wouldn't miss Sam this weekend, but she knew exactly what she was signing up for when she fell head over heels in love with her.

"Once I've signed off on everything, it'll all settle down."

"I know...and I'll be waiting for you."

"Come on." Sam tugged Luciana's hand, glancing back at Lucia's grave momentarily. "Let's get back to the car."

"Is Lindsay still coming over tonight?" Luciana asked, nonchalantly. If she asked once more, she would sound like a broken record. "You still haven't heard from her?"

"So far, I haven't. No reason why she wouldn't come over, though." Sam pressed the button on her car key, unlocking it. "Did you want to grab lunch in the city before we head home?"

"Lunch would be great." Luciana was spending every moment she could with Sam. Soon, she would lose her for the foreseeable.

Settled into their seats, Sam fired up the engine and backed down the path which led to Lucia's grave.

She'd recently made the decision to lessen her visits here to once a week, but it was enough for her. Lucia wasn't here, she never had been. This cemetery was just a place for Sam to visit to help her feel that closeness. Now that life was truly changing, so was her routine. Everything about this past year had been more than she could have hoped for—dreamed of—but she would never forget Lucia. She couldn't.

Luciana faced Sam and said, "Oh, the lads wanted me to thank you for the food you sent in with me the other night."

"I sleep better knowing you all eat well on shift."

"You really don't have to go out of your way, babe."

Sam shrugged as she pulled out onto the main road. "I like doing it. When you're working, I imagine you're eating instead of fighting fires."

"Well, we really appreciate it." Luciana slid her hand across the console, resting it on Sam's. She chose to refrain from going deeper into Sam's comment; it only left her feeling guilty. After last night, she already had enough guilt inside. She knew how anxious Sam felt when she left for work, knew Sam clung to her phone for twelve hours, but work was work…and she loved every minute of it. "Thank you."

"Any time." Lifting Luciana's hand, Sam pressed her lips to her skin. "How's Craig's wife?"

"At the moment, she's okay."

"No new tumours?"

"Not that I'm aware of. I can't imagine what they're going through." Just the idea of Craig sitting with his wife during chemotherapy sessions was enough to take Luciana's other worries off her mind. Janet didn't matter.

"No. It must be hard. They're lucky to have so much support from you and the boys at the station."

"Always. We're family."

Sam remained silent for a moment, appreciating just what kind of woman she had in her life. Luciana would drop everything if one of her friends was in need. No matter the time of day, she would be there, offering support in any way she could.

"Plans for next weekend while I'm non-existent?" Sam's heart weighed heavy with her words. "You really shouldn't sit around in this gorgeous weather."

"Thought I'd visit Mum and Dad on Saturday. Maybe spend a night or two. Catch up, you know?"

Sam nodded, her eyes fixed on the road in front of her. "That'll be nice."

"You know they prefer you being there, too."

Sam offered Luciana an apologetic smile. "It's not often we don't visit together. I am sorry."

"You have a shit tonne of work. Don't worry about it."

"Wish I didn't. Especially with this weather." Sam stopped at the traffic lights, looking up through the panoramic roof of her Range Rover.

"Maybe I won't stay the night in Manchester." Luciana side-glanced at Sam. "What do you think?"

"I think you should do whatever you feel like doing. Catch up with them. Friends. Whatever."

"Are you saying you don't want me around next weekend? Do you have another woman planned?" Luciana's eyebrow rose, a smirk playing on her lips.

"You were the only woman I could have *ever* planned, baby." The lights turned green and Sam put her foot down, revving away from the traffic behind her. As the familiar buildings in the centre of Liverpool came into view, memories of meeting Luciana came flooding back. It wasn't often they spent the day in the city anymore, only when work required either of them being here, but being back felt good. "If you don't want to stay, come home to me."

"Maybe I will."

Sam's hand fell to Luciana's thigh. "Maybe you *should*. You know I want you beside me."

"I know." Luciana smiled fully as her head turned, her eyes focusing on the dock to her left. "Where do you fancy eating today?"

"Tapas? Unless you had somewhere else in mind?"

"Tapas works for me, babe. Only the best, though."

Sam grinned, offering her girlfriend a wink. "The dock."

Luciana tore into a wedge of artisan bread, dipping it into a balsamic and olive oil combination before shoving it into her mouth. Sam sat quietly, sipping her glass of water, her eyes focused on the table between them. Work commitments were about to truly take over her life, but missing Luciana would be the hardest transition. Nothing about her business was glamourous, but the rewards she would reap at the end would be worth it. Another incredible complex of high-end homes. Couples beginning a life together, perhaps with the prospect of children. Sam could no longer plan her own future that way, so she would admire those who could from afar. She would provide the younger generation with beautiful, *safe* homes.

She looked up and a blonde caught her eye. "Is that Lindsay?"

Luciana's head shot up as she turned around. "What? Why is she here?"

"I'm going to be *really* bold and assume she's hungry, Luce."

"Right. Yeah." Luciana smiled, her eyes returning to the scrap of bread on her plate.

"Should I invite her over?"

Luciana shrugged. "She looks a bit dressed up. Maybe she has plans."

As much as Luciana wanted to be the one who broke the news of Lindsay and Janet's friendship to Sam, she couldn't. It didn't matter how awful she felt for keeping it to herself, no good could come from Sam knowing. Perhaps if she sat back and watched it all unfold, she wouldn't have to be the one.

"You think she's meeting someone?" Sam's eyes widened. "S- she's on a date?"

"Oh, I don't know. She could be here for any reason." Luciana hoped it wasn't a date.

"So, that's a no to inviting her over?"

"Um..." Luciana swallowed hard as she watched a dark-haired woman head towards Lindsay, her back to Sam and Luciana. "I-I, uh..." Lindsay embraced her date, their lips about to meet.

Sam noted the shock on Luciana's face; it mirrored her own. "Who the hell is that?"

"No idea." Luciana winced as the lie left her mouth. She hated this. Luciana couldn't recall a time she had ever lied to Sam. It certainly didn't feel good.

"She's into women?" Sam choked on her words. "Lindsay...my sister...is into women?"

"Looks like it." A sinking feeling settled in Luciana's belly. She had wondered last night if something more was going on, but she couldn't possibly believe it. Now, seeing it with her own eyes, something more was most certainly going on. *A lot* more than she had hoped.

Luciana still felt a genuine surprise. Lindsay had never given so much as a hint that she wasn't straight—and it didn't matter—but this wasn't the way to find out. Not for Sam, anyway. If or *when* Janet turned around, Sam would freak. Luciana knew Sam liked to be in control, to have the correct information at all times. This news...it was about to send Sam's head into a spin. Luciana could practically see the steam coming from her ears. It was one thing to find out your sister was sleeping with another woman, but Janet? This wasn't about to end well.

"Your bill, Sam." Xavi, the waiter, placed a leather wallet down in front of her. "It's been good seeing you both."

"Thanks, Xavi." Luciana took the wallet, slipping cash inside. She handed it back over, her eyes never leaving Sam's. "Babe?"

"Mm?" Sam frowned. "What?"

"Are you okay?"

Sam scoffed. "Why wouldn't I be? I've just discovered my sister is possibly gay...what the hell is there to worry about?"

"Um, you don't *sound* okay." Luciana lowered her voice as she leaned in, taking Sam's hand. "Is it really that big a deal to you?" Pushing Janet from her mind, Luciana was shocked by Sam's general reaction.

Sam nodded, her voice wavering. "That she didn't tell me, yes. How could she not tell me?"

"Maybe she wasn't ready to."

"Wasn't ready to?" Sam's stone-faced look didn't sit well with Luciana. She understood that her girlfriend wasn't expecting to see such a public display of affection from her sister today, but the attitude had to change. "Why wouldn't she be ready to? What are you trying to say?"

Luciana took her jacket from the leather seated booth beside her. "I'm not *trying* to say anything. And why are you behaving like this? It's not my fault your sister is fucking a woman!"

"Maybe if *I* wasn't busy *fucking* you, she would have felt like she could come to me." Sam's voice was low but held an element of anger. An anger Luciana wasn't prepared to accept.

"Is that right?" Luciana was taken aback by her girlfriend's comment. It felt like a punch to the gut. "Then I should let you get on with your day. Maybe you could tag along with Lindsay since you seem more concerned about her than enjoying your afternoon with me. The woman you're *fucking*! The woman you *supposedly* love."

Luciana slid out of the booth and pulled her jacket on. The hurt she felt by Sam's words was new for her. Sam had never spoken to her out of turn; she also wouldn't ever do it again.

If this was her reaction to Lindsay's sexual orientation, all hell would break loose when she discovered the woman with Lindsay was Janet.

"Luce—"

She held up her hand. "Don't bother."

"Fuck!" Sam gritted her teeth.

"I'm taking a walk. Let me know if you go home so I can make my own way back." Luciana looked down at Sam, bitterly disappointed. "Or maybe not."

Sam looked back at her sister standing at the bar. Guided to their table by another waiter, she couldn't see the facial features of the woman who now had her hand on the small of her sister's back, but she seemed vaguely familiar. *I doubt I know her.*

As much as she wanted to go over there and see Lindsay—to introduce herself—Sam couldn't. Luciana was walking the opposite way and out the door, and she didn't like it. How she had just reacted...how she had spoken to Luciana, it wasn't right. Sam had to fix it.

THE CALL

Luciana sat on a bench around the corner from the tapas bar she had just left Sam in. An ache settled throughout her body—a feeling she didn't ever wish to experience. She knew Sam was stressed with the work that was about to come her way, but she didn't deserve what she'd just received. The attitude. The nastiness in Sam's words. Luciana didn't understand what the problem was. If Lindsay was dating a woman, it was hardly the crime of the century.

But it's not just any woman. It's Janet fucking Mason.

Resting her head back, the sun beat down on Luciana's face. She could feel the tears forming in her eyes, but she wouldn't allow them to fall. She wouldn't sit here crying in public, not in this lifetime.

As a shadow cast over her face, Luciana opened her eyes to find Sam standing in front of her.

"I'm sorry." She crouched down in front of Luciana, her hands resting on her thighs. "Baby, please..."

Luciana sat up, squinting. "Please what? Please get over it while you speak to me like shit?"

"I didn't mean what I said. I don't know why I said it."

Luciana laughed. "You do. You wouldn't have said it if you didn't mean it."

"I just didn't expect to see Lindsay with another woman." Sam sighed, her forehead resting against Luciana's knee. Of all the scenarios in the world, Sam hadn't anticipated *that* one. "Surely you understand that?" She looked up at Luciana.

Luciana focused on Sam's dismal, deep brown eyes. "I understand that perfectly. What I don't understand is why you have an issue with me. With us."

Sam's brows drew together. "I-I don't. I don't have *any* issue with us."

"I find that hard to believe." Luciana lowered her eyes. "I think I'm going to just spend some time in town. I'll be home later." She climbed to her feet, almost knocking Sam to the ground.

Shocked, Sam fell back on her hands, then scrambled to her feet as tears welled in her eyes. She'd said silly things during their relationship, but this one topped them all. Luciana wouldn't forget this in a hurry, nor did Sam expect her to.

"What you said back there really hurt me. It's going to take a lot more than you telling me you didn't expect Lindsay to be there with a woman—"

Sam stepped closer to Luciana, taking her hand and cutting her off. It would take more than a simple apology on the dock, so Sam would ask what she really needed to ask. "Please, come home with me."

"Need some air." Turning and walking away, Luciana brushed a single tear from her jawline. She had no intentions of arguing with Sam, so she chose to remove herself from the situation entirely.

Sam sat facing her sister, unease evident in her body language. She'd thought about calling Lindsay earlier in the day but decided against it. They already had plans to spend the evening together, but Luciana was supposed to be involved in those plans. Sunday night usually included the three of them sharing a bottle of wine. Ever since Lindsay had made a comment to their mum about how she was worried for Sam, they'd made it a regular thing. This time…Sam had messed up.

"Is everything okay?" Sam cleared her throat, playing stupid. She knew when her sister appeared uncomfortable that Lindsay had big news. This time, she also knew what it was. "You seem different."

Lindsay shifted. "Of course. Why wouldn't everything be okay?"

"Well, I don't know…that's why I'm asking. How's work?"

"Work is work." Lindsay focused on her hands in her lap. Her palpable anxiety was close to blowing the roof off the house. "I just...I had something I needed to tell you."

"Oh?" Usually, Sam would worry. She would assume Lindsay was using drugs and needed her help. Thankfully, she had an idea where this conversation was going. Lindsay may not divulge everything, but Sam was satisfied that she wasn't using again. "Go on."

"I'm seeing someone."

Sam's eyebrow rose. She shouldn't be shocked, already knowing this information, but she was still surprised that Lindsay had finally said the words. Whatever her reason for not discussing it, it no longer mattered. Sam had no right to dissect her sister's relationship when her own was a mess this evening.

Lindsay sighed. "Say something. Anything."

"Honestly..." Sam ran her fingers through her hair. Today hadn't gone as planned, so her words were the last thing on her mind. She just wanted Luciana home. "I'm not sure I have anything to say."

Lindsay scoffed. "Oh, you *always* have something to say, Sam. You're never lost for words."

"First time for everything, I suppose." Sam fell silent. Truer words had never been spoken. Not only did she feel unable to comment on her sister's sexuality, but she often found herself lost for words around her own girlfriend. A year since she'd met Luciana, and life was as perfect as anyone could claim it to be. They'd been settled at the lake house for some seven months, and life flowed better than either Sam or Luciana imagined it could. Being out of the city meant that their evenings didn't suffer any interruptions, only planned nights with family once a week pulling them away from the confines of their safe space. Their beautiful home in the middle of nowhere. So why was she sitting here without her girlfriend? Why had she said what she did this afternoon? "I didn't know..."

"That's why I'm telling you now. Nobody knew I was dating anyone."

"I meant I didn't know you were into women."

Lindsay's eyes widened. "W-what? How did you know?"

"We saw you today at the tapas bar on the dock. I just didn't know..." Sam lowered her eyes.

"I didn't either. It just kinda happened."

Sam cleared her throat. "Right, okay. Well..."

"You think it's a phase."

Sam frowned. "I didn't say that."

"You didn't have to. I can see it in your eyes." Lindsay shifted forward, wringing her hands together. "I thought you of all people would be accepting."

"I *am* accepting." Sam gripped her sister's wrist, angry with herself. Luciana already hated her; the last thing she needed was for Lindsay to follow suit. "You *know* I am."

"So, what then?"

"I can't believe I didn't know it before now. I mean, you've never even given me an inkling that you were gay."

"Bisexual," Lindsay corrected. "Or maybe we don't even have to give it a name. A label."

Sam nodded slowly. "If that's what you want. This woman... how long?"

"About two months."

"Jesus Christ, Linds!" She really was out of the loop lately. That *had* to change. "How could you keep it from me for so long?"

"You've been busy."

And there it was. Sam had suggested that she'd been spending too much time with Luciana, and Lindsay had just confirmed it. The problem was, Sam no longer cared. Luciana was her girlfriend —one day maybe something more—so spending too much time with her wasn't possible.

"Not *that* busy."

"I didn't want to rush anything. You and Luciana have your

own thing going on here, and I guess I just let my own life take its course. I'm sorry."

"How did you meet?" Sam asked, showing an interest in her sister's love life. "Is she local, or?"

"She works out of town a lot but she's from around here, yes."

"I know how she feels working out of town." Sam smiled faintly. Nothing was more daunting than leaving the woman you love to work away. "So, you met where?"

"At work. She came in with a few friends."

"Nice."

"She is. And she's gorgeous." Lindsay's eyes lit up.

Sam rarely saw her sister looking so happy, or seemingly in love, but it looked good on her.

"I'd like you and Luciana to meet her."

Sam's heart sunk a little. Lindsay would hit the roof if she knew what she'd said to Luciana earlier. "We'd love to. I-I'll speak to Luciana when she's home."

"Where is she?" Sam was surprised it had taken Lindsay so long to enquire. She and Luciana were close. "She's always here on Sunday night with us. I thought after last night, she would definitely be here."

"She's out." Sam sighed, taking her wine glass from the coffee table and downing its contents. There didn't appear to be enough wine in the world tonight. "W-we had a disagreement earlier."

"Oh, I'm sorry. Nothing serious I hope?"

"Honestly, I don't know. I said something that has really hurt her." Sam's voice wavered.

"Do you want to talk about it?"

"No, thank you. We would *love* to meet...your girlfriend. Let me know when you're both available again and I'll cook dinner."

"Sounds perfect."

Sam held up her hand, her forehead creased as something hit her. "Wait! You said after last night you thought Luce would be here?"

"At the club," Lindsay explained. "When we bumped into each other, I told her I needed to speak to both of you."

"She didn't say she'd seen you last night."

"Maybe she just forgot."

"Yeah. I'm sure it just slipped her mind."

The sound of tyres on the gravel pricked Sam's ears, almost sending her head-first off the couch as she rushed to the door. Yanking it open, she stepped out onto the decking to find Luciana climbing from a taxi. Sam slowly approached her. "Hey, uh...I could have picked you up. You should have called."

"Didn't want to interrupt your evening." Luciana stepped past Sam, aware that her girlfriend was upset with her lack of contact this evening. As much as she knew she should care, in this moment, Luciana didn't. She was furious with Sam. Her words still hurt. "Lindsay here?"

"She is." Sam smiled. "She told me." Luciana knew Sam couldn't possibly be referring to Janet; her body language wouldn't be so relaxed...or happy.

Luciana sighed, no longer interested in whether Lindsay had told Sam who her girlfriend was or not. "Great. I'll just say hi to her and then I'll be out of your way for the evening."

"What? No, I don't want that." Sam gripped Luciana's wrist, catching her before she could walk away. Sam felt awful about today, but she couldn't fix it if Luciana refused to be in the same room as her. "Please, I haven't seen you since this afternoon."

"Mm, you made it perfectly clear how you felt earlier, Sam. You don't have to pretend you want me here."

Sam fisted her hand in Luciana's T-shirt and pulled her closer. "I do. I *really* want you here."

Luciana lowered her eyes, shrugging off Sam's grip on her clothes. "I should go and see Lindsay. Talking out here is rude."

She disappeared, leaving Sam standing alone outside. As much as she wanted to just forget about her girlfriend's comment earlier in the day, she couldn't. Those words had come from somewhere and it had played on her mind since the moment they were said. So much so that she wasn't sure she would come home tonight.

"Linds, hi. Good to see you." Luciana kicked off her pumps, pushing them aside with her foot.

"I believe you already saw me today."

Luciana shrugged. "Well, yeah. Sam said you've talked?"

"We have. Would have been nice if you were here, too."

Luciana filled a glass with water and rounded the counter. "Sorry, I'm laying low. You two should spend some time together. Sam is under the impression that I'm around too much, so..."

"What? She said that?" Lindsay's eyes widened. "But—"

"In much more offensive terms, yeah." Luciana cocked her head. "You're happy? With your girlfriend?"

"Very, Luce."

I really wish she wasn't happy with Janet. "I'm going to go and shower, okay? Just...be careful." It was all Luciana could offer right now. This required a discussion with Sam. As much as Luciana wanted to blurt out the entire truth, she really needed Sam's support *and* encouragement. More than anything else, Sam needed to be made aware of who Lindsay's girlfriend was.

Lindsay frowned. "Sure, okay."

Luciana turned, heading for the staircase. Sam blocked her path, but she wasn't doing this now. She didn't want to end the day fighting with her girlfriend, so she leaned in, pressed a kiss to Sam's cheek, and smiled. "Goodnight."

CHAPTER THREE

Sam focused on the plans in front of her, a Costa Rican blend of coffee sitting beside her. The sun shone down on the swing bed she'd commandeered some two hours ago, but Luciana showed no signs of waking. As much as she wanted her girlfriend to talk last night, it didn't appear to be on the agenda. Instead, she found herself climbing into bed quietly and lying awake for most of the night.

She didn't know where Luciana had spent most of her evening, but it no longer mattered. Today was a new day, and once she had apologised, she would pray that Luciana wanted to spend time with her. After all, she would be in full work mode by the end of the week. It may have been Monday morning, but Sam had no intentions of going to the office before the afternoon. Another routine she found herself slipping away from the more time she spent with Luciana.

Yesterday had troubled her. Yes, their relationship still felt new...but before she said what she had, it also felt settled. Luciana officially moved in two months after Sam returned to her home, and their combined routine blossomed. Everything blossomed. Now, it felt marred.

By Sam's words. Her attitude. An attitude that Luciana hadn't deserved.

Sam's behaviour yesterday may have shocked Luciana, but it shocked Sam more. She wasn't that woman. She loved Luciana with everything she was.

She set her plans to one side and took her coffee cup in both hands. Sam needed a moment before she tried to make amends. Luciana was strong headed, so she knew it wouldn't be easy, but the least she could do was try. This, her relationship, it meant too much to her to risk losing it because of her own stress. Because that's what it was that brought it on. Stress.

Luciana stood on the decking behind Sam holding a cup of coffee, wondering if today could possibly be better than yesterday. Fighting with Sam was one of her all-time hates, she wasn't sure she could bear it for a second day in a row. "Mornin'. Do you mind if I sit out here for five minutes before I get dressed?"

"You're asking me if you can sit with me?"

Luciana's brow furrowed. "Well, yeah."

"Have we really come to that?" Sam's voice broke, her eyes closing momentarily.

"You're busy working," Luciana said. "I just want to enjoy a cup of coffee in the sun before I head out."

Sam sat upright, straightening her back as her eyes followed Luciana. "You're going somewhere?"

"I'm meeting with Shannon. Midday." Luciana sat in the deep chair facing Sam.

"Oh." Sam nodded, disappointed that she wouldn't have much time with Luciana today. "Shannon...you were only with her Saturday night."

"She's my friend. You know that." Luciana wouldn't say it, but Sam gave off the impression that she was accusing her of something. Deep down, Luciana knew Sam would *never* accuse her of anything, but their relationship was strained this morning and Luciana was reading into things that weren't there.

Sam gathered the plans beside her. "I know. I'll just go to the office then."

"You weren't planning to?"

"Not until this afternoon and only for an hour. But you're busy so I should use my time when I can."

Luciana studied Sam's face. The hurt was clear to see, but she didn't know where to begin with how she was feeling. To hear the woman you love suggest that she could have been doing other things instead of being with you hurt. In some way, she understood Sam's concern for Lindsay and the fact that she hadn't disclosed her new relationship, but it was the way in which Sam went about explaining that didn't sit well with Luciana.

Luciana sipped her coffee. "I'm going to leave for Manchester on Friday night instead of Saturday. I'll be back Sunday afternoon...or night. I don't know. Or if you want, I can stay until Tuesday and I'll head back before my shift starts. You'll be busy with work anyway."

"O...kay." Sam noted the lack of emotion in Luciana's voice. She really had hurt her yesterday. That much was clear by her girlfriend's lack of interest in being here. Honestly, Sam was devastated. This wasn't how their relationship worked. They *never* fought. It looked like change was coming whether Sam wanted it to or not. Between the tension in the house and Lindsay coming out, Sam wasn't sure what day it was.

"You should invite your sister to stay at the weekend."

"I'd rather you were here with me." Sam's voice betrayed her, trembling. "Look, I really hoped we could talk this morning."

"About what?"

"You know what." Sam looked pointedly, removing her glasses. "I never meant to hurt you yesterday, Luce. You know I love you."

Luciana sat forward, setting her cup down. "That may be true, but you sounded pretty adamant. Do you really believe that I'm too much? This is too much?"

"No. Never. You've *never* been too much." Sam spoke barely above a whisper.

"Do you think we need a break so you can be there for Lindsay?" Luciana pressed. "I mean, she doesn't look like she needs any help, but maybe you need a break from *me* anyway..."

Sam's heart constricted. The idea of time away from Luciana wasn't something she had *ever* thought about. This woman made her incredibly happy. "No."

"Think about it." Luciana leaned forward, squeezing Sam's knee. "Think about all of this. If it *is* too much for you, I can do whatever you need. If you need me to take a step back, I can do that. I don't want to, but I want you to be happy. If that means less of me in your life...say the word, Sam."

A shiver rolled down Sam's spine.

Her heart fell into her stomach.

Luciana stood up and headed towards the folding doors. She had to tell Sam who Lindsay's girlfriend was. Once she knew, this would probably crumble anyway. After all, she'd known for two days now and hadn't breathed a word of it to Sam. That couldn't possibly be a good sign.

"It's been a year, Luciana."

Luciana turned around to find Sam standing on shaky legs. Her arms wrapped around herself. Devastation in her usually gorgeous eyes.

"It's been a year, and I don't want you anywhere other than here."

"The most incredible year of my life." Luciana offered a heavy-hearted smile. "But you said what you did and now you have to decide if it came from somewhere deep inside you." Without another word, Luciana disappeared inside and took the stairs. She didn't want this to be her life. She didn't want a relationship like this. Everything would blow over, she knew it would, but Sam still had decisions to make. Luciana couldn't bear the thought of her being a burden, or too much. She couldn't bear the thought of Sam wishing she was alone for the night or out with friends. This was her life now and Sam would be the one to decide which direction it took.

"Didn't expect to see you so soon."

Luciana glanced up at Shannon. "Mm. Needed to talk."

"Everything okay?" Shannon asked, handing over a mason jar of brown sugar cubes. "You seemed okay on Saturday night."

"Janet..." Luciana cleared her throat and sat up straight. "She's dating Sam's sister."

Shannon shook her head. "What? No! She can't be."

"She is."

"And how do you feel about that?" Shannon asked. "How does *Sam* feel about it?"

Luciana's hand trembled. "She doesn't know."

"You haven't told her? You really have to. If she finds out you knew all along, she's going to—"

"Yeah, I know what will happen. You don't have to tell me." Luciana sunk back into her seat, clasping her hands together. This really was turning into one huge mess. Luciana was beginning to wonder how it got to this point. "We're already not really speaking."

"Oh."

Luciana relayed her fight with Sam yesterday afternoon at the tapas restaurant. The more she thought about it, about what was said, the less she was beginning to care. Could she really not accept that Sam was sorry? She seemed to be sorry this morning when Luciana dismissed her and left the house, but something still niggled away at her. A hurt she hadn't expected to ever feel when she was with Sam.

"It sounds to me like you both need to talk," Shannon said. "I'm sure she never meant it."

"Still...she said it."

Shannon arched a dark eyebrow. "Don't we all say things we don't mean? I'm sure you've made mistakes before."

Luciana nodded. "I have. Many. And I know I should just forget about it, but it seems I can't."

"So, what?" Shannon asked. "You're going to leave her?"

"What? Don't be ridiculous."

"Then what? You're going to hold it against her forever?"

"Fine, I get it." Luciana held up her hand. "Bite the bullet and forget it happened. I know."

"Well, I wouldn't say to just forget about it. But at least speak to Sam. Tell her how you feel."

"I think she knows how I feel. That was quite obvious this morning when I didn't even kiss her as I was leaving."

Shannon smirked. "You two are sickly sweet. Go home to her, Luciana. Sitting here with me and drinking coffee isn't going to solve your problem."

"I still have to tell her about Janet."

Shannon nodded, reaching for Luciana's hand. "You can do it. She wouldn't want to be kept in the dark and have it sprung on her unexpectedly. If you tell her, you can figure it out together."

Luciana ran her fingers through her hair, blowing out a deep breath. "Lindsay can't be with Janet. She just can't."

"Agreed."

"What am I supposed to do? Sam is going to hate me for not telling her sooner. I won't blame her."

Shannon smiled. "I'm sure she won't."

"I should go, shouldn't I?"

"Before you change your mind, yes."

"Okay, well if this all goes wrong...can I call you? If she kicks me out." Luciana stood up and slipped her jacket on.

"She's not going to kick you out."

"If she does?"

"I'll have my phone by my side all day."

Luciana slowly walked towards a familiar glass building. Her heart weighed heavily in her chest, but she needed to see Sam. She needed that connection with her. That smile. Those intense eyes. Her soft lips. She needed Sam and there was no more to it.

Of course, they had things to discuss, predominantly Janet, but she'd spent the last hour walking aimlessly around town, and now she was done with being worried. She was also done with being angry. Yes, she had every right to be, but Sam meant more to her than a petty argument. Her words stung, they always would have, but her girlfriend was about to take on one hell of a project and stress had ultimately prevailed.

Walking through the double doors, she found Cheryl at her desk, a smile waiting for her. "Luciana, hi."

"Is Sam here?" she asked, clearing her throat from the unexpected emotion that seemed to have lodged itself there. "Is she busy?"

Cheryl checked her boss' schedule. "No, she's free as far as I can see."

"Right, okay."

Cheryl shifted awkwardly in her seat. "She asked me not to disturb her. I don't believe that included you, though. Go through."

"Thanks. I won't keep her long." Luciana shoved her hands in the front pockets of her jeans.

"She wasn't supposed to be here today so I don't expect you to be interrupted by anything that can't wait."

"Still, she has a lot going on." Luciana walked towards the glass-walled corridor.

"Luciana?" Cheryl called out. "Is everything okay?"

"Yeah, everything is fine." Luciana gave Sam's assistant a full smile. Cheryl nodded and returned to her desk.

She reached Sam's office door and knocked lightly as she turned the handle. Finding Sam with her arms folded across her desk and her head down, Luciana quietly closed the door and approached the desk. "Sam?" She crouched down, taking her girlfriend's hand. "Babe?"

"Mm?" Sam's eyes opened slowly, a tiredness evident in them. "Oh, I didn't know you were coming here."

Luciana smiled weakly. "Me neither. You look tired."

"I didn't sleep last night."

Luciana sighed. "Because of me."

"No." Sam sat up and cupped Luciana's face. "Because of me. The stupid things I said."

"Can we forget about it? Can we just be us and happy again?" She leaned into Sam's touch, a heat spreading throughout her body.

"It's all I want." Sam's thumb trailed her girlfriend's bottom lip. In the last twenty-four hours, she'd missed the sensation of Luciana's skin against her own. Her kisses. Holding one another in the night. Last night, for the first time in a year...she felt alone. "I'm *so* in love with you, Luce."

Luciana's eyes closed. "I know."

"And I will never hurt you again." Sam leaned in, her lips gently caressing Luciana's. "God, I never want to so much as look at you the wrong way again."

"What you said hurt, but I love you too much to fight any longer. We shouldn't be like this."

"Let me make it up to you. Come home with me right now and just lie with me."

It's all I want. Luciana loved that idea, but she swiftly remembered that she had *other* things to say.

"Babe, you don't have to make it up to me. So long as we're okay, I can live with that." Her hands fell to Sam's bare thighs, smoothing the skin beneath her palms as Sam's black pencil skirt rode up ever so slightly. "Everything is going to be okay."

"Lindsay was mad at me last night, too."

"Why? She seemed fine when I left you both alone."

Sam glanced up through her long, dark lashes. "I told her what I'd said to you. She went crazy."

"You didn't need to tell her."

"I did." Sam sighed. "I needed someone to tell me how much of a bitch I'd been."

"And are you over that now? I mean, if you do think we're together too much...you know, intimately—"

Sam gripped Luciana's jacket, pulling her in by the lapels. "No. No, I don't think anything of the kind."

"You're sure?"

"More than sure." Sam leaned in, her lips desperately attacking Luciana's. As much as she wanted to partake in what was about to happen, Luciana couldn't.

She pulled back. "Babe, I need to tell you something."

"Can't it wait?" Sam sighed, her forehead pressing against Luciana's as she attempted to shed Luciana's jacket. "I'm kinda busy..."

Luciana sat back on her knees, looking up at Sam. "No. It can't wait. You're probably going to hate me when I tell you this, and that's fine, but I didn't know how to say it."

"Say what?" Sam's heart throbbed hard.

"Saturday night...I saw Linds at the club."

"Yeah, she told me." Sam's forehead creased.

Blue eyes widened. "Wait! You know? She told you?"

"About seeing you at the club, yes."

"But nothing else?" Luciana asked, rubbing her hands down her denim-clad thighs. "She didn't say anything else?"

"No."

Luciana scoffed. "Great. I thought she may have been honest with you since it's her who should be telling you this." Luciana was looking for someone to be mad at in all of this. The truth was, nobody was at fault. Lindsay had no idea who Janet was or that they had a past.

"Telling me what?"

"I-I saw Lindsay's girlfriend at the club on Saturday." The longer this conversation went on, the more Luciana wanted to throw up. "I *spoke* to her."

"You did?" Sam beamed. "Tell me about her. I need to know whatever you think I need to know. I've invited them to dinner, and I *have* to get this right. First impressions count, Luce."

"Maybe you could hang fire on the enthusiasm."

Sam laughed. "Why? This is great. Maybe we should go home now and prepare. I can call Lindsay and see if she's available with her girlfriend tonight. Can you believe she thought I was pissed off with her for dating a woman?"

"No, that won't work." Luciana shook her head, bypassing Sam's latter comment. This was all too much at once. "It's probably best if you don't invite them at all. Ever."

"Lindsay really wants us to meet her."

"Janet Mason." The words flew from Luciana's mouth faster than the speed of light.

"What about her? Is she back in town?"

"She's back, and she's sleeping with your sister." Luciana's knees gave out underneath her, sending her back onto her arse. "I only realised they were together at the tapas bar."

"Janet Mason..." Sam's voice changed. Hatred. A deep *deep* hatred. Janet Mason was back? And dating Lindsay? No. Not in this lifetime. Sam's stomach lurched. She suppressed the bile rising in her throat, instead focusing on her anger that bubbled away at the surface. "Why the *fuck* is Janet Mason anywhere near Lindsay?"

Luciana studied Sam's eyes. The fury she found burning deep in them was enough to terrify anyone. Luciana included. "I-I don't know. Do you want me to leave?"

"Janet Mason," Sam whispered, her eyes closing as she pinched the bridge of her nose. Of all the things Luciana could have told her, this had to be the worst. "No. Not happening."

"I wanted you to know but I didn't know how to tell you." Luciana took Sam's hand, but she pulled away, breathing deeply. "Babe, please don't hate me."

Sam's eyes opened suddenly. "I-I don't."

"What are we going to do?"

"I don't know but I'm certainly going to figure it out." Sam stood, rounding her desk. "Lindsay cannot *possibly* be in love with Janet." She paced the floor back and forth. "How could anyone love a woman like that?"

Luciana exhaled. "Love happens, babe. Even to the worst people."

"I can't let her do this." Sam clenched her fists. "I can't let either of them fall in love with one another. I mean, is Janet even capable of love?"

"I thought she wasn't..." Luciana lowered her eyes.

"But?"

"I don't know. Lindsay seemed really happy on Saturday night."

"You said you spoke to Janet."

Luciana scratched the back of her neck. "Yeah...I went outside to call you and she was there."

"And?" Sam folded her arms, looking expectantly at Luciana. This was new information. Why was Sam only just learning about this? If Janet had been around—communicating with Luciana—Sam *should* know. Along with the relevant authorities.

Luciana got to her feet. "And what?"

"Well, how did the conversation go? Friendly?"

A laugh fell from Luciana's mouth as she shook her head. This attitude Sam seemed to have developed really needed work. It needed it quick. "If you're trying to say something...say it."

"I'm not, but I want to know what *the hell* is going on around here lately!" Sam approached Luciana, taking her hand and squeezing it. Curling her fingers under Luciana's chin, Sam offered a small smile. "I'm sorry."

Luciana shrugged her shoulders slightly. "Seems to be all we say to one another lately. I just...I don't know what you want me to do. Lindsay and Janet are together."

"Not for much longer."

CHAPTER FOUR

Two days had passed since Sam discovered her sister was dating a woman she sometimes had sleepless nights over. Lindsay had called to arrange the dinner they were supposed to plan, but Sam had cancelled, explaining that something had cropped up at the office and she would be in touch once everything had settled down. Two days on, there were still no intentions of inviting Janet Mason to her home on Sam's part. Two days on, she hadn't said much about it at all.

Luciana watched Sam quietly from across the table. Dinner was over with little conversation, but she understood that Sam was processing Lindsay's news. Okay, it *was* huge...but Sam's silence was uncomfortable tonight. Luciana could see the wheels turning —she could see it in her deep brown eyes. Pensive. Confused, perhaps. As much as she wanted to know what was going on in Sam's mind, Luciana felt the weight of their day slowly pressing down on her. A lead weight. Something about Janet being back in town made Luciana angry, but she didn't know why. She wasn't any of her concern anymore, she hadn't been for a long time. Still, something felt awkward between Luciana and Sam.

"How was dinner?" Sam asked as she glanced up, knowing Luciana's eyes were boring into her. "Satisfying?"

"Always is, babe."

Sam's eyes narrowed; her hands clasped under her chin. "You look tired. Did you want me to clear this away while you take a bath?"

"Depends…"

"On?"

"Whether you'll be joining me." Luciana took her beer from the table and sipped, her eyes never leaving Sam's. "It would be the perfect end to this day."

"Oh, I have some things to do. Work stuff." Sam loved the thought of relaxing, but her mind wasn't in a good place. Everything whirred around, a jumbled mess of emotions. That wasn't a good combination, Sam needed space.

"I'm already going to lose you in three days. Are you sure I can't steal a little of your time and attention tonight?"

"Maybe later. You should head up and relax." Sam offered a weak smile as she stood, clearing the plates from the table. If Luciana could just let this lie for a few more hours, that would be fantastic.

Luciana followed Sam into the kitchen. "I'm fine here, thanks." The plates clattered on the counter. Luciana wasn't sure if it was accidental or caused by anger. She struggled to read Sam lately.

"Okay, well I'll load the dishwasher and get out of your way. I don't want my paperwork strewn all over the place."

"Why? It usually is…" Luciana caught Sam's wrist as she brushed past her. "Hey…"

Sam sighed, deciding that playing stupid would be her go-to method this evening. "What's up?"

"We have to talk about this sometime, you know."

"Talk about what? Work?"

"Lindsay. Janet. The mess they've gotten themselves into."

Luciana knew Sam had thoughts about it all. She couldn't not. But not discussing it wouldn't help anyone. And as it appeared tonight, it also wouldn't help *their* relationship.

"I'll handle it," Sam said. While she was panicking about Lindsay, Sam was dismissing the concerns Luciana probably had. After all, it was Luciana who had once been devastated by Janet Mason. Hurt. Bruised. "Don't worry. Janet won't get anywhere near you."

Luciana curled her fingers under Sam's chin as she dropped her head. As this all unfolded, the one worry Luciana didn't have was herself. Janet wouldn't lay a finger on Luciana *ever* again. "I'm not worried about that. I'm worried about you burning yourself out *and* worrying about Lindsay."

"I can handle Janet Mason." Sam stared, stone-faced. "And I'd appreciate it if you could trust that."

"I trust you one hundred percent, babe. Don't ever doubt that."

"Then this conversation is over." Sam cleared her throat, backing away from Luciana. The more she thought about Janet Mason, the more Sam seethed.

"No. Wait." Luciana tightened her grip. "Please, stop pulling away from me."

Sam sighed, aggravated by her girlfriend's questioning. Janet had interfered with their lives enough over the last year; she wasn't about to allow that to continue. Once Sam had fixed the Lindsay situation, Janet would once again no longer exist. Blocking her from her mind was how Sam had coped, and that was how it would remain. "I have things to do, Luciana. If I don't get this work done at home, I'm going to be at the office until God knows when."

Luciana dropped her hand, her stomach lurching, and stepped away. This was becoming a common theme between them lately. With Sam's words at the tapas bar swimming around her head, Luciana couldn't help but wonder if Sam *was* growing tired of her. Of having her here. As she rounded the counter, she glanced back at Sam to find her with her head in her hands. "I'll just get out of your way, Sam. It seems like the best solution for you right now. N-not having me 'round. If I can get you anything, give me a shout."

"Wait! Come here." Sam sighed, her voice hoarse with emotion.

Luciana's shoulders sagged, exhaustion setting in. "I don't want to fight with you, Sam."

"Come here, please?" Sam leaned back against the counter, holding out her hand. Over the last couple of days, she'd continued to push and pull with Luciana, and she didn't want it to be that way. Whatever the outcome of this was, she and Luciana *had* to stick together. They *had* to be okay at the end of all of this. Work. Janet. The shitstorm of life.

Luciana approached Sam. "I know you're stressed. You don't have to apologise."

"I'm not stressed enough to behave this way." Sam closed her eyes as Luciana's hand slid into her own. "This, all this work…it's been a long time since I've had someone at home with me while I work on a big project."

"I understand that." Luciana chose to agree, deciding against the mention of Janet's name for the time being. This attitude, this anger, *wasn't* only work related for Sam. Not in a million years.

Sam shook her head. "But that doesn't excuse all of this. Let me make it up to you."

Luciana lowered her eyes, her fingertips toying with Sam's. "Honestly, I just wanted to spend the evening with you."

"Then that is what we will do. Don't ever think I don't want to spend time with you. It's *all* I want to do." Sam squeezed Luciana's hand, pulling her closer. Sam couldn't imagine how Luciana must be feeling. She really had been awful to be around lately.

"I know how busy you are, babe." Luciana appreciated Sam's willingness to drop everything, but the work would still be there in the morning…unfinished. "You do what you have to do, and I'll go out for some snacks. We can have a late film and then call it a night."

Sam arched an eyebrow. "You're sure? I can drop all of this if you need me to."

"I don't *need* you to do anything." Luciana's hand found its way to Sam's cheek. "I'd never expect you to drop work for me."

"Well, you should. I'd drop everything for you." Sam drew her into a kiss, her lips passionately enveloping Luciana's. This *was* what she wanted to be doing. It was exactly where she needed to be. In Luciana's arms, kissing her until the sun began to rise.

"Later," Luciana replied breathlessly. "Finish what you're doing and then you're all mine."

"I love you." Sam's forehead rested against Luciana's. "So much."

"I love you, too."

Luciana watched Sam descend the staircase, her gorgeous dark hair pulled up on the top of her head. Evenings with Sam usually left Luciana in a state of euphoria, and tonight wouldn't be any different. She wanted no talk of Janet and Lindsay; the office could take a backseat, too. Just Sam, in her arms, loving one another. It couldn't be that hard to do, it was their norm after all. Sam's stress was becoming more obvious by the day though, and it was only going to get worse.

Maybe I should de-stress her. Luciana smirked as she followed Sam's every move. Her body responded to the white boy shorts barely covering her girlfriend's ass cheeks, a baby blue racer back hiding perfect breasts.

"Do you need anything before I join you?" Sam called out from the kitchen, turning around to find Luciana staring at her. She loved that look Luciana gave her. A look that could unravel

Sam in a matter of moments. A look of complete want. Arousal. "See something you like?"

"Oh, very much so."

"I thought we were watching a film?"

"We are. It's ready." Luciana's eyes darted to the screen of the TV before returning to Sam.

Sam's dark eyes narrowed. "Except I know that look. You have *no* plans to watch that film."

"Are you saying I have no self-control?" Luciana quirked an eyebrow.

"Yes. That's exactly what I'm saying."

"Fine." Luciana shrugged, turning her back on Sam. "Let's see just how wrong you are."

"Oh, baby." Sam leaned over the back of the couch, taking Luciana's earlobe between her teeth. "We both know," her voice dropped lower, "that you'll be fucking me on this couch within ten minutes."

"In your dreams. And just hurry up, anyway. I'm waiting to watch this." Luciana's voice remained even, but inside she was dying. Her hands itched to touch Sam.

"Coming..." Sam smirked against the side of her neck. "All. Night. Long."

Luciana squeezed her thighs together, closing her eyes briefly and calming herself. When Sam spoke like that, her body went into overdrive. *This* was the Sam she knew and loved. Luciana hated seeing Sam stressed, so this, the sultry voice and the teasing, was the perfect end to what could be considered a terrible couple of days. This version of Sam would always be the one she wanted to spend her evening with. Sex or no sex.

"So..." Sam dropped down beside Luciana, moving painfully close to her. "What are we watching?" She reached for a melon ball and popped it into her mouth, moaning as the juice slid down her throat. This may be the ideal night after all.

"J-just something I found on a streaming service." Luciana

fixed her eyes firmly on the TV, her heart almost beating out of her chest. "If you don't like it, we can look for something else."

Sam's hand slid to Luciana's thigh. "Perfect."

"I like seeing you less stressed. You know I hate it when work gets on top of you." Changing the direction of the conversation, Luciana felt Sam smile beside her.

"The life of a businesswoman, Luce. It won't be forever."

"No, I know." Sighing, Luciana's head rested on Sam's shoulder, a faint hint of her perfume still present. "Just wish I could whisk you away for a week so you could forget all about work."

"A week alone would be ideal. Maybe when this is all over... that could happen." Sam pressed a kiss to Luciana's hair, smiling as she did. A week alone sounded extremely inviting.

"I'd love that, babe."

"So, about that film?" Sam cocked her head towards the TV. "You have the controller."

"I do." Luciana pressed play, a smirk playing at the corner of her lips.

As the opening scene played, Luciana side-glanced at Sam... noting the confusion on her face. "Um, we've seen this. Like, two weeks ago."

"I know." Pushing her down onto the couch, Luciana straddled Sam's legs and met her lips frantically. "But when you come down dressed like this, what do you expect from me?"

"No self-control," Sam teased, breathlessly. "Wouldn't have it any other way."

"No?" Luciana took her bottom lip between her teeth as her hands found the hem of Sam's racer back. "You wouldn't?" Lifting it up and over her head, Sam sunk deeper into the couch, her hips thrusting up to meet Luciana's.

Gasping, Sam delighted in the lips now enveloping her nipple. "N-never. Fuck."

"I hate fighting with you, babe. It's not us." Luciana palmed Sam's other breast.

"I know." Sam's hand found Luciana's hair, grasping at it and pulling her face closer to her chest. "N-no more," she said, moaning and writhing. "This. This is what we should be doing."

Luciana smiled as her hand slid down Sam's bare stomach. "Mm, it is. This is exactly what we should be doing."

Sam's insides tightened. "Oh, God. T-touch me."

Pushing her hand into Sam's boy shorts, Luciana's fingers glided through swollen, wet folds. Aroused and needing much more, she removed her hand, took her fingers between her lips, and sucked. "Shorts off!" Luciana demanded, the taste of Sam on her lips almost too much to take. As she tugged Sam's shorts over her thighs and threw them to the floor, her legs fell open, revealing exactly what Luciana wanted. "God, I don't even know where to begin with you..."

"I'm all yours. You know that." Sam's hand travelled down her own stomach, separating slick lips.

Every time Sam touched herself, all oxygen disappeared from Luciana's lungs. Marvelling in the scene before her, her breathing became laboured and her body begged to be touched. "B-babe."

"Mm?" Sam's fingers continued to tease Luciana from afar.

Luciana moved closer; her knees almost buckling. "Shit. You have to stop doing that. I-I should be doing that."

"Then come and join me..."

Climbing back on top of Sam, Luciana gripped her wrist and brought Sam's fingers up to her lips. Trailing her tongue over them, she sucked them into her mouth, moaning in pleasure as Sam's arousal took over her entire world.

Sam dragged Luciana's body down against her. "I need you. Right now."

"Where?" Luciana's lips worked the skin of Sam's neck, her pulse throbbing. "Here?" Her hand rolled over a nipple. "Or here?" It slid lower, garnering the response she expected.

"Mm, definitely there." Sam's back arched, two fingers suddenly slipping inside of her. "Oh, fuck." Her mouth fell open as Luciana sunk deeper. This was the evening she had been praying for since they'd exchanged words in the restaurant. This side of Luciana was what she'd craved in the days that followed. Their connection. Their love. Their responses to one another's touch.

Luciana trailed her tongue across Sam's bottom lip. "You feel so good. You're so beautiful."

Sam took a sharp breath, and a sudden rush of warmth spread through her like wildfire as her orgasm approached. "F-fuck, I'm close."

"I know." Luciana pushed in and out slowly, her thumb gliding over Sam's clit as her walls squeezed her tight. "I can feel you."

"O-oh." Sam's eyes slammed shut, her thighs trembling as Luciana brought her to the peak. "Yes, right there." Her hips bucked but Luciana didn't stop. She didn't slow. "Shit." Gripping her back, Sam sunk her nails into Luciana's skin, eliciting a hiss from her. *Pain with pleasure.* Sam smirked. It had become their thing over the last several months, something neither of them ever imagined they would enjoy. As her body trembled, craving more, Sam relaxed and took the weight of Luciana's body on top of her. "I love you."

Luciana kissed Sam slowly. Softly. Nights like these...she never wanted to leave the house again. Take away Janet, the daily grind, and nothing mattered more than moments like this. "I love you, too."

CHAPTER FIVE

"Okay, Mum." Sam relaxed back in her seat, a cool summer evening breeze whipping around her.

"You'll promise to visit?"

"Yeah, I'll arrange for us to come over next weekend. Luciana is working on and off until mid-next week. She's visiting her parents this weekend."

"Okay, well keep in touch. Love you."

Sam smiled. "Love you too, Mum."

Ending the call, Sam set her phone down beside her, taking her glass of red wine from the holder on the swing bed. Luciana was due home in the next ten minutes—her shift unexpectedly running over this evening—but Sam appreciated this time alone. Of course, she would choose Luciana over any time alone, but the events of the last couple of days were beginning to take their toll on Sam's mind.

A few days on, and she still had no idea what she was going to do about Lindsay and Janet. If she could, she would leave her sister alone to figure it out by herself...but she couldn't. She couldn't be responsible if or *when* something went wrong. It was inevitable, but it didn't make her decision any easier.

She'd thought about discussing it with her mum, but this wasn't only about Sam and Lindsay. This involved Luciana, too. In order to give her mum the full picture, she would have to explain her girlfriend's past. While Sam had no issues with the fact that Luciana was once an escort, she couldn't be sure that her mum would feel the same. Understandable in some way, but also none of her business. It was best for everyone concerned if Sam kept her parents out of it. She knew it would only complicate things further and neither she, nor Luciana, needed that right now. It would always be Luciana's decision if the time ever came to discuss her past and Janet with anyone else.

The familiar sound of Luciana's Audi rumbled up the gravel path, Sam's eyes landing on the vehicle as it slowly came to a stop beside her own car. Tonight would likely be a quiet night for them but she'd prepared a bottle of wine for Luciana's arrival since something about Luciana's tone during a call they'd shared some thirty minutes said it would be needed.

Smiling as Luciana climbed from her car—that familiar navy-blue uniform sending Sam wild—Sam got to her feet and moved towards the edge of the decking. The late evening sun bounced off the lake as it slowly disappeared behind the trees, pink and purple hues dancing in the sky above them.

"Hi, babe. Sorry I'm late." Sam noted the collapse in Luciana's shoulders as she approached.

"You're right on time." Sam drew Luciana closer, kissing her softly. "Everything okay?"

Luciana squeezed Sam's hands, not willing to get into this conversation right now. "Yeah, of course."

"Busy day?"

Luciana slung her rucksack to the floor, falling down onto the swing bed. Busy was an understatement. "Always is."

"Well, I have wine or if you wanted something else?"

"Wine. Large. Thank you."

Sam studied Luciana's body language. Something about her

seemed different tonight. Her first thought was that she may have bumped into 'she who shall not be named' but that was quickly erased with the possibility of a hard shift. "Did you want to talk about it?" Sam reached for a glass, pouring a large measure of wine into it. "You look like you need to."

Luciana sat up on her elbows. "You know the rules. I don't bring work home with me."

"That's *your* rule." Sam handed the glass over as she tugged Luciana into an upright position. She really wished Luciana would open up to her. "You know I'm here to listen whenever you need it."

"And I appreciate that but it's easier to block it out."

Sam exhaled deeply, sitting beside her girlfriend. "That's not healthy, Luce. I know something is on your mind...I can see you're hurting."

"But I'm home with you and that's what matters. I'm where I should be and I'm okay." Luciana took Sam's hand, resting her head on her shoulder. She'd waited for this moment all day.

"At least tell me what happened."

"You didn't see the news?"

"You know I don't watch the news." Sam hadn't paid any attention to news channels since Lucia died. If something was going on nearby, someone would call her. She watched the building Lucia was in crumble before her eyes; she wouldn't allow that to happen again. "Sorry, but I just can't."

Luciana lifted Sam's hand, pressing a soft kiss to the back of it. "I know." She paused. "We've been tackling a blaze at a house outside the city for the last seven hours."

"That doesn't sound hopeful."

"Someone called it in soon after the fire began." Luciana scoffed, shaking her head. "I was too late. We arrived and it seemed pretty straight forward. We made entry and I knew whoever was in there, we would save. We had to get them out; we couldn't *not*."

"Take a breath, baby." Sam's voice remained soft as Luciana's increased in speed. This story wouldn't have a good outcome, Sam felt it in her gut. A heaviness. A sorrow. "You don't have to rush this."

"I carried the three year old out in my arms." Luciana lowered her eyes as she cleared her throat. If this job had taught her anything, it was that she couldn't cry. As much as she wanted to drop to her knees and sob, she wouldn't. You deal with what's in front of you, and then you move on. That had always been her motto. Luciana knew it wasn't healthy, but it's how she got by. "I carried her out...lifeless."

"Luciana..." Sam's heart broke. Not only for the family, but for the woman sitting beside her, a shadow of who she usually was. "I'm so sorry."

Luciana gritted her teeth. "I should have saved her. It doesn't make sense."

"Some things never make sense." Sam wrapped her arm around Luciana's shoulder, pulling her against her body. "You know you did everything you could. You would never go into a call unprepared."

"We got word of a leak in the kitchen when Jack was clearing the lower level," Luciana said. "I'd just made it outside with the deceased and handed her over to paramedics. Next thing I know, Jack's running out behind me, pushing me face first into the grass verge on the street."

Sam had nothing to offer. Her heart sunk. In her mind, she imagined Luciana trapped in that house with nowhere to go. This...*this* was her recurring nightmare.

"The windows blew out, partial roof collapse."

Sam focused on the lake in front of her, Lucia's death playing over in her mind. The original pain she'd once felt came back tenfold, the devastation of reliving Lucia's death now tearing her in two.

"We got everyone out. Jack was the last..."

Sam shuddered, tears falling from her eyes as they searched the water before her. What she was looking for, she didn't know, but she couldn't bring herself to look at Luciana. She couldn't attempt to speak. The possibility of her past becoming her future made her want to heave. Would she one day lose Luciana, too? Sam blinked back tears, her throat thick with emotion.

"Can I have a refill?" Luciana nudged Sam as her arm fell away from her shoulder. "Babe?"

Sam wiped the tears from her jawline. "One moment. Just...I need a moment."

"Sam, I'm okay. It comes with the job." Luciana's hand settled on Sam's thigh.

"Yeah, well, I'm not okay." Sam shook her head, her eyes closing when her voice betrayed her. How could she put her foot down in this relationship if she couldn't even stop the tears? "Y-you can't go back. You have to leave. You don't even need to work. I'm bringing in *more* than enough for the both of us."

Luciana laughed. "What? You're not serious." Sam finally looked at Luciana, her eyes telling her she was, in fact, serious. "I can't just leave my job."

Sam nodded. "Y-you can. Please?"

"Babe, I understand that my job is hard for you, but it's who I am. If I don't do what I love, I'd be miserable." Luciana's hand found the side of Sam's face, her thumb caressing her cheek.

Sam leaned into Luciana's touch, her breathing slowing when the touch reminded her that she was okay. Alive. Luciana was breathing and sitting right beside her. "At least you'd be alive."

"Sam..."

"Say you'll think about it?"

"I can't do that," Luciana replied. "It's not something I've *ever* thought about...I'm not going to start now."

"I can't lose you, Luciana. I *won't* lose you." Sam turned away, picking up her wine glass and draining its contents.

"You know that's not going to happen." Luciana's stomach clenched, disappointment rolling through her. She thought Sam understood. Her career was her life. Of course, Sam took precedence over that to some extent, but she wouldn't leave her job because of something that would likely never happen. Luciana had been in harder situations than this before, ones that Sam *didn't* need to know about. "Hey, look at me." Luciana gripped Sam's wrist as she attempted to stand.

Dull brown eyes found hers, heartbreak written all over Sam's face.

"I'm *not* going anywhere."

With a half-hearted smile, Sam pulled away from Luciana and headed inside their home. "Yeah. You're right. I'm just overreacting."

Tiptoeing through the kitchen, Luciana prepared morning coffee for both her and Sam, and then leant back against the counter. Last night had worn her out—emotionally and physically—but the sun was shining and she'd had the woman she loved beside her all night long. Sam had tossed and turned, Luciana was aware of that, but this morning she would put an end to the ridiculous idea of her quitting the brigade, and life would move on. Sam would realise that it wasn't an option…at least, that's what Luciana hoped for.

She took her phone from the kitchen counter, poured herself a cup of coffee, and pulled back the bi-folding doors. Another glorious day sparkled outside, but Luciana wasn't feeling the summer spirit. Not this morning. Finding numerous missed calls from her mum on her phone, she brought up her number and waited for the call to connect.

"Hi, Mum."

"You didn't call. I saw the news and you didn't bloody call!"

"Calm down, I'm fine." Luciana sighed. "Christ, you should come and live here with Sam."

"What's that supposed to mean?"

Luciana giggled. "*You're* losing the plot and *she* wants me to quit my job. I know you all think I'm literally going to go out in a *blaze* of glory, but I'm not."

Luciana was deflecting from how she truly felt with humour. It wasn't ideal, it was also anything other than funny, but if she allowed Sam's or her mum's words to hit home, the guilt would trickle in and she would consider if what they were saying was true. Should she leave? No. She couldn't.

"That's not funny, Luciana!" Jackie spat. "You think this is easy for the people around you? The people who love you? Because it's not. It's painful…terrifying." Jackie's voice broke. "All I wanted was a call and all Sam probably wants is to know that you're safe."

"I am safe. I'm sitting on the decking enjoying a cup of coffee. Can't be much safer, Mum."

"No! Lose the tone."

"Okay, I'm hanging up now," Luciana said. "I know you all worry, and that's understandable, but it's my job, Mum."

"Sometimes I wish it wasn't," Jackie cried. "Sometimes I wish you would just change careers, so we all sleep better at night."

"You do realise that I could go out tomorrow and get hit by a bus, right?"

"That doesn't make me feel any better."

Luciana sighed. "But it's true. I do what I love, and I try to be the daughter you want me to be. I don't know what I'm supposed to do. Sam went to bed last night and broke her heart crying."

"That woman loves you more than life itself and *you* think it's a joke. I'll bet you had some smart-arse comment to come back with when she was begging you to stop."

"Actually, I didn't." Luciana's shoulders slumped. Her defence mechanisms were dwindling by the second. She knew exactly how terrified Sam was as she relayed her shift to her, but it didn't change anything. Fighting fire was what Luciana was born to do.

Nothing else could ever come close. "Sam will be waking up soon; I should go."

"Please, don't turn this into a joke, love."

"A joke?" Luciana scoffed. "I carried a dead three year old out of a house last night, Mum. This is *anything* but a joke."

"I'm sorry, love."

"While everyone worries about the job I do, I'm worried about how I'm supposed to just get on with life when I can't save them. So, the next time you call me ranting and raving about how I don't see it from other people's perspective, think about me!"

Luciana cut the call, throwing her phone on the table in front of her. She was more than done with people talking *at* her. They had no idea how she felt. Of course, that was sometimes because she didn't tell them.

"Good morning." Sam's sleep-filled voice turned Luciana's head. Sitting on a kitchen stool with her legs crossed and a robe covering her body, she offered Luciana a small smile. "Can I get you some fresh coffee?"

"No, thank you." Luciana gauged Sam's mood, but found nothing. She really didn't have the energy to justify her career this morning.

"Some breakfast?"

"Not really hungry, but thanks." Luciana turned around, taking her coffee cup in her hands. Tears pricked her eyes, but they'd never fall. She knew that. *Trained not to cry. I've trained myself not to fucking cry.*

A soft hand rested on her bare shoulder, comforting Luciana when she hadn't known she needed it. "I'm sorry about last night."

She lifted her hand and settled it over Sam's. "Don't be. You're entitled to your opinion like everyone else."

"I overreacted."

"No, you were honest with me. Which I appreciate."

"But it still doesn't change anything," Sam said. "You'll still go to your next shift."

"I will."

"Then I just hope you'll be safe." Sam bit back a sob, a single tear falling down her cheek.

Luciana hated seeing Sam like this, but she didn't know how to change it. She *couldn't* change it. They'd been through this before. She wouldn't quit.

Luciana squeezed Sam's hand when she whispered, "Always am."

"I should get showered and call Lindsay." Sam cleared her throat. "I think you should relax today."

"I'm fine." Luciana glanced up at Sam, motioning for her to come closer. "Sit." She pushed her chair back and pulled Sam down into her lap. "I'm fine and I always will be."

"I heard everything you said to your mum."

"Then I don't have to repeat myself." Luciana smiled, cocking her head. "When I was twenty-two, I lay in intensive care. Job just got the better of me. The *only* time." Luciana really didn't know how Sam would react to that news, but she hoped she would listen. "I had Mum on one side of me, and Dad on the other. No girlfriend. No friends. Just my parents." Luciana knew how pathetic that sounded, but that was the life of a firefighter. Nobody wanted to get tied down with someone like that, but she understood. "I lay there wondering if I would ever have someone by my side who loved me if it ever happened again."

Sam listened intently, her unease not quite settling yet. While she hated the idea of Luciana being loveless, Sam was grateful that *she* was the one who snapped her up.

"I knew I was fooling myself. Someone like me was unlovable. Someone who ran towards danger couldn't possibly have a wife in her future. Kids. Probably not even a girlfriend." Luciana toyed with Sam's fingertips, her eyes focused on her soft, tanned hands. Her perfectly manicured nails. She knew she could tell Sam anything, but this honesty still took a lot of courage. Luciana felt a slight hint of embarrassment. This was weak. "All I ever wanted was for someone to look at me like they couldn't live without me. Someone who would be waiting at home, knowing I'd never let them down."

Sam attempted to speak but Luciana held up her hand.

"I knew I'd never find the woman I wanted to spend my life with…she didn't exist. I knew that no matter how smart I was, how hard I tried to look good when I went on a date, it was useless. One word about my firefighting career and they never called me back. Whether it was the hours I worked or the danger, I don't know. So, I joined the agency. I didn't have to worry about being blown off. No knock in confidence. It was just a job."

"I'm sorry."

"And then I met you." Luciana beamed. "God, I met you and you turned my entire world upside down, Sam. Nothing made any sense, but it didn't matter. It didn't *need* to make sense." Luciana brushed a tear from Sam's jaw. "I've never believed in love at first sight, it's ridiculous…but I fell in love with you the moment I met you, I truly did. I fell in love with everything you are, everything you've been through, and everything I want in life with you."

Sam wrapped her arms around Luciana's neck, kissing her softly.

"Please, don't make me choose," Luciana whispered against Sam's mouth. "I'd give up everything for you, my career included, but please don't make me choose. Let me have all of it…"

"I wouldn't ever make you choose," Sam said, her forehead pressing against Luciana's. Sam may have felt uneasy whenever Luciana left for a shift, but she was still incredibly proud of her.

Luciana cupped Sam's face. "You are the reason I fight every day. You are the reason I come home feeling proud. *You* are the reason that I'm madly in love."

"Promise me you'll be safe…"

"I know exactly what you've been through, Sam. It breaks my heart every day, but I'm here. I'm staying. I would fight until my last breath for you to know how much I love you."

"Promise me?"

"I'd move heaven and earth to be with you, babe. I don't need to promise you."

"Please...I need you to say it."

Luciana caressed Sam's cheek and smiled as she said, "I promise."

A comfortable silence filled the air around Sam and Luciana, only the birds chirping in the trees keeping them grounded. Their morning had been unexpectedly emotional, but Luciana felt better for it. She felt lighter. Sam hadn't moved from her side since breakfast, but she could live with that. Having Sam by her side would always be the kind of day she wanted.

Sam's comment about calling Lindsay earlier hadn't fallen on deaf ears; Luciana was just finding it hard to let go of the relaxed environment they'd found themselves in. She was struggling to let go of the serenity. Lindsay being around meant that everything would be up in the air again.

Lindsay *was* a priority, she always would be, but would it be the worst thing in the world to turn off their phones and forget about real life for the rest of the day? It wasn't possible, not with Sam's business, but Luciana would take this time and relish in it until Sam's phone started to ring. It was inevitable—her phone was nonstop—but she was incredibly lucky to have someone like Sam in her life, so constant calls and emails was the least she could accept in their relationship.

"How is work coming along? Everything ready for next week?" Luciana's fingertips ghosted up and down Sam's stomach, eliciting a soft sigh.

"Pretty much. Not much more can be done before my meetings on Monday."

"You don't seem to be worried."

"I have you in my arms. What the hell is there to be worried about?"

"Smooth." Luciana pressed a kiss to Sam's shoulder. "But still...you *were* worried."

"Trying to let it go while I'm here with you."

"Let what go?" Luciana sat up on her elbow, her forehead creased.

"Work. Lindsay. Everything that is pulling us apart."

Luciana offered Sam a sad smile. "Nothing is pulling us apart, Sam. We had a moment, one that would have been hard to just ignore, but we're good. Amazing."

"I know."

"So..."

"I thought I'd invite Lindsay tonight," Sam said. "What do you think?"

"With Janet, or?"

"No. Alone. I need to speak to her. What she does with the information I offer is her own business."

"You do realise it could all go wrong, don't you? Lindsay may not like us getting involved."

"I'm her sister. I *always* get involved."

Luciana grinned. "I love it when you get protective. Something very arousing about it."

"Will you behave for five minutes? Lindsay needs our help."

Luciana sat upright, crossing her legs beneath her. Sam needed her full attention. Her support. "I know, I know. So, what's the plan?"

"I think she should hear it from you."

"O-oh, right...uh..." Luciana nervously scratched at the skin of her arm.

"Unless you don't want her to know about Janet? I can't really tell her anything she needs to know without your history with her."

"No, I know. I get that." Luciana ran her fingers through her hair.

She had to do this. She didn't even have to think about it. Janet had weakened her last time, but Luciana was totally over that now. She would *never* allow that woman to make her feel worthless again.

"If you don't want to be a part of this, I completely understand."

Luciana shook her head. "I have to. I don't like this either, and I want to help."

"Okay, so we tell her about Janet and see how it goes?" Sam asked, unsure about what she was doing. "I'm not foolish for doing this, am I?"

"For wanting to protect your sister? No. No way."

Sam took Luciana's hand. "Do you ever regret going to the police? I know how hard it was for you and how much strength it took, but do you ever regret it?"

"I thought I would." Luciana focused on their hands. The reminder of discussing her personal life with a complete stranger still riled her up; she shouldn't have ever had such a story to tell. "I thought it would ruin me, I don't know why, but no...I don't regret going to the police."

Luciana didn't know what it was that led to her calling the police, but once they'd taken her statement—listened to her—a weight lifted from her chest. A weight she hadn't known she'd been carrying. The process was by no means easy, and she didn't know what the outcome would be, but Janet Mason now had a charge against her name and a suspended sentence. Her lawyer had explained that Janet may never see the inside of a prison cell with no prior convictions under her belt, but Luciana made peace with that. So long as she had told her story, she had done her job. She had called Janet out on her shitty behaviour, and for a year, she'd felt free. She still did, to some extent, but she wouldn't take this lying down. Whatever was about to come, Luciana would face it head on. She was done allowing Janet to believe she had a hold on her.

"I still admire you for doing it, you know."

"I had to. If I was ever going to be rid of her, I had to do it. For myself *and* for us."

"For us?"

"I didn't want you to see me as weak. One thing I've never been is weak."

Sam's heart tore. "That's not what I thought of you, Luce."

"No, I know. But I still had to do it."

Sam had been shocked when she received a call from Luciana, explaining that she had just left the police station. They'd discussed Janet one evening when Sam had moved back into the house, but no more was said on the matter. They talked over a bottle of wine, both cried, and that had been the end of it. To know that Luciana had taken it upon herself to tell her story…Sam couldn't have been prouder.

"You did the right thing."

"Do you think maybe she *has* changed?" Luciana asked. "I mean, one of the reasons for her suspended sentence was that she'd started anger management therapy of her own accord."

"I really don't know. Would it change anything for you if she had?"

Luciana frowned. "Change anything for me?"

"Could you be her friend?"

"No. Not in a million years. What she did to me…I could never forgive her."

"Okay." Sam pulled Luciana close, holding onto her. "And if anything changes…if she makes you uncomfortable, you tell me."

"She won't have the chance to, babe."

"No?"

"No. I'm done taking her shit!" Luciana said with conviction. "Completely one hundred percent done."

"That's what I like to hear." Sam winked, curling her fingers under Luciana's chin. "Hey. I love you."

Luciana's eyes closed momentarily before a smirk curled on her lips. "Tell me about that time you had her against the wall again..."

"Nope." Sam rushed from the swing bed. "We both know what happens when I tell that story."

Luciana shot from the bed, catching Sam by the waist and swaying their bodies. "Babe, please?" She took her own bottom lip between her teeth. "It's my favourite story."

Sam's hand slid up the back of Luciana's T-shirt, her nails gently dragging down Luciana's skin. "Mm, I know. But I'm still not telling it."

Luciana stuck her bottom lip out. "Please? My hero..."

"Hero?" Sam's eyebrows rose. "That's what you think I am?"

"Uh, yeah. Always."

"Then you should probably fireman's lift me up to the bedroom and I'll tell you *all* about it."

Luciana lifted Sam, her upper body now resting over her right shoulder. Carrying her towards the spiral staircase, Luciana's hand connected with Sam's ass, a moan falling from both of their mouths.

Sam held onto Luciana's body. "You're my hero, too, you know."

"Keep talking like that and I'll never let you leave this house again."

Arousal coursed through Sam. "Mm, wouldn't be the worst idea in the world."

"No, babe." Luciana caressed Sam's thigh. "No, it wouldn't."

Sam stroked Luciana's soft, strong back with her fingertips, their love making tipping over longer than they had imagined it would. Silence. Contentment. Love. That's what she felt as she lay with

Luciana against her, her breathing slowly returning to normal. They'd needed this. Of course, they'd had a quickie on the couch since their fight a couple of days ago, but this, sweaty and tangled up in one another...this was what they needed.

She knew Luciana had a lot on her mind; she could see it in her body language as she relaxed around the house. But as with every other time, Luciana chose to let it fester. Sam wasn't sure it was the best thing for them at the moment. It was one thing to have Janet on your mind, but to have the death of a child eating away at you... that had to be tough.

"Mm, that was something kinda beautiful." Luciana's lips curled as she tilted her head, kissing Sam's jaw. She could go another round, maybe two, but lying against Sam like this was perfect. Her full breasts just there and begging to be touched; Luciana had to refrain from doing so. She needed a refreshed Sam tomorrow, not a broken one. "You okay, babe? You look like you're thinking pretty hard about something."

"I'm perfect."

"Well, I know that."

"How are you?" Sam blurted out the words before she'd had the time to decide if she actually wanted to say them. This could go either way.

"Me?" Luciana propped herself up on her elbow, a devilish grin on her mouth. "I'm just bloody great."

"I don't mean the sex. I mean, just how are you in general?"

"Well, I could do with winning the lottery. It's one hundred and seventy million this weekend. I can't really be arsed to leave the house ever again after the night we've just had, but other than that...good."

"And work?"

Luciana cleared her throat. She knew where Sam was about to take this. As much as she wanted to change the subject, Sam deserved her honesty. "What about work?"

"Are you feeling okay since your last shift?"

"I've been better." Luciana sat upright, bringing her knees to her chest. As much as she tried to push it from her mind, the death of a child would always remain there. In twenty years' time, it would still be there.

"You know, I'm here if you need me."

"It's a funny thing to explain." Luciana focused on the wall ahead of her, a shiver coursing through her body as the early morning air hit her bare skin. "I've actually never tried to explain it. I've just always pushed it away. But, it's not nice. It's not nice at all."

"No, I don't imagine it is." Sam mirrored Luciana's position, shifting closer and settling a comforting hand on her arm.

"They offer us all these sessions and debriefs after something like that happens, but it doesn't really do much. It takes the edge off, it helps you to come to terms with it in some way, but that kid is still dead. Whatever the shrink tells us...it's not going to bring her back."

"No, I know."

"But I also know that fire is life changing once it takes hold. Soul destroying for those caught up in it. We do our best, but we're only human. Nobody judged that situation wrong, nobody thought it would be so devastating when we got inside...but it was. I can't change that, but I can remember that little girl for the rest of my life."

"Remember her, or feel guilty?" Sam asked.

"I always have some kind of guilt there immediately after we get back to the station. I think it's only natural. You know...why am I here but that child isn't? That kinda thing."

"Yeah." Sam's head fell to Luciana's shoulder.

"But then common sense ultimately prevails and once I get home, I know I did what I could. After I've taken a bath and wound down for the night...I move forward. I put it to the back of my mind and hope it doesn't happen again. And often, it doesn't.

I've been to more fatal road accidents than I have house fires. Christmas is always a bad time..."

"Christmas?"

"Faulty tree lights. People insist on leaving them on overnight and before they know it, the entire living room is up in flames. It happens more than you would think."

"You know one of the things I love about you most?"

Luciana glanced at Sam, offering her a questioning look. This would be interesting. Heroism would always score points in the bedroom with Sam. Luciana couldn't help the grin that spread across her face. "What?"

"How you come up to bed five minutes later than me almost every night because you're going around the house turning *every* plug socket off. I'm surprised you let me charge my phone overnight."

"*That's* what you love most about me? Christ..."

"I said *one* of the things. You know there are many others."

"TVs left on standby are another no-go. And I guarantee almost every fucking house in the country has one. Deadly!"

"I'm so proud of you, Luce." Sam leaned up, kissing Luciana's cheek. "I may not show it all the time and I know I go on at you to be careful, but I am. I'm the proudest woman in the world having you by my side. The things you do, the danger you put yourself in...it takes a special kind of person."

Luciana hadn't realised she needed to hear those words from Sam, but after her last incident at work and the reception she received when she got home, she did. She really needed to hear it. "Thanks. That means a lot coming from you."

"I am supportive of you, I promise." Sam cupped Luciana's face.

"Babe, I don't expect you to be fully on board with it. Most people aren't and they didn't lose their wife in a fire. I completely understand that it's hard for you, I really do, but just knowing that you don't hate me for doing what I do, that's good enough for me."

"H-hate you?" Sam pulled back, almost choking on her words as they slid from her lips. "People like you are the reason Lucia's body was returned to me. If it wasn't for those firefighters, I'm not sure I'd have ever had a real burial. They risked their lives to save who they could, and they did their best to recover those they couldn't. I have so much respect for the job you do. Don't ever forget that."

"Thank you," Luciana whispered against Sam's lips.

"When you came home a few nights ago, I couldn't see sense. I panicked, saw red, and in that moment...I couldn't imagine the thought of you going back to your job. That doesn't mean I don't still love you and admire you for everything that you do, Luce. I just didn't think I would be faced with something like that so soon, or maybe even ever again."

"I know." Luciana straddled Sam's legs, wrapping her arms around her shoulders. This woman and her honesty made Luciana feel a particular kind of way, a way nobody else could ever come close to. "You have every right to feel how you do. Always remember that."

"I love you." Sam whimpered when Luciana's hand slid down her stomach, her fingertips inching through the tiny tuft of dark hair. "You're my everything. I don't ever want to lose you."

Luciana pushed two fingers inside Sam, slick and throbbing as ever. "Never going to happen, baby."

CHAPTER SIX

Sam leaned against the window frame in the bedroom, a sense of discomfort swirling around in her belly. Lindsay was due any moment now, but Sam didn't know where to begin with anything. Should she come right out and say what she had to say? Should she serve dinner and wait a while? Should she...mind her own business? Sam sighed. *I can't. She has to know.*

Pushing off the frame, she turned around to find Luciana watching her.

"Stop worrying." Luciana held out her hand, guiding Sam to their bed. Sam repeatedly but subconsciously rubbed her eyebrow as she moved around the bedroom, a clear sign to Luciana that she was terrified about what this evening may bring. It pained Luciana to see Sam this way, but it was just another little quirk she loved about Sam. "I'll be by your side the entire time. If you don't feel like you can do it, I'll step in."

Sam sat beside Luciana, their skin connecting and making her feel marginally better. Truthfully, Sam wasn't sure anything could take her mind off the panic she felt inside. "I can't let you do that. That's the one thing I *cannot* do."

"We do this together," Luciana said, her tone leaving no room for hesitation. "Side by side."

"You're amazing."

Luciana quirked an eyebrow. "Me? There's nothing amazing about me. I'm just doing the right thing."

"No. You are," Sam pressed. "This is personal to you. It was your experience. To willingly open up to Lindsay about it...that's amazing to me."

"Good thing only your opinion matters then."

Sam froze at the sound of Lindsay's car approaching. The gravel beneath the tyres sending a wave of anxiety through her entire body like electricity.

"Come on." Luciana stood, pulling Sam up with her. There was no use in worrying. Neither she, nor Luciana, could possibly hazard a guess as to how this evening would unfold. "Let's have some dinner."

"I'm suddenly not very hungry." Sam's stomach churned. Nothing positive could possibly come from this night, but once she'd planted the seed, she could only hope that Lindsay would reconsider her relationship with Janet. "You're sure they're definitely together? It wasn't just a friendly kiss?"

Luciana was aware of the fact that Sam was trying to make this anything other than it actually was. Luciana had done the same since she found out about Lindsay and Janet. "Looked cosy to me at the restaurant last weekend. But hey...maybe I did get it wrong."

"No, I don't think you did." Sam steeled herself as the doorbell sounded around the house. "I think you're right on the money."

"What makes you say that?"

"Because I have a bad feeling about all of this."

"Who knows...they might not be together anymore." Luciana knew she was trying to settle Sam. In her heart, she was sure Lindsay and Janet would still be together. Life couldn't be that easy, surely. "Why don't you get us all a glass of wine and I'll get the door?"

"Would you?" Sam shifted uncomfortably.

"No problem." Luciana approached the door, surprised by how severely Sam seemed to be taking tonight. She was a successful businesswoman who could make men drop to their knees and beg for her time, but this? This was an entirely different situation. This was family. This was what mattered to her more than any business venture ever could. Lindsay was her life.

Luciana opened the door. "Linds, good to see you."

"You too." Embracing one another, Luciana felt a hint of what she knew Sam was feeling. "Is our Sam okay?"

"Of course, why?"

"Just...thought she might have invited my girlfriend over, too." Lindsay shrugged as she pulled back. "She did say she would arrange dinner with us both."

"She's been really stressed with work. I think she just wanted to be alone with you tonight."

"You're not leaving, are you?" Lindsay placed her bag down by the door and removed her jacket.

"No. I'm here for the night."

"And you've sorted out your differences?" Lindsay smirked. "I mean, you seem calmer."

"Of course we have. It was just something and nothing."

"She does love you. It's impossible to deny."

Luciana smiled. "I know."

"So, where is she?" Lindsay moved into the open plan space, no sign of her sister in the kitchen. "Oh, there she is."

Luciana followed Lindsay, anxiety kicking in when she found Sam standing by the fireplace, her arms folded across her chest. "Linds, hi."

"God, you look awful."

"Thanks." Sam scoffed, running her fingers through her hair. "Don't hold back, will you?"

Lindsay held up her hands. "Sorry. You look like you need a break."

"We need to talk," Sam said, disregarding her sister's observation. Lindsay was being honest; Sam *did* look like shit.

"Now, babe?" Luciana cut in, her heart sinking into her stomach. The time would come, that was inevitable, but she didn't feel prepared. "Like...right now?"

"Yes, right now." Sam nodded. "I cannot bear this any longer."

"Uh, what's going on? I feel like I'm about to be told off." Lindsay's eyes darted between them both.

"Don't be silly," Luciana tried to reassure Lindsay.

"I have something I need to talk to you about." Sam's blood ran cold, her body shivering as she opened her mouth to speak. "I need you to listen to me, okay?"

"No," Luciana stopped Sam, approaching her and taking her hands. "I should do this. You're stressed enough and this is not your problem."

Sam smiled faintly. "Baby...she's not our problem anymore."

"Still. I should be the one to do this." If Lindsay was going to hate anyone at the end of this, Luciana would prefer it to be her. Sam was too close to her sister to lose her over another woman, but Luciana could accept that fate. After all, she was the one who once involved herself with Janet Mason. This all lay on her.

"What's going on? Just spit it out." Lindsay slumped back on the couch, looking up at Luciana with confusion.

"Last year..." Luciana took a breath. "I-I filed an accusation with the police. S-something happened to me."

"What?" Lindsay sat forward, her voice barely audible. "What happened?"

"I used to see a client. On and off for a few years..."

Sam placed her hand on the small of Luciana's back, comforting her. Sam may not know it, but it was reassuring.

"After a while, she changed. She wanted more from me...sexually." Luciana wrung her hands together, lowering her eyes. "When I met Sam, she contacted me. I didn't want to see her anymore, so I arranged to meet her and explain that I'd left the agency."

"D-did she hurt you?" Lindsay's voice quivered. "Luce?"

"She did. One final time, she hurt me. Thankfully, Sam trusted me. She trusted that I didn't want any of what happened to me. When she came to my apartment to find me bruised...she was there for me and told me everything would be okay."

"There's a reason why I love her so much." Lindsay smiled. "Sam has a heart of gold." Switching her eyes to her sister, Lindsay focused on Sam. "You do, Sam. I'm so proud to call you my sister."

"S-she hasn't finished yet," Sam croaked out, closing her eyes.

"It took me a couple of months to build up the courage to go to the police, but I did it. I walked in there and I told them what she did to me."

"A lot of people wouldn't do that," Lindsay said. "You were brave to do what you did."

Luciana laughed, shaking her head. Janet had always held Luciana in some way. There was no particular reason for it—she didn't owe her anything—but Luciana always felt small in Janet's company. Insignificant. The woman who ran towards flames...felt worthless. "No, I was stupid for not doing it sooner. But the point is, I did it." Luciana approached Lindsay, sitting beside her. "The woman who did that stuff to me...she isn't a good person."

"No, she sounds like a complete bitch." Lindsay's jaw clenched. "How could anyone do that to another person?"

"I don't know." Luciana sighed, shaking her head as Lindsay's hand found hers.

"You didn't deserve any of that. I love you like a sister, Luce. If I'd known..."

"It was Janet." The words fell from Luciana's mouth unexpectedly. Although she couldn't gauge Lindsay's reaction, she felt lighter for saying it. "The woman who did it was Janet."

"J-Janet who?" Lindsay's hand trembled as she let go of Luciana's.

"The woman you're dating. *That* Janet."

"No." Lindsay stood up, laughing. "You must have got it wrong. Janet wouldn't *ever* do something like that."

Sam snorted. "And how would you know? You've only known her for five minutes."

"Why are you doing this, Sam?" Lindsay's voice broke. "I know you can't get past the idea of me being into women, but this?"

"I couldn't care any less about who you sleep with, Linds. Man, woman, I don't care!"

"You clearly do," Lindsay spat, rounding the couch and backing away from her sister. "And you…" She pointed at Luciana. "Why would you spread lies like this?"

"L-lies…" Luciana almost choked as the word left her mouth. "You think I'm lying?"

"Yeah, I do."

Luciana's world slowed. She had an idea how this conversation would go, but to be called a liar…it stung. She wouldn't show it, but she was devastated. This was the reason she'd took the lead when Sam opened her mouth to speak a short while ago. This backlash. The anger. Luciana wouldn't allow Sam to be spoken to like this, not when Luciana was the one who didn't have the balls to stop Janet in her tracks long ago.

Lindsay wiped a tear from her jawline. "You always promised you'd be there for me, Sam. You always said you'd have my back."

"I do," Sam said, Lindsay's reaction shocking her to the core. Her heart tumbled into her stomach, a cold sweat forming across her body. "Why do you think I'm telling you this? To protect you, Linds."

"No. You just don't like seeing other people happy!" Lindsay roared. "Since Lucia died, you've turned into an absolute bitch. And I thought having Luciana in your life had changed you, but you've turned out to be just like her." Lindsay focused on Luciana who was now sitting on the couch with her head in her hands. "I'm glad you're both so happy together. Nobody else would want to be around this."

"Excuse me?" Sam held herself, her forehead creased. "What

the hell are you talking about?"

"You think you have the perfect life, Sam. You think that nothing and nobody can touch you. It's sickening."

"Y-you don't mean that," Luciana whispered, looking up through hooded eyes. "You don't mean any of what you've just said."

"Except I do."

"Then you should leave," Sam cut in. Lindsay was always going to be unsure about what Sam was saying, but this? This cut deep. "If that's what you truly believe, after everything I've done for you..." Sam shook her head, willing her tears to fade. "I've always been there for you, and this is what I get?"

"Yeah, you're always the hero." Lindsay rolled her eyes. "Saint Fucking Sam."

Clearing her throat, Sam squared her shoulders and crossed the living room. She couldn't listen to any more of this, not right now. Lindsay was angry, which was in some way understandable, but Sam hadn't done anything wrong. The longer she thought about Lindsay's past, the less this all made sense.

"You should leave." Sam opened the door. "All I've ever wanted is for you to be safe, Lindsay. Protected. I'm sorry you feel like I haven't done that. I was doing my job as your sister. We've been through so much together, but those things you've just said to me..."

"I don't need protecting." Lindsay glanced back at Luciana before stepping out onto the decking. "And I certainly don't need protecting with lies."

Sam disappeared outside with Lindsay, closing the door behind her. Luciana no longer needed to be a part of this. Janet had interfered with her life enough. "That night when I went to Luciana's apartment...I found handprints around her neck. Rope burns on her wrists." Sam's stomach flipped. "The following night, I contacted Janet and met with her. She didn't have an ounce of remorse. You know what she said to me?"

"I'm not interested. It didn't happen."

"She told me it was her word against Luciana's." Sam leaned in close, her breath washing over Lindsay's face. "You may choose to be pissy about this and take the side of a woman you barely know, but don't you fucking dare come into my home and call my girlfriend a liar! *She* was the one who had strike marks down her back. *She* was the one who begged me not to hold her because of the pain it caused. *She* was the one who was assaulted."

"If Janet had done this...I would have known about it. You wouldn't keep something like this from me."

Sam searched her sister's eyes, shocked by the change in her. "It wasn't my story to tell."

"And Janet wouldn't be walking the streets if it was true."

"Why don't you go back to her and ask her, Linds? Ask her about the charges. The suspended sentence. The anger management therapy."

"I'm leaving."

"Because you know I'm right. You know everything we've just told you is true."

"No, I'm leaving because I cannot look at you any longer." Lindsay turned on her heel. "When you see how happy she makes me, you'll realise this was all a mistake."

The silence in the room lulled Sam into a world of her own. A time when everything was okay with her life, her sister's too. Lindsay had left almost two hours ago, but nothing made sense in Sam's head. The anger, the hatred in her eyes. Lindsay wasn't that person. She never would have said those things to Sam, so why had she? Why had she purposely hurt Sam and Luciana with her words when they both only wanted to help her?

Love was a strange thing, Sam knew that, but it didn't excuse her sister's behaviour. She wasn't sure it ever would.

In the hours since Lindsay had left, Sam had watched Luciana. She watched as she tried to refrain from crying, her bottom lip trembling. She watched as Luciana tried to make sense of things in her own head, coming up blank every time. She watched the heartbreak written all over her girlfriend's face, a lack of understanding for the position they now found themselves in.

Luciana was never this quiet. She always had a joke about something or a smart-ass comment to make. But tonight, she was distant. Understandable, but worrying for Sam. She didn't like seeing the woman she loved so far away mentally. She didn't want this to come between them. In an ideal world, Lindsay would still be here and asking questions, trying to make sense of things herself, but nothing about this situation was ideal. Nothing about Janet Mason was normal. The longer Sam sat thinking, the more her heart hurt.

She looked up at Luciana, her blue eyes glued to the plate of barely eaten dinner in front of her. "I thought maybe we could go out to dinner tomorrow night."

"Okay."

Sam lifted her wine glass and sipped. "There's a new Italian that's opened in the city. It's had some great reviews."

"Yeah, sounds good." Luciana looked up briefly, managing a smile. Lindsay's voice played over in her mind; it didn't make sense.

Shock and disbelief plagued Luciana, her thoughts spinning as she tried to make sense of what had happened tonight. Since Lindsay left, she felt as though time had stopped, the anger of Sam's sister suspended above her, waiting to drop with an almighty thud. And then her mind began to race, searching for answers she wouldn't find.

Lindsay believed she was a liar. Luciana opened her mouth to speak, but nothing came. She was truly perplexed.

"I mean, you're not leaving for your parents' until Sunday now and I'll be stuck in the office for the foreseeable future. Makes sense to spend some time together while we can." Sam had been thrilled this morning when Luciana decided to change her plans and leave for her parents on Sunday morning rather than Friday. And after this evening, having some time together could only be a good thing. Sam wanted to steal every possible second with her.

Luciana nodded. "Dinner would be lovely."

"Did you want to talk about it?" Sam asked, setting her wine glass back down.

"Nothing to say, babe." Emotion welled in her belly, threatening to rise up her throat, but Luciana managed to suppress it. "Your sister thinks I'm a liar."

"She's just angry," Sam said. "It doesn't excuse what she said, but I know it's only anger."

Luciana's fork clattered on her plate, startling Sam. "Yeah, I'm not so sure about that. She looked pretty certain when she was tearing us both a new one."

"I'm sorry she said those things." Sam didn't imagine this being the outcome. She hadn't for one moment anticipated Lindsay's reaction. Confusion, maybe...but anger? No.

"I'm more concerned about what she said to you." Luciana relaxed back, toying with the edge of her napkin. "You don't seem bothered."

"I'm trying not to think about it. I'm trying very hard."

"Tell me how you really feel." Luciana sat forward, her hands clasped under her chin. Sam didn't need to be strong in front of Luciana. Not when she was hurting. "It's just me and you here, babe. Tell me how you feel."

"Honestly?" Sam set her cutlery down, giving herself a moment to think about her words. "Hurt. Disappointed. Devastated."

"Understandable."

Sam's emotions bubbled to the surface. "I mean, how could she say those things about me? I don't understand. Is that how she's always felt? Does she hate me, Luce?"

"I don't think anyone could ever hate you. I don't know why she said it, but I'm not happy with her. Not at all." Luciana reached forward, taking Sam's hand.

"Don't worry about it. This one's not on you."

"This is *all* on me."

"I thought I was doing the right thing. I couldn't sit back and say nothing."

"Me neither."

"I'd never forgive myself if Janet hurt her one day," Sam cried, burying her face in her hand. "I'm already to blame for the time when she attacked you."

"What?" Luciana furrowed her brow.

"If I'd come to you when you called me, the attack wouldn't have happened."

Luciana climbed to her feet and approached Sam, dropping to her knees. "No, we're not doing this again. None of what happened was your fault, babe."

"Still feels like it was."

"I know you would have been there if you knew what would hap—" Interrupted by a knock at the door, Luciana furrowed her brow and got to her feet.

Sam rushed from her chair, praying it would be Lindsay, but when she opened the door, she found Janet standing there instead. "What do you want?"

"To talk," Janet said, shifting uncomfortably from left to right. "Lindsay showed up at mine an hour ago crying."

"Don't you dare come here talking to me about my sister."

"I love her."

Sam saw red, lunging at Janet and gripping her by the lapels of her suit jacket. "You're not fucking capable of love. You're nothing but a fucking monster."

Luciana pulled Sam back, holding her around the waist. "Babe, don't. She's not worth it."

"You lay one finger on her and I'll kill you!" Sam snarled.

Janet stumbled back as Sam loosened her grip. "P-please...I'm not here to fight with you, Sam. I'm here to beg you *both* for forgiveness. Lindsay...I don't want to lose her."

"You deserve nothing from me. You don't deserve anything from either of us."

Janet nodded, straightening out her suit jacket. "I know. But we have to work together on this project, and I don't want *this* to disturb that." She motioned between the three of them.

"What? I haven't signed you onto any project."

"The contractor you're using for the interior design..." Janet paused. "I work for them now. I'm their head designer as of yesterday."

"Then I'll find another contractor."

"You really want to put everything on hold while you find someone else?" Janet's eyebrow rose, her raven black hair falling down one side of her body. "I know you hate me, but do you really want to stop everything for something that is already available to you?"

"If it keeps you out of my life, yes."

"Reconsider." Janet stepped back. "I'm ready to go with this project as much as you are. And as for Lindsay...I'd never hurt her."

Luciana remained quiet, unsure why Janet couldn't possibly hurt Lindsay when she was quite happy ruining her life. It cut like a knife, but Luciana no longer cared for the reasons why Janet did what she did. She had Sam and nobody could ever come close to that.

"Lindsay will see you for who you are soon enough." Sam gripped the door, pushing it until it slammed shut. "If she doesn't, she's a fool." Sam's final words were spoken barely above a whisper, said to nobody in particular.

"Wow..." Luciana breathed out.

"I need to lie down." Sam turned on her heel, pushing past her girlfriend.

Luciana gripped Sam's wrist, holding her in place. "Do you think she knew? That Lindsay was your sister?"

Sam pondered that possibility. "I-I don't know."

"Then maybe she's telling the truth."

Sam's eyebrows rose, a laugh falling from her mouth. "You're defending her? You're defending the woman who once *beat* you?"

"No, not at all." Luciana shook her head. "I'm just wondering if she's genuine about Lindsay. If she knew who she was, I'd say she was doing it to get at you, but if she didn't...she could really be in love with her."

"Whatever the reason, I cannot have that woman in my life."

"And I fully understand that. Maybe you have to give it some time. See how this plays out."

"And when Lindsay shows up here, beaten and bruised...then what?"

"I...I don't know." Luciana couldn't give Sam the answers she needed. Only Lindsay could make the decision as to whether she wanted to be with Janet or not. They could tell her, but then they had to step back. It wasn't their business, however hard they tried to make it exactly that. "I really don't know."

"And the business at the office?" Sam asked. She couldn't comprehend the thought of working with Janet. She may be good at her job, but Sam had no qualms with booting Janet off her development. "Am I supposed to just let that happen, too?"

"I can't tell you what to do. Only you can decide if you can work with her or not. It's business, babe. It's not personal."

"I know."

Luciana kissed Sam's head. "Sleep on it, okay? Tomorrow is a new day and things may seem a little clearer."

"Mm, I doubt it."

"Still...you should sleep. Right beside me, while I hold you all night long."

Sam lifted her head, guiding Luciana back towards the staircase. "Couldn't ask for anything better."

CHAPTER SEVEN

Sam woke to the sound of a lawnmower rumbling outside. What she didn't understand was why her gardener was here. It was Saturday; he never worked Saturday. Had she slept through an entire day? What the hell was going on?

Climbing from the bed, she immediately noticed the lack of Luciana beside her, but she didn't panic. They'd gone to bed last night on good terms, neither of them blaming one another for Lindsay's behaviour. How could they? Lindsay was free to form her own opinion. Sam just wished it was a different one.

Checking the clock beside the bed, Sam shot up, not realising how long she'd slept. Almost eleven on a Saturday morning, and she was lying in bed without a care in the world. She had things to do, problems to fix. If she was being honest, she hoped she would go downstairs and Lindsay would be waiting for her. It wasn't likely; she'd heard nothing from her sister since last night. But she could still hope.

Pulling on an oversized T-shirt, Sam took the stairs two at a time, the scent of fresh coffee hitting her immediately. Luciana wasn't anywhere to be seen, but she couldn't be far. Sam felt her presence, her love. Pouring coffee, she approached the open doors leading to the decking and furrowed her brow. Luciana waved at her in the distance, sitting atop a ride-on lawnmower. *This is why I love her so much.* Regardless of what happened last night, Luciana still made her world spin. She still made her laugh. Luciana waved Sam over to her, flailing her arms about as she neared her on the lawnmower.

"What the hell are you doing?" Sam's voice rose over the sound of the engine, laughing as she brought her coffee cup to her lips. "You're mad!"

"I'm being a domestic goddess."

Sam pointed at the lawnmower, and Luciana powered it off. "And where did you get this from? I know I don't have one of these hidden away somewhere."

"Bought it a few days ago. It was just delivered this morning."

"You bought it? But we have a gardener." Sam's forehead creased.

"Wanted to do my bit. Fancy a ride?" Winking, she powered the engine back up, holding out her hand to Sam. "Come on…you can sit right here." Patting the leather seat between her legs, a smirk played at the corner of Luciana's mouth. "You know you want to."

Yes, I definitely do. "Five minutes and then I have to shower."

Sam set her coffee cup down and straddled the seat in front of Luciana, smiling as her girlfriend's arms wrapped around her waist. Resting her head back on her shoulder, Sam hummed as soft lips caressed her neck.

"You make everything feel better." Sam's hands fell to Luciana's, sitting perfectly on her stomach. "Just spending a moment with you makes everything seem less worrying than it is."

"It's what I'm here for, babe." Luciana cut the engine on the lawnmower again.

"Thank you. Everything is going to be okay. It has to be." Sam turned her head, capturing Luciana's lips.

"Five more minutes." Luciana smiled against Sam's mouth, a

burning passion building in the pit of her stomach. "Five more minutes before we worry, okay?"

"Mm, okay." Sam closed her mind, willing her worries to disappear. In this moment, it was her and it was Luciana. Nobody else around for miles. In that moment, she felt a tremendous amount of love. A love that only the woman wrapped around her could provide. Security. Protection. "Are we still on for dinner tonight?"

"We are." Luciana lifted her hand, settling it against Sam's face. "Dinner with you before you disappear, and I forget what you look like."

"Never going to happen. And don't forget I want you to come home sooner than Tuesday night."

"How could I forget? I don't even want to leave." Luciana sighed, holding Sam.

"Still...you should. It's just a couple of days. And with a certain someone back in town, it could be good for you."

"I know, I know." Luciana hated to admit it, but avoiding Janet was for the best. She should report it to the police, but that would only hurt Lindsay, and potentially, Sam's business. Luciana loosened her grip, sliding her hands up and down Sam's naked thighs. "Maybe you could make breakfast while I finish here. Then we will take that shower you mentioned...together."

Sam climbed from the seat. "I can work with that. Anything in particular?"

"Anything with bacon. *All* the bacon."

"I wonder how you keep in shape with the crap you eat." Sam rolled her eyes, moving up the decking. "Really wonder."

"Just got one of those bodies, babe. Which is kinda good considering I should be about four-hundred pounds by now."

Sam lifted her coffee cup, draining its contents. "And you'd still be beautiful."

Luciana stared across the table at where Sam's little black dress enveloped her body in every way imaginable. The very same dress she'd worn the night they met continued to arouse Luciana; it always would. Thick, dark hair fell down Sam's back, the caramel highlights she once sported no longer present. Luciana would always remember their first encounter. After all, it was the night she fell in love with Sam.

Of course, that sounded stupid, but it was true. That night, Sam stole her breath and her heart. All in one fell swoop, Luciana would never be the same again.

Luciana's eyes followed her every move. They landed on the fingers holding the dessert menu. Delicate. Slender. Manicured to perfection. Those fingers…God, the things they could do. Luciana lifted her eyes once more, finding Sam staring back at her with a smirk on her lips. She knew that look all too well, but dinner wasn't over and she wouldn't fall for the teasing she knew was about to ensue.

"You're staring," Sam said.

"You're gorgeous." Luciana shrugged her shoulders, clearing her throat and picking up her own dessert menu. "See anything you like?"

Sam shifted in her seat, the toe of her six-inch heels running up the back of Luciana's calf. "Not on this menu, no."

Luciana closed her eyes, shaking her head ever so slightly. "Babe. You really shouldn't do that."

"I could leave dessert. Could you?" Sam placed her menu down, folding her hands on top of it as she cocked her head.

Luciana salivated as Sam's eyes darkened. "Y-yeah. I mean, if you wanted to leave?"

"I think it's best if we do." Sam nodded, taking her credit card from her purse. "You get the bill while I use the bathroom."

"Don't be long." Luciana lifted her hand, calling for the waiter's attention. Motioning that she would like the bill, he turned on his heel and headed for the nearest cash register. Sam stood in front of her, eyebrow arched. "Seriously, Sam. Don't be long."

"I'll be as long as it takes, beautiful." Bending at the waist, Sam leaned in and pressed her lips below Luciana's ear. "And you should know...I'm not wearing any underwear."

Luciana exhaled slowly through her nose, her voice barely audible when she breathed, "Sweet fucking Jesus."

"I'll meet you outside," Sam whispered. "You could use a moment or two to cool down."

"Hard to do when you're talking like this..."

Sam smiled as she pulled back. "Oh, here comes the waiter. Outside. Two minutes."

Luciana watched Sam walk away, fixing her dress on her thighs as she did. Sam had legs that women could only dream about, but Luciana had the pleasure of enjoying them every moment of the day. As the waiter cleared his throat, she snapped out of her arousal and glanced up at him, offering a crooked smile. "Sorry." Handing over the credit card, she finished up at the table and gathered her own belongings by the time the waiter returned. "Thank you." Putting Sam's credit card away safely, Luciana almost fell when she rose, managing to save herself on the back of someone else's seat.

Focus, Luce. Her eyes scanned the room; Sam was nowhere in sight. Deciding to take her girlfriend's advice, she moved through the busy restaurant and out onto the street. The temperature was cooler this evening, but the sunset...wow. The sunset was one of the best she'd ever witnessed. Staring out between the buildings and towards the dock, all thoughts of a naked Sam beneath her faded. The view was absolutely breathtaking.

"You ready?" Sam settled her hand on the small of Luciana's back.

"Y-yeah. Look at that." Pointing towards the water, Luciana turned to find Sam's eyes wide. "How gorgeous is that?"

"Come somewhere with me?" Sam asked, her hand sliding

around Luciana's waist. This sunset was too good not to view in its entirety.

"Anywhere."

Holding hands, they crossed the street and headed down toward the dock. Luciana wasn't sure what Sam had in mind, but she didn't care. So long as they spent the evening together, she would follow Sam to the ends of the earth.

"Where exactly are we going?"

"To the office," Sam said, picking up her pace.

"Um, I'd rather we just went home."

"Just...trust me. You're going to want to see this." Rounding the corner, Sam took the office keys from her purse, checking the traffic as she rushed across the main road.

Stopping outside the building, Luciana frowned when she could no longer see the sunset. Whatever Sam had in mind, it had better be good. "Why are we at the office?"

"You remember I always told you Lucia installed the windows in my office for a reason?"

"Yeah."

"You're about to see exactly what that reason is." Sam smiled as she glanced over her shoulder, unlocking the door and turning off the alarm. "Just close it behind you; it'll automatically lock."

Sam strode down the hallway, a woman on a mission, and flung her office door open. Grinning as her eyes focused on the floor-to-ceiling windows in front of her, Luciana stepped up behind her, gasping as she did.

"You see?"

"I-I see." Luciana's voice wavered. "Oh, wow."

Sam took Luciana's hand, aware that the view was overwhelming. "Come inside. Just watch it."

Luciana slowly made her way inside the office, moving closer to the window and shoving her hands in the pockets of her jeans. "Come and join me."

Sam followed, the office door closing behind her.

"Something else, isn't it?"

"It certainly is. Quite incredible."

"This office space has one of the best views of Liverpool and the river," Sam said, wrapping her arms around Luciana's waist, the burnt orange sky setting her eyes ablaze. "And Liverpool has some pretty amazing sunsets."

"It does." Luciana turned in Sam's arms, holding her close. This was where Luciana wanted to be. Her and Sam...alone, in love, and in one another's arms. Nothing and nobody could touch them here. Nobody could hurt them. "Thank you for bringing me here to see this."

"I'd hoped to do it sooner."

"Just had to wait for the right moment. Everything is about waiting for the right time." Luciana's lips met Sam's softly, slowly.

Sadness settled over Sam, and, with a sigh, she said, "I wish you weren't leaving for Manchester."

Luciana smiled, the tip of her nose touching Sam's. "Say the word and I'll stay."

"No, I can't do that. You should spend some time with your mum. I'll be no use to you for the next few days at least."

"Yeah."

"You're only down the road. If you want to come home, you know I'll be lying in bed waiting for you."

"Or here."

Sam nodded. "I'll be close by, you know that."

"And if for any reason you have a day off, you can come and visit."

"You know I'd love to."

Luciana guided Sam backward towards her desk. "I think we should rest a minute."

"Rest?"

"Mm. Rest..." Luciana's lips trailed Sam's neck, sucking and nipping at the sweet spot below her ear.

"Rest sounds like a good idea." Sam wrapped her legs around

Luciana, trapping Luciana against her body. Arousal built deep within her, Luciana's slender fingers touching her in all the right places. "I have to spend the next two nights alone," Sam murmured, moaning in delight as Luciana's hands forced her dress up her thighs. "Baby..."

"Yes?" Luciana pulled back, her blue eyes deepening.

"I really need you tonight." Sam lifted one leg, resting her heel on the edge of her desk.

Luciana stepped back, salivating as Sam's glistening sex came into view. Two nights would be too long, she knew that, but these moments alone in the office late at night, they were the moments she craved. Moments when their love was so heightened, they needed one another without a second thought. The world could be watching, and it wouldn't matter.

Dropping to her knees, Luciana's fingertips ghosted up Sam's leg. The silky, smooth skin beneath them left her wanting more, craving Sam's arousal on her tongue. Dipping her head, Luciana's mouth followed a familiar path up Sam's thigh, both women shaking with anticipation. As much as Luciana wanted to draw out this moment, she couldn't. Sam hadn't been lying when she told her she wasn't wearing underwear at the restaurant, and now she had to act on it. She had to have her girlfriend, in every way imaginable.

Luciana blew gently against swollen lips, heat settling in the pit of her stomach. Her own arousal gathered by the second, but Sam needed her...and that was exactly what she would get. Separating velvety folds, Luciana's tongue found Sam's engorged clit with ease. The moan that fell from Sam's mouth was almost enough to tip Luciana over the edge of her own desire, rumbling through her entire being with no signs of slowing.

"Fuck, I need more." Sam's words ignited every nerve in Luciana's body. As Sam pressed herself down against her tongue, Luciana drew back and climbed to her feet.

"Turn around." She guided Sam down from the desk,

turning her in her arms and placing her hand between Sam's shoulder blades. Luciana slowly lowered the zipper holding Sam's dress in place, watching it gather at her feet. Luciana would forever hold this image in her mind. Sam, naked before her. Sam, ready and waiting for her next move. "Bend over." Her lips brushed Sam's ear, smirking as she felt the heat radiating from Sam's body.

Gasping as the cool wood pressed against her stomach, Sam closed her eyes and took her bottom lip between her teeth. "Luciana, please..."

"Begging will get you everywhere." Luciana's hand slid up the back of Sam's thigh, pushing her legs apart. "God, you look so beautiful like this." Placing kisses up Sam's spine, Luciana's fully clothed body pressed against her back, her fingers teasing Sam's entrance as she whispered, "Feel good?"

Sam whimpered, telling Luciana everything she needed to know. Gripping the edge of her office desk, all breath left Sam's body when two fingers slid inside her. Slowly but surely sending herself towards the peak, Sam pushed back against Luciana's hand, delighting in the sensation of her fingers working her deeper. Harder.

"Touch yourself, Sam." Luciana pressed a kiss to Sam's shoulder blade, sinking deeper with each movement. Smiling when Sam weaved her hand between her own legs, the gasp that fell from her mouth could be considered heart stopping.

"S-shit." Sam's body tensed, her fingers working her to the edge of one hell of an orgasm. "H-harder," she pleaded, her voice hoarse with emotion *and* arousal. "Oh, God."

Luciana obeyed, sinking deeper and hitting the spot which she knew would drive Sam wild. Fresh arousal coated her fingers, the palm of her hand, and as Luciana's name tore from Sam's throat, she felt Sam's legs buckle. Wrapping her arm around Sam's waist, Luciana held onto her, pulling Sam upright and against her body. "Hey, I've got you."

"O-Oh." Sam's head fell back against Luciana's shoulder, her legs trembling.

Luciana smirked against Sam's neck. "That was hot. And why exactly have we never done that before?"

"I-I don't know. But wow…it'll be added to the list."

"Good to know." Luciana turned Sam in her arms. "I love you."

"I love you, too. Just…come home to me on Tuesday, okay?" Sam leaned in, caressing Luciana's lips.

"Counting down the hours."

CHAPTER EIGHT

Sam walked towards the dock, determination and control in her stride. She never imagined she would be in this position, but here she was...about to meet with Janet Mason. It was no secret that Janet was good at her job—Sam had chosen her over others many times before—but Sam wasn't sure she could stick this one out. When Janet worked for her previously, it was under different circumstances. This woman she knew now wasn't the Janet Mason she once had on her payroll.

She had a lot to think about. Sam *never* delayed projects; if she did with this particular one, it would only mean Janet had won. Sam couldn't win whatever decision she made. If Sam kicked Janet off her development, Janet would be controlling her. If she didn't get rid of her, Janet would be around for the foreseeable future. Sam was torn, but she had a plan.

By keeping Janet close by, she could watch her. If something was going on within Janet's relationship with Lindsay, Sam would surely sense it. If there was a hint of a threat to Luciana's *or* Lindsay's safety, the police would be called.

With Luciana gone, Sam had thought hard about the choice she was making. She didn't want her girlfriend to feel uncomfortable in any way—Luciana was her priority—so one wrong move from Janet and she *would* be gone. Sam only hoped Luciana wouldn't hate her for the decision she was about to make. When everything was said and done, Luciana mattered most in all of this. Yes, Janet had already breached her injunction, but would she worm her way out of the consequences? Probably. For the time being, Sam was satisfied that Janet was here to work. The best she could do for Lindsay was to look out for her.

God, I could be making the biggest mistake of my life.

She reached the door to the coffee shop and steeled herself. Before she could even think about asking Janet to join her at tomorrow's meeting, Sam wanted to lay down some ground rules. She pushed the door open, spotting Janet immediately. The first thing that pissed Sam off was knowing that Janet would be the one to comfort Lindsay. She still hadn't had any contact with her sister since they had argued, but she wouldn't ask Janet about Lindsay. Not now. Not ever.

Janet stood, her dark eyes watching Sam as she moved through the tables. Instead of joining the interior designer, Sam walked straight past her and to the counter. Sam placed her usual order with the barista, moving to the end of the counter to collect her order. She glanced back to find Janet sitting, tapping her fingernails against the table. Sam simply laughed, shaking her head at the audacity of this woman.

"Thank you." Sam offered the barista a smile as she took her cappuccino and approached the table. "Been here long?" Sam sat down, placing her briefcase on the table, her coffee cup beside it. The reality was, Sam didn't care how long Janet had been waiting.

"Only five minutes," Janet said.

"Oh, well..." Sam focused on the lock of her briefcase. "So, let's get down to business."

"Right, okay." Janet cleared her throat, sitting forward and clasping her hands on the table in front of her. She appeared eager.

"First of all, this is business. I don't want you in *any* other aspect of my life. You're *not* welcome at my home. You still have an injunction in place."

She finally looked at Janet. A shiver worked its way through Sam's body.

"Sam—"

"And, Lindsay has made it clear how she feels about me." Sam's voice remained level. "That's her choice."

Janet's eyes lit up. "You're okay with us dating?"

"I'll never be okay with anything that involves you. Lindsay stupidly worships the ground you walk on, so it's no longer any of my business."

Janet relaxed. "I won't hurt her, Sam. I know you have no reason to believe me, I understand that, but I do really like Lindsay. And Luciana doesn't have to worry; I won't approach her again. I had no idea she would be at the club."

Sam wouldn't sit here discussing Luciana. Janet had no right to speak her name.

Sam narrowed her eyes. "Did you know?"

"Did I know what?"

"That Lindsay was my sister."

"Y-yes," Janet replied, "but I'm not dating her because she's your sister."

Sam snorted. Her disgust for this woman was unrelenting. "Something tells me you're full of shit. But I'm not here to discuss Lindsay with you. I'm here to finalise details."

"I won't let you down."

Sam wasn't sure what Janet meant by that comment. Was it business, or was it personal? Either way, she'd already spent too long in this woman's company. The sooner she discussed what was necessary, the sooner she could go home and shower any trace of Janet from her body. Just being in the same room as her left Sam's skin crawling.

Sam took her glasses from her bag. "Right. You've seen the blueprint?"

"I have."

"You're up to date with the style I want? Sleek. Minimal. The way we used to work."

"It's my area, Sam. You have nothing to worry about."

Sam's head shot up, her brow furrowed. "I asked if you've seen it?"

"Briefly." Janet nodded. "I've been...busy."

"Right, well I want you to familiarise yourself with it. Know it inside out. I don't care what plans you have coming up, this takes precedence. You know how I work; you know what I expect. Work to the specifications I've given you."

"Of course."

Sam handed over a stack of papers to Janet. "Meeting tomorrow. Midday at the bistro."

"I'll be there at eleven-thirty."

Sam shook her head, finishing her coffee. "Don't over enthuse. It doesn't suit you."

"Can I get you a refill?"

"No." Sam frowned, eyeing Janet. "Take the papers I've given you and do the job you're here to do." Sam slammed her briefcase shut. "Your contract is in there. Everything you need...you'll find in that pile."

"O...kay."

Sam stared, unable to comprehend how she had come to be sitting across a table from Janet Mason. "You can go now," Sam said, her tone cold and harsh. "Unless you needed something else?"

"Is this how the entire project is going to be?" Janet asked. "I mean, I know you hate me...but I can't work with you like this."

Sam took her belongings from the table, pulling them in front of her and preparing to leave. "Then find me someone else or put up with it. Now, I have a life to live. One that doesn't need to include you for a moment longer."

Sam climbed to her feet, taking her briefcase from the table. She could have enjoyed another coffee, but it wasn't a good idea to do so in the same building as Janet. *What the fucking hell am I doing?* Sam scolded herself inwardly, the idea of going ahead with this needing to be mulled over with a glass of wine. Luciana would settle her mind once she had time to call her, Sam was sure of it.

Sam settled down on the couch, blueprints and specifications scattered all over the coffee table. She'd gotten a lot done today, surprisingly, and now she was waiting for Luciana to call her. Sam hated this time away from Luciana. Yes, she was used to sleeping alone when Luciana had a night shift, but this was different. Her body—it knew this was different. If it really called for it, Sam could easily hop in her car and take the fifty-minute journey down the motorway, but work was preventing her from doing so. What she would give to fall asleep in Luciana's arms tonight, wrapped up and safe.

Her phone rang, Luciana's beautiful face lighting up the screen. It was Sam's favourite picture, a shot of them relaxing on the swing bed outside—Luciana in Sam's arms.

"Hi."

"Hi, babe. Missing you." Luciana's voice instantly washed away the stress of Sam's day.

"I miss you, too." Sam lay back on the couch, her eyes closing. Luciana's voice was soothing. "A lot, actually."

"I didn't expect anything less."

"How's your mum and dad? Did you apologise for me?"

"I did. Not that an apology was necessary."

Sam exhaled. "Still. I should be there with you."

"Babe, it's fine. Honestly."

"I had a meeting today," Sam said.

"The first of many. I bet you can hardly wait for the next one."

"With Janet."

The line went silent, no sign of Luciana or her breathing.

Sam cleared her throat. "I'm going to work with her. Business, nothing more."

"Okay."

"She is to remain business and she knows that. She isn't welcome in this home, Luce. She will not bother you; I won't allow it."

"Hey, I'm not worried about that." Luciana's voice softened. "You do whatever you think is best for your company. I'll be by your side the entire time."

"I appreciate that, but she shouldn't be anywhere near you." Sam didn't want this to come between her and Luciana. That woman had a criminal record for a reason...a very good reason. "If it becomes too much for you, just say the word and I'll pull her."

"If you hate her so much, why did you agree to work with her?"

"Because while she's close by...she can't hurt Lindsay. She also can't hurt you. Knowing she's back in the city...it's making me feel uneasy. She has no reason to be in the same space as you, Luce. And I'll make sure she doesn't."

"Babe, I'm not concerned about me. And as for Lindsay, she's made her bed. She kinda has to lie in it now."

Luciana appreciated Sam's worries. Janet wasn't allowed near her, but Luciana also wouldn't be the reason for Lindsay having her heart broken. If Luciana contacted the police regarding Janet's injunction, their relationship would be no more. As much as Luciana *loved* that thought, it wasn't her place to split them up. She had no idea who the woman Janet was now. If she had, in fact changed, Lindsay would be the one who got hurt.

"And I know how much you want to protect her, but she hasn't even bothered to call you and apologise for the things she said to you."

Sam was already torn. She didn't need Luciana making her feel worse. As much as she wished Lindsay would contact her, Sam would have to wait for it to happen naturally. Lindsay was stubborn. "Do you want me to take Janet off the project?"

"No, I'm just saying that what her and Lindsay have isn't our business."

"O...kay."

"The last thing I want is to see Lindsay get hurt. Unfortunately, we have no way of stopping that from happening. Janet may have changed; she may not. You can't work with her just to keep an eye on her though, Sam. She's manipulative and sly. Do you really think she would give you any hint of something untoward between her and Linds?"

"No, I suppose not."

"And I know I should call the police, but it's not my place to get involved in Lindsay's business. Can you imagine what she would think of me if I sent Janet away? I know her coming to the house the other night was against the law, but Lindsay would never speak to me again. Other than her showing up, she hasn't actually done anything wrong. The club just happened by chance."

Sam understood Luciana's reasoning. Even if she didn't like it.

"If you want to work with her because she's good for the business, okay. But if you're doing this to try to protect your sister, I'm afraid it's probably not going to be as simple as that."

"Thanks."

"For what?" Luciana asked.

"Telling me what I guess I've been needing to hear."

"You do what you think you should," Luciana said. "If I wasn't around, you wouldn't be any wiser to Janet's behaviour."

"God, I wish you were here with me right now." Sam's eyes glazed over, the thought of never meeting Luciana too much to take. She was right, though. If she'd never made the call to the agency, this wouldn't be her present. Terror tore through her at the prospect of Luciana still being in the hands of Janet. "I really wish you were here."

"I'll be home before you know it."

CHAPTER NINE

Luciana tapped her fingers against the steering wheel of her Audi, bopping her head along to the music playing from the radio. She'd left Manchester a day early, planning to surprise Sam at the office after her late-morning meeting at a local restaurant on the dock. As she exited the motorway and reached the city centre, her heart swelled at the prospect of seeing Sam. A year on, she still felt as though their relationship was brand new, those butterflies ever present when she thought about Sam. Luciana felt more in love than she ever thought possible. Of course, over the last week or so they'd had their differences, but ultimately, Luciana remained head over heels in love with Sam. That kind of love that hurts. Aches. The love that hits you square in the chest at the mere thought of being apart.

Since yesterday morning when she'd reached her parent's home, Luciana had thought hard about Janet and Lindsay. She'd wondered if her ex-client had actually changed. She appeared different—less agitated with life—but in Luciana's mind, someone like Janet could never change. As much as she wanted Lindsay to be happy, Luciana wasn't sure it was possible with Janet. That saddened her, it truly did, but she knew the kind of woman they could be dealing with and she didn't like that possibility. Lindsay was free to make her own decisions, but Luciana had voiced her opinion and her experience; now she had to sit back and pray that the woman who once tried to break her didn't repeat her actions.

The music cut out as Luciana's handsfree sounded around her car. Glancing at the screen, her brow furrowed when she didn't recognise the number. "Hello?"

"L-Luciana, hi."

Janet?

She cleared her throat. "Who is this?"

"It's me. Janet."

"Why are you calling me and how *the hell* did you get my number?" Luciana asked, her jaw clenched. "You really are beginning to push your fucking luck!" She was now close to calling the police. Just like she should have a few nights ago.

"It's Sam. S-she, uh…we're down at the dock."

"Yes, I'm aware of my girlfriend's schedule."

"No, you don't understand." Janet's voice wavered. "Something happened. An explosion."

Luciana's heart shattered. She couldn't have possibly heard Janet right. She pulled over and turned on her hazard lights. "What? What did you just say?" Her entire body shook with terror. "Janet?"

"We had a meeting. Sam was already there."

"You mean you're not with her? Is that what you're saying?" Luciana's eyes closed, career mode about to kick in. This couldn't be happening.

"Y-yes," Janet said. "I'm not with her."

Luciana checked her mirror and sped off down the road. "I'm on my way. Look for her. *Find* her."

"They won't let me past the cordon," Janet cried. "I've tried to find her, Luciana. It's the least I could do for you."

Luciana frowned when Janet's voice filtered through her hands-free. "No, we're not doing this. You're not going to look for her as some way of forgiveness. It doesn't work like that. Just find her Janet. Forget about me. Forget about us...forget what happened and find her."

"I'm trying."

Luciana ended the call, the dock coming into view. As her hands gripped the steering wheel tighter with each second that passed, tears fell hard and fast. Luciana had seen a lot during her career—some of the most harrowing scenes anyone could imagine—but nothing could prepare her for this. She never thought she would receive 'the call,' but now she had to decide how she dealt with it. Did she fall apart, or did she find Sam? Pray that she was alive? Hold her and never let her go?

She couldn't think about the possibility of Sam being hurt right now; it would only create a mess inside her head. A mess she didn't need, and quite frankly, a mess she couldn't handle. And then it dawned on her...

What if Sam was dead?

Reaching the gates of the dock, she pulled up away from numerous emergency vehicles, catching sight of Jack Bridges, her colleague. She cut the engine and rushed from her car, almost losing her footing on the cobbles beneath her feet. "BRIDGES!"

"Foster, what are you doing here? We didn't call you," he asked, confusion etched on his face as he held his helmet against his hip. "We've got it here. It's your weekend off."

"S-she's here. S-Sam." Luciana's lungs burned, every emotion toppling over the edge of what would be considered normal.

The colour from Jack's face drained, only terrifying Luciana more. "What? Your Sam?"

"Yes. She's here. Please, you have to let me through." Luciana's voice begged Jack as she brushed tears from her jawline. "I have to find her." If Sam was lying hurt somewhere, she would want Luciana to be with her. Holding her.

"The boss won't let you through. You know that."

"Yeah, that's not going to work for me." Luciana scoffed,

pushing off on her right leg and sprinting towards the impact zone. Her boss' commands had gone right out the window the second Luciana answered Janet's call.

As she rounded the corner, she was met with complete devastation. Rubble. Carnage. Her eyes scanned the various forms of enforcement, a sea of emergency services milling about surveying the damage behind the cordon put in place. The dock looked like something from The Blitz, blue sky trying to force its way through the thick, acrid smoke and dust in the air.

"Hey, Foster!" a familiar voice called out. Luciana glanced to her right to find Craig coming her way. "Your girl...she's here."

Luciana stood on shaky legs. "Y-you've found her? She's alive?"

"You think I'd let one of our own down? No chance."

"Oh, my God." She collapsed in his arms, dust and debris covering her once pristine white shirt. Luciana's heart pounded, slamming against her ribcage with every breath she took. "Where is she? Is she hurt?"

"Paramedics are bringing her out in a minute or so." Craig ran his hand up and down Luciana's back. "She's going to be okay. She's going to need you."

"She's got me. She's got me now more than ever," Luciana cried.

"I should get back. I wanted to see you myself; your friend there has one hell of a temper." He motioned towards Janet who stood at the side of the barrier, shifting from left to right.

Luciana stared, undecided as to whether she should shake Janet's hand or rip her head off. The latter seemed more appealing in this moment, but this wasn't about Janet. She was insignificant.

"You have good people around you."

"She's not my friend." Luciana wiped her tears away, releasing her grip on Craig. "You, on the other hand...you're my fucking saviour."

Craig nudged Luciana's shoulder. "Just doing my job, mate.

Stay here. She'll be out in a minute. I'm sure you'll want to go to hospital with her."

Luciana nodded as she watched her friend and colleague walk away. Was this deliberate? "Hey, Craig!"

He turned around. "What's up?"

"Cause?"

"Pointing towards a gas explosion."

"Fatalities?"

"Zero...so far." Craig sat his helmet on top of his head.

Luciana breathed a momentary sigh of relief, the tension in her shoulders releasing as she felt a hand on her back. As she looked to her left, she found Janet standing by her side. Shrugging that hand off her, Luciana turned to face the woman who had once been the cause of her suffering. In what universe was Janet going to be the hero today? In all honesty, it wouldn't have surprised Luciana if Janet *had* saved Sam. She had always been the kind to come up smelling of roses.

"Are you okay? Did you need a hug?" Janet asked, studying Luciana's face.

"No, thank you. Thanks for calling me, but you can go now. You shouldn't be here; it's dangerous."

Janet shrugged her purse higher up on her shoulder. "I'm fine. I'd like to make sure Sam is okay."

"Why?" Luciana may have sounded harsh, her question laced with a scoff and a hint of hatred, but she had no reason to accommodate Janet. None whatsoever.

"Because she's my boss on this project...and I'm dating her sister."

"This, what I have with Sam...you'll never be a part of it, Janet. You're not *in* this family. This bond."

"That's a little harsh."

"No, it's the truth," Luciana sighed. "I'm not going to stand here and argue the toss with you, I have no desire to do so, so please stop trying to insert yourself into our lives."

Janet squared her shoulders. "I feel very strongly about Lindsay. Please, let me continue with that."

"You do as you please; I really don't care at the minute. But please, stay away from me. For your own sake." Luciana turned her back on Janet, her heart pounding as two paramedics approached the cordon with a stretcher. "Babe?" Luciana rushed to the side. "Sam, I'm here."

Nothing.

Sam's head was held in a brace, her eyes open, but no words came from her mouth. Nothing to indicate that she was happy to see Luciana by her side.

Luciana squeezed Sam's hand and her eyes darted to the right. "Sam?"

Sam's hand instantly turned over, her fingers lacing with Luciana's. In the moments after the explosion, Sam had lay flat on her back, praying that Luciana would somehow find her. Be with her. Hold her. As the minutes passed, that hope faded. Luciana couldn't possibly come to her rescue when she was some thirty-odd miles away in Manchester. To now have her by her side, a weight lifted from Sam's chest. Holding her hand, Sam knew she would be okay.

"You're going to be okay, Sam. I'm not leaving your side."

"You are?" a paramedic interrupted.

"Her girlfriend." Luciana glanced up briefly before her eyes returned to Sam's. "She's my life."

"Then you'll be coming with us in the ambulance?"

"Y-yes, of course."

The paramedic smiled. "Perfect. You should know that your girlfriend can't hear you."

"What? She can't hear?"

"At the moment, no."

"B-but it'll come back?" Luciana's voice broke. "It has to come back..."

Luciana stood back as Sam was manoeuvred into the back of

the ambulance, only releasing a breath when she was invited inside. So long as Sam was alive, everything else could be figured out. She approached Sam, leaned down, and kissed her head. "Hey, I know you can't hear me...but I'm going to marry you someday."

Sam lay in a side room, a humidity in the air that came with being in a British hospital. She'd never planned to wind up in a place like this, but she was thankful for the help and care she had so far received. Unable to open her eyes for fear of what she would find when she did, Sam enjoyed the sensation of Luciana running her fingertips up and down the side of her wrist. She knew it was Luciana beside her; she would know that touch and that scent anywhere. She would know the undeniable feeling of love radiating from her body whenever Luciana was close by. She felt it every second of the day, but today it was heightened. Every emotion, every touch, felt different to any that had come before. Something about lying in a hospital bed, her body aching and tired, changed everything for her.

I could have died today. I could have died, and I'd have never seen her again.

Emotion welled in Sam's throat, tears pricking her eyes as she attempted to open them slowly. The room spun, her body buzzed, but as she turned her head to the left, she found the bluest eyes staring back at her. Red and swollen, but still so very beautiful.

"H-hi," Sam said, unsure if any words had come from her mouth. "Are you okay?"

Luciana's lips moved, but no sound reached Sam's ears. Muffled, yes...but nothing she could make out.

"What?"

Luciana's mouth continued to move, her lips parting, a slight smile curling on her mouth.

"Baby, I don't know what you're saying."

Luciana stood, gathering a notepad and pen from table beside the bed.

I love you

"I love you, too." Tears fell from Sam's eyes as she held the piece of paper, running her index finger over the black ink. "I thought I'd never see you again."

I was coming home to surprise you. Looks like I'm the one who got the surprise.

"I don't know what happened." Sam sighed, turning on her side and facing Luciana. She hadn't ever felt physical pain like this, the grimace on her face alerting Luciana to that fact. Sam breathed deep through her nose, just about managing the intense ache she felt. "I was about to walk into the restaurant, and something threw me back. Out the door and onto the pavement."

I spoke to Craig. They think it was a gas explosion.

"Did everyone get out okay? I knew I shouldn't have gone there earlier than usual. I just...I thought I'd finish some paperwork before my contractors arrived."

Luciana had discovered there had been three fatalities, but Sam didn't need to know that right now.

You didn't know this would happen, babe. Nobody could know that.

"I hate not hearing your voice." A tear rolled down Sam's cheek, hitting the pillow beneath her head.

Doc says it's the trauma from the blast.

"Will it come back? I don't think I could go on not hearing your voice."

Of course it will.

Luciana would normally never just tell somebody something they needed to hear, especially not under these circumstances, but the devastation in Sam's eyes was too much to watch. The fear in her voice sent a shiver down her spine. She couldn't add to it. Today, as she left Manchester, she imagined the happiness in Sam's eyes as she walked through the office door. Today, they should have been sharing a late lunch together and planning the week ahead. But now? Everything was a mess and Sam was lying in a hospital bed with a nasty gash to the forehead. Still, she looked beautiful.

I need to call the boss later. See about taking some unpaid leave until you're back on your feet.

"You don't have to do that. I'll be fine."

Wrong answer.

"As much as I want you at home with me, you have a job." Sam lifted Luciana's hand, pressing a kiss to her knuckles.

Luciana could only watch Sam, relieved that she was not only alive but also awake.

"Do I look terrible?"

You look drop dead gorgeous.

Luciana leaned over, her lips settling beside the sutured cut above Sam's eyebrow. "So fucking gorgeous." She breathed against Sam's skin. "And I swear I'm going to look after you. I'm never letting you out of my sight again."

Sam sighed, aware that Luciana's lips were moving. This was going to be a big adjustment for them both. "I still don't know what you're saying."

Sorry. I was talking to myself.

"Any idea when I can get out of here? No use wasting a bed when I can be at home."

Let me go and check for you.

Luciana got to her feet and disappeared out the door. Approaching the nurse's station, she saw a familiar face coming towards her. Lindsay. She'd taken it upon herself to call her while Sam was being admitted but hadn't had the opportunity to update her girlfriend. Yes, they were in a bad place with one another, but this surely took precedence over everything else. "Hi, Linds."

"Is she okay?" Lindsay cried. "Can I see her?"

Luciana pulled Sam's sister into a hug. "Of course you can. Don't worry, she's going to be okay."

"She could have died, Luce. She could have died, and she'd

have done so hating me." Lindsay sobbed in Luciana's arms. Her body weakening, Luciana held her up, soothing Sam's sister.

"She doesn't hate you." Luciana held Lindsay at arm's length, squeezing her shoulders. "You've fallen out over a woman. It happens."

Lindsay shook her head. "But it shouldn't. She's my sister and we shouldn't have fallen out."

"Nothing we can do about it now."

"Do you think she's going to tell me to leave? I don't think I could handle that. I need to see her."

"No, I don't think she will do anything of the kind. Second room on the left."

"Luciana..." Lindsay backed away, teary eyed. "Is it bad?"

"Not as bad as it could have been. You should know...that she can't hear you." Luciana offered Lindsay a small smile. It was brought on by nerves, but Lindsay wouldn't know that. Nobody would know how anxious Luciana felt.

"She's lost her hearing?"

"Trauma from the blast. It'll return."

"You're sure about that?" Lindsay's eyes brightened. "You can one hundred percent say it'll come back?"

"Y-yeah."

"If you don't think it will...you have to tell her, Luce." Lindsay shoved her hands in her pockets.

Not now, Linds.

"She wouldn't want you to lie to her. You should know that by now."

"I'm not a medical professional. I'm simply telling you what *I* believe."

"Still..."

"It's Sam," Luciana pressed. "If anyone can get back up and running...it's her."

"Yeah, you're right."

"Now, go and visit your sister while I try and bail her out of here." Winking, Luciana turned on her heel and made her way towards a nurse. In her heart, she wanted Sam to remain here until she was feeling better, but at the same time, she wanted to be at home with her where they both belonged. Whatever the outcome of this conversation was, Luciana would be by Sam's side. If she had to sleep in a plastic chair for nights on end, she would.

The dull thrum in Sam's ears was beginning to get on her last nerve. It had been mere hours since she'd quite literally been blown away, but the sound was already interfering with her life. Her sleep. Her mental health. Honestly, she felt as though she was going insane.

When she opened her eyes, Lindsay was staring at her from the seat across the room, her gaze burning through Sam. She remained on her left-hand side, the pain in her right causing too much discomfort at the moment. Luciana wasn't around; Sam knew she was giving them space. What that space was for, though...she didn't know. It wasn't like she could hear if Lindsay had some kind of apology up her sleeve.

Sam rolled onto her back, sharp pain travelling the expanse of her body. This didn't feel good. Nothing about the last several hours could feel anything other than miserable. Sam didn't know if anyone had been seriously injured; the bistro had been pretty quiet for a Monday morning, but she couldn't think about it for the time being. If someone had been injured or worse...Sam wasn't entirely sure how she would deal with it. The blast had hurt her enough; she couldn't imagine what the inside of the bistro looked like.

Her eyes focused on the ceiling above her, the thrum and whooshing leaving her feeling nauseous. The nurse had been by twenty minutes ago with anti-sickness meds, but they didn't appear to be working. Sam would have to wait this out; there was no more she could do.

Sam's eyes landed on her sister, sitting in the corner of the room with her head now in her hands. As much as Sam wanted to work everything out with Lindsay, it was difficult. Given the circumstances, Sam wasn't able to discuss Janet or Lindsay's relationship with her. Truth be told, she wasn't sure she wanted to.

Sam had always looked after Lindsay. When her sister hit rock bottom, Sam was there like a shot. And she would be, time and time again. Lindsay's words still hurt, though. They cut deeper than Sam imagined they could. While she didn't plan to dwell on what Lindsay had to say a few nights ago, Sam did wonder if it was how her sister truly felt. Insinuating that Sam had the perfect life was so far from the truth that she was beginning to question whether Lindsay knew her at all.

Losing your wife unexpectedly—cruelly—really does do a number on you. Sam thought Lindsay understood that, but it was apparent that she didn't. She couldn't. Lindsay was merely a bystander through Sam's hardest times, assuming to know what her sister was going through. She would always be grateful to Lindsay for being there, for helping her through those times, but Lindsay couldn't begin to imagine what Sam felt in those moments after Lucia's death. Not really. She could hazard a guess, but unless someone has been in that position, that dark void of not knowing if you can go on, nobody knows how hard it is.

"You don't have to sit here with me. I'm sure you have other places to be."

Sam spoke, Lindsay's head slowly lifting.

"Please, you can go."

Lindsay reached for the notepad sitting at the end of Sam's hospital bed, scribbled onto a blank page, and handed it to her sister.

You're my sister. My life. I should be here.

Sam nodded slowly, stifling the scoff that works its way towards her mouth.

"Luciana will be here if I need anything. But I don't. I'm fine for the time being."

What you're saying is you want me to leave?

Sam shrugged.

I have a lot to talk to you about. So many apologies, Sam.

"No." Sam sunk down in the bed. "I'm not doing this with you. Not now."

Lindsay slunk back in her plastic hospital chair, watching Sam intently. Sam noted the tears in her eyes, the tremble of her bottom lip, but she struggled to sympathise. How could she when Lindsay may as well have told her she hated her? Actually, 'I hate you' feels like it would have been less hurtful than everything else that had dripped from her mouth with such venom.

"I should try to sleep a while longer." Sam groaned as she turned on her side, tears pricking her eyes with the pain coursing through her body.

Sam needed Luciana. Their hands in one another's.

"Where's Luce?"

Lindsay appeared at Sam's side, notepad in hand.

She's sitting in the coffee shop downstairs. She said we needed time alone.

"Can you get her for me? Or hand me my phone so I can text her?"

Do you need something? Let me help you with whatever you need.

Sam's eyes closed as she brought the sheet up under her chin. "I just need Luce. Can you please just ask her to come back...?"

"Shit, that hurts!" Sam winced as she was helped from Lindsay's car. Everyone knew she'd had a lucky escape this morning, but now that she was home...it was really beginning to sink in. While at the hospital, Luciana had received a call from Craig. Luciana had been reluctant to update Sam, but she needed to know. Three fatalities in total with multiple critical injuries had been the outcome of the explosion.

So now, as Sam moved up the decking towards the front door, her complaints seemed irrelevant. She hadn't lost her life. She hadn't been maimed. She was about to sleep in her own bed, with the love of her life beside her.

"Thanks." She cleared her throat, shrugging Lindsay's arm from around her waist. "You're both too good to me."

"Can I get you anything?" Lindsay asked, forgetting that her sister couldn't hear her. "Maybe a cuppa? Some pain medication?"

"She can't hear you, Linds." Luciana took Lindsay's hand and pulled her into the living room with Sam. "Notepad, remember?"

Lindsay smiled half-heartedly. "Oh, yeah. Notepad."

"You help her get comfortable and I'll get the last of our stuff from your car."

"I can do it."

"No, you can sit with her. The more time you spend together, the sooner everything will blow over."

"Mm, I'm not so sure about that." Lindsay sighed. "Luce?"

"Yeah?"

"I'm sorry I called you a liar." Lindsay's voice broke, but her eyes told Luciana that she still chose Janet over everything else.

Luciana could only pray that Lindsay was doing the right thing. That Janet had turned her life around. She still felt cold all over at the mere thought of Janet Mason, but Lindsay had made it clear where she stood on the matter. Luciana felt paralysed in this situation.

"That's your decision, Linds. I just hope it all works out for you."

"It will."

God, I hope for your sake that's true. Luciana walked back to the car. It was no longer her priority to watch Lindsay's every move. Sam needed her, and her mind was fully focused on exactly that. If Janet had changed, great, but Luciana's past would be her truth regarding Janet. It always would.

Luciana locked up Lindsay's car and took a moment to allow the day's events to hit her. Coming back here today could have been a completely different story. Coming home...she could have been alone. No Sam. No life together. No nothing. As she leaned back against the bonnet of Lindsay's car, she released a deep breath and allowed her emotions to hit her hard. Tears fell faster than she anticipated but rather than hold back like she usually would, Luciana let them flow. She needed this. A moment to realise how lucky she was. A moment to cry for her girlfriend. A moment to breathe. Nothing could have prepared her for today. No matter how emotionally strong she was.

"Hey, come on." Lindsay appeared and wrapped her arms around Luciana's shoulders. "Come on, Sam is okay."

Luciana sobbed, "I know, but this could have ended differently."

"She's asking for you," Lindsay whispered, holding Luciana closer. "She needs you, and she's asking for you."

Luciana cleared her throat, wiping away her tears. "I-I'll be right there."

"I know you will."

"Just needed a minute, you know?"

Lindsay sighed. "I've needed a few of those lately."

"Is everything okay?" Luciana found Lindsay's eyes and pressed, "If something is wrong, I need you to speak to me."

Lindsay shook her head as she stood upright. "Not now, okay."

"Then when?"

"Maybe later."

Sam slept soundly beside Luciana, her breathing slow and even. As much as Luciana wished to close her eyes, she couldn't. Watching Sam, listening to her breathe as her chest rose and fell, seeing her eyelashes flutter, was the one moment Luciana hadn't realised she needed today. Sam would be knocked out for a few hours at least, her medication taking care of that, but still...Luciana couldn't pull herself away. She couldn't bring herself to leave their bright and airy bedroom, for fear of returning to find Sam gone.

It was ridiculous to feel that way, Luciana knew that, but this was new for her. This crippling terror she felt. The idea of losing the one you love more than life itself.

When she received that call earlier today, a million and one thoughts flashed through her mind. What would Sam's wishes be regarding a funeral? Would she want to be buried with Lucia? Could Luciana face life without her? All of those thoughts evaporated once Sam held her gaze, but that moment still occurred, and Luciana felt lost. For the first time in her life, she didn't know what to do.

Luciana had always prided herself on controlling her life and its destiny, but since she'd met Sam, all control had been relinquished. Willingly, of course, but this was a lack of control she'd never imagined she would be faced with. This feeling of helplessness was a feeling Luciana never wished to be a part of. She was supposed to be strong, determined. And while she still felt those things, today they were lacking.

Just like they were a year ago when Janet showed up at her apartment, demanding and receiving exactly what she'd expected. All strength inside her vanished, leaving a weak and apprehensive Luciana. Everything she had ever known, gone in a split second. Instead, she was reduced to a shuddering wreck...a silhouette. The two situations couldn't be compared, she knew that, but that lack of control still felt the same regardless of the reasons for it.

A light knock on the bedroom door startled Luciana. As she

turned her head, looking over her shoulder, she found Lindsay watching her.

"Did you want some coffee? I can bring it up for you if you want?"

"No, it's okay." She climbed from the bed, kissing Sam's hand as she did. "I'll come down and sit with you for a while."

"You don't have to do that."

"You're here. The least I can do is catch up with you." Luciana smiled faintly. Something about Lindsay's comment earlier had unsettled Luciana, and now she wanted to know what it meant. Was Lindsay having trouble in her personal life, or was Luciana inwardly overreacting? "Put the kettle on, I'll be down now."

Lindsay nodded, backing up down the hallway. "Okay."

CHAPTER TEN

Luciana poured two fresh coffees and approached Lindsay. She hoped this conversation would be cut and dried—nothing to worry about—but the atmosphere in the room had changed and she didn't quite know how to interpret that. As much as she wanted to just cut to the chase, Lindsay deserved more than Luciana demanding answers. If something was bothering her, Luciana knew better than most that Lindsay would have to be given the time to get it out of her system. As she took a seat beside Lindsay, she hoped and prayed that everything was good.

"So, what did the doctor say about Sam?" Lindsay asked, smiling as Luciana handed her a cup of coffee. "I didn't think she would be home so soon."

Luciana set her cup down, relaxing back against the couch. Small talk, to an extent. This would work for the time being. "Honestly, I didn't either. I don't know how she didn't have any other injuries. That place looked like it had been demolished."

"So, it's the hearing and that's it?"

"She has some cuts and bruises. The doctor said she's going to be sore for quite a while, but it's the hearing that worries me most."

"There's nothing there at all?"

"Not that I know of." Luciana closed her eyes briefly, willing her emotions to take a backseat for five minutes. "I just...what if it doesn't come back?"

Lindsay sighed. "Don't. I can't even begin to imagine that possibility."

"But it *is* a possibility, Linds. And I know, I know people lost their lives, but Sam is who I'm concerned about. Her health."

"Me, too. We have to stay positive." Lindsay reached for Luciana's hand.

Luciana lowered her eyes. "I'm trying."

"She seemed a little unsteady before. Is that related to the hearing problem?"

"Yeah. Doc says she's not to be left alone until her balance improves." Luciana lifted her cup and sipped her coffee. "I've spoken to my boss. I'm off until things improve dramatically around here."

"I can stay with her. It's the least I can do."

Luciana squeezed Lindsay's hand. "Thanks, but I need to be here. I won't be able to concentrate at work if I know she's not okay. If I can't concentrate, I can't do my job to the best of my ability."

"Mum and Dad said they would come around later."

"Do you think maybe you could ask them to come tomorrow instead?" Luciana shifted in her seat. While she appreciated everyone's help and support, Sam was her focus. She needed to rest, and she couldn't do that while people were faffing around her. "I'm not sure Sam will be in any state to have people 'round. Not tonight, anyway."

"I did say that to them. But you know what Mum is like. It's useless trying to explain."

"That's understandable."

Lindsay scoffed. "It's also annoying. Sam won't be in the mood for Mum's company tonight. I don't want her upset because Mum doesn't know why she can't hear her. You know how it'll be. She'll just push and push and Sam will freak out."

"I'll speak to her," Luciana said. "You know...Janet was at the dock this morning." It was now or never. It appeared Luciana *couldn't* mind her own business.

"That's nice." Lindsay smiled weakly. It didn't go unnoticed by Luciana, not at all. "She's working with Sam, but I don't know if Sam knows that yet."

"Oh, Sam knows *exactly* who she's working with. If Janet was due at that meeting...Sam knew."

"How did she seem?"

"Who? Janet?" Luciana's forehead creased. "She seemed perfectly fine."

Lindsay remained quiet. As the seconds passed, Luciana became increasingly concerned that her quietness was for a particular reason.

She steeled herself, facing Lindsay fully. "What's going on?"

"N-nothing."

"Please, don't lie to me."

Lindsay cleared her throat. "She just...she's very full-on. And I'm sure she means well, but I don't like being told what to do."

"You'll have to give me more to work with."

"When I left here last week, I went to her place. She asked where I'd been, and I told her I'd been with you and Sam."

Luciana nodded, giving Lindsay time while quietly, she was bracing herself for the worst.

"I explained that I knew you and her were once together."

"We've never been *together*. She was my client. That's where it ended." Luciana knew it didn't really matter, but she wanted Lindsay to know exactly what kind of relationship they'd had.

"Yeah, well...I just said I knew you'd been together."

"Right, okay."

"She seemed a little bit off after that," Lindsay explained. "I went to shower and when I came back, she had my phone. She wanted to know why it had a passcode on it."

Luciana breathed, "And so it begins..."

"I can see her point, but I wasn't trying to hide anything from her. I don't *have* anything to hide."

"You don't have to explain yourself to me." Luciana held up a hand. "And whether you see her point or not, she had no right to even pick up your phone."

"She was looking for your number. Said she wanted to run something by you."

"Did you give it to her?"

"Yes. It seemed like she wasn't going to stop talking about it until I did."

Luciana squared her shoulders. "She's not supposed to have my number. She's not supposed to be *anywhere* near me."

"You mean...legally?"

"Yes, legally. I know I gave you bits and pieces last week Lindsay, but I meant it when I told you not to get involved with her."

"She said she's changed."

Luciana's eyebrows rose. "You told her what I told you? That was brave of you."

"No, not exactly. She said that whatever you'd told me, she'd changed, and she wasn't that person anymore."

"Could be true." Luciana tugged her bottom lip between her teeth. Could Janet truly change? Luciana wanted to believe that *anyone* could redeem themselves; she always thought people deserved a second chance. The problem was that every time she thought about Janet Mason, anger tore through her. If Luciana was being completely honest with herself, she imagined it always would. "I don't think she could ever change, but I can't say for certain that she won't."

"I told her I wanted to see less of her. It just feels like too much all at once."

While Luciana wanted to believe Lindsay, she couldn't. The

seed had been planted regarding Janet's behaviour; Luciana could see the worry in Lindsay's eyes. It wasn't her intention to literally frighten Lindsay into ending their relationship, but Luciana could see the doubts. The apprehension. Last week everything was great between Lindsay and Janet—or so Luciana believed—but now Lindsay wanted out of the relationship? This had to be related to their heated conversation. Luciana would usually apologise for getting involved in someone else's business, but she couldn't. She was secretly happy that Lindsay was considering kicking Janet out of her life.

"And how is that working out for you both?" Luciana asked, intrigued. "I mean, Janet is an all or nothing kind of person."

"She's been calling me daily," Lindsay said. "I haven't answered."

"Why not?"

"I don't like the neediness. The jealousy."

"Jealousy?"

"If I tell you something, I need for you to not tell Sam."

"I don't know if I can promise you that, Linds. We have a very open and honest relationship. If something happened and she finds out I knew, she'd never forgive me."

Lindsay chuckled. "It's nothing bad. It's just something I never thought I'd tell her. Something I agreed with the *other* woman involved."

"Okay, you've got my attention." Luciana sat up straight, desperate for more information. She was partial to a little dose of gossip. Being at the station and surrounded by men usually meant gossip was lacking. "Spill."

"Six months ago, I had a thing with Cheryl."

"*Cheryl* Cheryl?" A grin spread across Luciana's mouth. "I fucking knew it!"

"What? You knew?"

"I had a feeling. Sam told me I was out of my mind, but I just knew something was going on with you two."

Lindsay placed her head in her hands, seemingly embarrassed by Luciana's observation. "Great. My sister is going to think I'm just sleeping my way around Liverpool."

"No, she won't."

"Anyway, we got really close, and I really liked her. I suppose in some way, I still do." Lindsay's eyes lit up as she spoke about Cheryl. "Sam has always made it clear that business stays business, so I took a step back. I didn't want her to feel uneasy around the office and Cheryl was already worried that Sam would fire her when she found out."

"Sam wouldn't do that."

"Deep down, I knew that," Lindsay agreed, "but I'd never felt that way about a woman before and I didn't know how to begin telling my sister. So, we decided to call it a day."

"This doesn't explain Janet and her jealousy."

"We were out at the bar three nights ago. Cheryl came in."

"Okay..."

"She spotted me while Janet was at the bar. She got a bit touchy feely and danced with me, then Janet appeared out of nowhere. She wasn't happy."

"Oh, I'll bet she wasn't."

"Once we got back to her place, I explained that I'd had a bit of a thing with Cheryl and she told me I wasn't to see her again. If Cheryl came into the bar, I was to call Janet."

"Doesn't surprise me," Luciana spat. "You should be with Cheryl. I can see how much you regret ending things with her."

"I know. I should have faced the music six months ago and we *would* be together now."

"So, why the hell are you dating Janet Mason?"

"She just appeared when I needed someone. Cheryl kept coming to the bar with that woman she was dating last year. It's just a friend with benefits kinda thing, I think. I hated seeing her with her though, so I looked for someone myself," Lindsay admitted, fidgeting with the sleeve of her jacket. Once again, she seemed embarrassed by her behaviour. "And I know that makes me sound like a shitty person, but I somehow got attached to Janet, too. Not how it was with Cheryl, but there was still an attraction there."

"Was?"

"I'm not sure I want to continue this with Janet." Lindsay wrung her hands together, glancing up at Luciana through hooded eyes. "After what you told me though, I'm not sure how to let her down without all hell breaking loose."

"You don't want to be with her?"

"No."

Luciana gripped Lindsay's knee, squeezing it. "Then you tell her it's over. She knows that I've told you about her past. If she has any brain cells left, she will accept that and move on. Janet knows she is being watched."

Luciana didn't want to think about it, but the thought had crossed her mind that Janet was simply using Lindsay to get to her. The reason she didn't worry too much was because Janet had the chance to get to Luciana this last year if she'd wanted to. Why wait for Lindsay?

"You really think that will be the end of it?"

"I can't promise you that, but the first sign that she seems aggravated, I'll call the police."

"What about Sam?" Lindsay asked, her shoulders relaxing slightly.

Luciana waved off Lindsay's concern. "Don't worry about Sam. I'm pretty sure she would rather know you had a thing with Cheryl than worry about you one day marrying that fucking Janet Mason."

"I don't know what I was so worried about. I should've just told you."

"Not important now. It's done."

"I should head home." Lindsay tugged the cuff of her hoodie. "And I suppose I have a call to make."

"You want me to be with you when you make that call? We can do it here if you'd feel more comfortable."

"No, I'll be fine. Thanks, Luce." Lindsay climbed to her feet slowly, glancing down at Luciana and smiling. She could do this; Luciana was sure of it. Sam may be the strongest of the two of them, but Lindsay still had a similar personality when it came to protecting herself.

"You want me to let Sam know all about this?"

"Maybe once she's better. I doubt she will be worrying about me and Janet while she's in pain."

"If you need anything, you call me." Luciana pulled Lindsay into a strong embrace, letting her know she wasn't alone. "I mean it, Linds. If you don't feel comfortable, you call me, and I'll be right there."

"You said she can't be anywhere near you…how did that happen?" Lindsay stepped back, studying Luciana's face.

"I spoke out, finally. It took me too long, but I finally did it."

"You went to the police."

Luciana smiled. "I did. I had no other choice. She was out there living her life and I couldn't be sure she wouldn't do it again."

"Do you think she has done it again since?"

"Honestly, I don't know." Luciana blew out a deep breath, shoving her hands in the back pockets of her jeans. The thought of Janet continuing her ways always weighed firmly on her mind. "She has a suspended sentence behind her name so I'd hope she wouldn't be stupid enough to do it again."

"I can't believe what she did to you."

"No, me neither."

Lindsay smiled softly, her eyes gentle. "I mean, look at you. You're Luciana Foster. Nobody messes with you."

Luciana had never quite understood what people meant by that. Was she supposed to be invincible? Just because she had a strong and demanding job, it didn't mean she could hold her own twenty-four-seven. "We're not all strong all of the time, Linds. Janet Mason was my biggest moment of weakness, but she'll never hurt me again."

"I know."

"Don't avoid this place, okay? Sam loves you."

"Look after my sister, okay?" Lindsay reached for the door and pulled it open. "You'll have me to deal with if you don't."

"Always."

CHAPTER ELEVEN

Sam groaned. Finding herself face-down against her pillow, the cut to her forehead throbbed. As she slowly lifted her head, wincing as she did so, fresh blood seeped through the white Egyptian cotton pillow slip. Raising her arm from beneath her pillow, she lightly touched the cut, hissing as her fingertips connected with the damp, sticky wound. She didn't have time for this; she had a business to run and plans to finalise with her contractors. *How am I supposed to do that when I don't know how to communicate?*

Sam sighed, gingerly rolling herself over in bed. Luciana's side was cold and empty. As much as she wanted to maintain the ability to look after herself, Sam's head spun. Her body ached, but that was always going to happen. Being thrown through the air would always have a traumatic effect on the body, no matter how fit and healthy someone claimed to be.

Sam sat upright, her stomach churning as she swung her legs over the edge of the bed. Right now, she was torn between throwing up and calling out for Luciana. This was the last thing she expected as the week began. She couldn't ever expect Luciana to look after her; it wouldn't be necessary as the day wore on, but she did need her this morning. She needed support—mentally and physically.

Sam attempted to stand, falling back down onto the bed as her balance faltered. *No. This cannot be happening.* She tried again, reaching for the corner of the bedside table to her left. Losing her grip, the belongings on top of it came crashing down against the hardwood floor as it wobbled. *Shit!*

Sighing, Sam remained seated on the edge of the bed, watching as the smashed glass of water on the floor spread to the rug beneath her feet. She should be on her hands and knees cleaning up the mess but instead Sam simply watched the water. A sudden hand on her shoulder jolted Sam from her stare, frightening her to within an inch of her life.

"Shit!" Sam placed her hand against her chest, panic rushing through her entire being. She turned to find Luciana standing beside her, worry etched on her beautiful face. "S-sorry, I'll get this cleaned up."

Luciana handed her a notepad.

No, you won't.

"It's going to get into the floorboards if I don't."

Leave it. I'll do it. Why are you up out of bed?

Sam glowered. "Because it's time to get up. I'm not lying in bed for the foreseeable. No way."

You shouldn't be up.

Luciana hated this. She should be able to hold a conversation with her girlfriend. It was only two days on from the accident and she was already over the whole writing-on-a-pad thing. Luciana sat beside Sam, offering her a sympathetic smile.

Sam held up her hand, sick to death of the overwhelming amount of sympathy seeping from Luciana. "Don't. Don't do that stupid fucking look."

I know you're frustrated. I am, too. This will all get better.

"When, Luce? Tomorrow...next week? Next month?"

I don't know, babe.

"I don't want to lie in bed all day." Her ears whooshed as though she was under water. "And I don't want you sitting around here waiting for me to need something from you."

"I'm supposed to be here. I'm supposed to look after you and do whatever it is that you need."

Sam rolled her eyes. "I can't hear you. Believe it or not...I haven't *quite* mastered lip reading since I went to bed last night."

Sorry. I forget sometimes.

Luciana wasn't sure how she could forget. She was sitting with a notepad in her lap and a pen in her hand. God, this was hard work.

"Don't you have somewhere to be today?" Sam asked. "Anything that is remotely more interesting than sitting around this fucking house all day?"

Nope. I've been doing laundry. I've already prepared lunch so it's one less thing to worry about later. And your parents are coming over in a few hours.

Sam read Luciana's handwriting. While she loved the effort her girlfriend had put in, this wasn't the life Sam wanted for them. What if her hearing didn't return? What if this was their future now? Sam wouldn't ever expect Luciana to stay. *Nobody* signs up for this when they fall in love.

Sam smiled dimly. "Luce...i-if this doesn't get better, you know?"

No, I don't know.

"You wouldn't have to stay...I'd be fine." Sam's stomach lurched at the thought of losing Luciana.

I've told you I'm not going anywhere until you're better. Work understands.

A tear hit the paper in Sam's hand. "That's not what I meant."

Luciana's brow drew together. Was she suggesting what Luciana thought she was? That she could leave. Not just for the day but for good? Luciana's heart ached in her chest. She wouldn't discuss this with Sam while she couldn't hear her. She wouldn't for one second entertain the idea that Sam would let her go.

We're not talking about this. Not now, not ever.

"We should."

You're going to get better. And even if you didn't, I still wouldn't leave you. I love you.

"I love you too, but what kind of life would this be?"

The most beautiful life.

Sam studied Luciana's features, hurt radiating from her soft, blue eyes. She couldn't imagine a future without Luciana, but it was one she had to consider. If this was going to be their life, Sam seriously had to consider being alone. Luciana deserved so much more than a woman who couldn't even hold a real conversation with her.

"I'd like to go downstairs for a few hours."

Anything you want.

Luciana lay back, the sun warming the skin of her face as Sam lay sleeping beside her. The temperature was ideal today. Not too hot and not too humid. Summer was beginning to wind down, autumn almost visible around them, but the days were beginning to roll into one. Only two days in and Luciana felt lost.

Sam was so worn out and despondent, she wasn't sure her girlfriend would be the same woman again. Luciana wasn't sure how to make things seem better for Sam. She could use a friend—someone to talk to—but she didn't know who she could turn to. Lindsay hadn't been in touch, and Sam's parents had their own stuff going on worrying about their daughter.

Luciana quietly sat up, taking her phone from the swing bed beside her.

L: Hey, you working?

Figuring that she could use a phone call from Shannon, Luciana waited as Shannon responded to her message.

S: No. Two days off. Did you and Sam work things out?

L: Yeah. All good on that front. Could use a friend for a moment though...

S: What's up?

L: You heard about the explosion down at the dock?

S: Yeah. Did you work it?

L: No, but Sam was caught up in it.

Luciana's phone started to ring in her hand, Shannon's name flashing on the screen. She glanced back at Sam, her chest rising and falling beautifully as she slept.

"Hey."

"What do you mean Sam was caught up in it?"

"She was on her way to a meeting," Luciana explained. "It happened as she was headed into the restaurant."

"Oh, my God. Is she okay?"

Luciana watched Sam, her belly aching from the vision in front of her. Sam was nothing like the woman she was just a few days ago. Confident. Fun-loving. The woman Luciana fell in love with. Of course, Luciana still loved her, more so now than ever before, but nothing felt the same. Nothing felt as though it would improve. "Define 'okay'..."

"Luciana."

"She's lost her hearing." Luciana closed her eyes momentarily, tears pricking her eyes. How the hell had this happened? "They say it should only be temporary, but what if it's not?"

"S-she's deaf?"

"Yeah."

"Oh, babe." Shannon's voice held an element of sympathy. Luciana didn't want sympathy, though. She just wanted someone to tell her it would all be okay. "Is there anything I can do? Do you want me to come over?"

Luciana laughed. "I've been trying to get you over here for the best part of a year, Shan. I've got more chance of seeing a chair walk than you showing up."

Shannon hesitated. "I could, if you want me to."

"Would you?" The idea of holding a conversation with someone who wasn't related to Sam seemed quite appealing. "It would be nice to chat."

"Send me your address. I'll get ready to leave now."

"Thank you." A relief settled inside Luciana that she wasn't aware she needed. Shannon would always be considered a good friend, but they didn't have the kind of relationship most friends did. They didn't sit drinking wine together on weekends. They didn't shop together. They just had an understanding of one another that many people outside of the escort business didn't. "See you soon."

"See you, Luce."

Luciana shifted from the swing bed, waking Sam up in the process. She froze, hoping Sam would drift back off to sleep. As pained brown eyes opened, Luciana winced. "Sorry, I didn't mean to wake you up."

"Mm?" Sam stretched, her T-shirt riding up her stomach, a now common discomfort on her face. "Notepad."

"Fuck sake," Luciana muttered, reaching for it beside Sam.

I'm sorry for waking you.

Sam waved off Luciana's apology, smiling as she slowly sat up. "It's okay. I didn't really want to sleep."

You should sleep whenever you can. Your body will heal better.

Sam sneered. "And then you won't have to sit here entertaining me. Why don't you go and visit your parents or something?"

Because I need to be here with you.

"You don't. I'll call Lindsay. She can come and stay with me out of guilt." Sam rolled her eyes, climbing from the swing bed and losing her balance in the process.

"Whoa." Luciana rushed to her side, scooping one arm around Sam's waist and holding her upright. "I've got you."

Sam shrugged Luciana's arm from her body. She wouldn't allow her girlfriend to become her nurse. "Let go of me, Luce. I'll have to figure this out at some point. You can't babysit me."

Luciana stepped back, dropping her head on her shoulders. Not only was Sam frustrated, but she was now beginning to take it out on the people who cared about her. Luciana wouldn't worry, that's what she was here for, but she did hate seeing Sam like this. Incapacitated. Angry. Reliant on others.

Sam struggled across the decking, but Luciana followed behind her. She may want to do this alone—that was perfectly fine—but Luciana would still be by her side. As Sam reached a stool at the breakfast bar, Luciana quickly sent off their address to Shannon. She couldn't be sure that Sam would like the idea of having Shannon here, but Luciana really needed some verbal interaction. The longer she spent writing out her words on a notepad, the quicker she would lose her mind.

"Um..." Luciana slid her phone into her pocket, scribbled on the notepad, and handed it to Sam.

I invited Shannon over. Is that okay?

Sam climbed down from the stool, her legs unsteady, and moved towards the staircase. If Shannon was coming over, Sam would lock herself away in the bedroom. What use was it sitting around downstairs? She couldn't exactly hold a conversation with Luciana's friend. They hadn't even met before, and that certainly wouldn't happen today.

"Babe?" Luciana called out, following Sam. "For the love of fucking God!" She gripped Sam's wrist, turning her around as carefully as she could. Luciana frowned, giving Sam a questioning look.

"What? You think I'm going to sit here while two *gorgeous* escorts talk about their latest plans?" Sam scoffed. "What planet are you on, Luce?"

Escorts? Sam had never referred to Luciana as an escort. Not since they became exclusive. While she wasn't embarrassed about her old profession, it still hurt. Did Sam still see her that way? *Wow.*

Sam gave Luciana a knowing look. "Don't look so surprised. Look at the state of me, Luciana. You think it's okay to invite people over who I don't even know while I look like this?"

Luciana lowered her eyes, nodding slowly. "Okay, fine."

"Stop talking to me!"

Closing her eyes for a brief moment, Luciana pinched the bridge of her nose. She hadn't thought this through. Sam had always taken pride in her appearance; of course she wouldn't like this idea. Instead of fighting with Sam, Luciana took her by the hand and guided her into the living room. Sitting Sam down, she took her phone from her back pocket and typed out a new message to Shannon.

L: I'm sorry. Change of plans. Sam isn't feeling too good. I'll catch up with you in a few days if you're free.

Luciana's phone buzzed as she set it down on the coffee table, but she could deal with it later. She'd made one foolish mistake and she accepted that, so now they moved forward.

Luciana powered on the TV, sat beside Sam, and kicked her feet up onto the coffee table. Sam remained silent, her bruised hand occupying the sliver of space between them. Taking it in her own hand, Luciana ran her thumb across Sam's knuckles, releasing a deep breath and allowing the soft leather of the couch to envelope her.

"I'm sorry," Sam said quietly. "I-I didn't mean to lash out at you."

Luciana simply nodded, remaining silent. There were two reasons for her silence. One, she didn't want to get into another discussion right now; and two, she didn't have the energy to get up and collect the notepad from the kitchen island. So long as Sam was comfortable, that was the only thing that mattered.

Sam's phone buzzed where it sat against her thigh, her eyes flickering closed as she focused on the TV, no sound reaching her ears. Luciana was beyond pissed with her—understandable—so she only had herself to blame for sitting alone. Perhaps it was for the best. Luciana deserved more than sitting in a house with nothing other than a toxic atmosphere. It wasn't as though Sam could entertain her.

Lately, Sam was useless to everyone. Herself included. Her plans once this project was in place and running smoothly involved taking some time off to relax, hopefully with Luciana. Now, she had no choice but to relax. While Sam loved a day off, she didn't want a forced day off. Or a forced month off. This wasn't how her plans were supposed to go.

Her phone buzzed again, reminding her that she had a message waiting. She lifted the handset, a message from Lindsay on her screen.

L: How are you feeling?

S: Sore. Tired. Uninterested in sitting around.

L: I know you hate sitting around. Please don't do too much, Sam.

S: I'm sure I'll live.

L: But we want you to heal.

Sam scoffed. How could Lindsay suddenly become her best friend again?

S: Really? Because for a moment, I thought you'd be happy to see me in this condition!

That was harsh. Sam was more than aware of it. Still, she found herself sending it without a second thought. Once again, her anger was prevailing.

L: I never want to see you hurt, Sam. I can't believe you would think otherwise.

S: We both know how you feel about me, Linds. Do yourself a favour and lay off contacting me. Don't pretend that

I'm the first thing on your mind. You and I know that's not the truth.

Tears pricked Sam's eyes. She hated fighting with her sister but sitting alone only meant her thoughts whirled around her head. Thoughts that predominantly included Lindsay's opinion of her.

Three little dots appeared beneath Sam's read message.

Then disappeared.

Sam shook her head, throwing her phone down on the couch beside her. Today had been one big huge success. First, she had pushed Luciana away, now it was Lindsay's turn. If she continued on this roll, Sam would be without *any* family by the end of the week.

She turned off the TV, turned her body towards the back of the couch, and sobbed. Not only for how she was feeling, but for what she knew she was losing. The woman of her dreams. Her family. Even the loss of her hearing paled in comparison to everything else. If Sam could wake up when this nightmare was over, she would choose that over living through it. Sam pulled the blanket from her feet and wrapped it around herself. Sleep. She needed to sleep. As she closed her eyes, her phone buzzing against the cool leather, Sam allowed tiredness to take over, her breathing beginning to even out. *I have to snap out of this.*

CHAPTER TWELVE

Sam glanced around, watching as her mother spoke animatedly to Luciana. She hated this, sitting around with no idea what was going on. This amount of downtime wasn't what she was used to; she couldn't begin to imagine it becoming a common occurrence. Sam wanted to work, come home, share dinner with Luciana, and relax. Not sit at home all day, attempting to lip read.

Luciana looked as though Susan was boring her to within an inch of her life—forcing a smile whenever Sam assumed it was the right time to do so. She appreciated that Luciana was accommodating her mum, but she really didn't have to sit around playing the good wife. If she had other things to do, Sam would be perfectly fine.

She sighed, allowing her head to fall back against the massive slouch chair she'd commandeered some two hours ago. Her ass was numb, her right side aching where it took the most impact from her fall, but she didn't have the energy to move. The last few days had quite literally taken all of the excitement out of her life. Okay, things hadn't been great between Sam and Luciana before the explosion, but Sam felt as though they could have been improving.

Slowly, yes, but improving, nonetheless. Sam's eyes landed on Luciana as she turned her head. She was watching Sam.

She offered Luciana a slight smile. It was all she could do. Her hearing didn't feel as impaired as it had the first half of the week, but everything was still a mess. She'd woken this morning to a piercing sound in her right ear, and now she was back to the whoosh she'd experienced the last few days. But that had to be an improvement, right? Sam could make out her mum's voice better, and the sound of her destroying the kitchen an hour ago, but it wasn't anything worth getting excited about. When she could hear Luciana fully, that would be when the excitement would kick in.

Sam's eyes switched to her mum. Susan was laughing. "Mum?"

Susan's eyes fell to Sam's.

"You do realise people died, don't you?"

Susan frowned.

"While you're sitting here laughing and joking...while *we* are sitting here drinking coffee, people died!"

Luciana got to her feet, removing the space between her and Sam. She understood her anger, it was completely acceptable given the situation she found herself in, but Susan was simply lightening the mood. Sam may not know that—she couldn't hear Susan—but Luciana was sure Sam's mum knew exactly what had happened down at the dock. The news continued to report it.

"Babe." Luciana took Sam's hand, reaching for the notepad on the coffee table.

Your mum is just helping us through the day. She knows how lucky we all are to have you sitting here with us.

Sam dropped the notepad to the floor, taking the blanket from the side of her and climbing to her feet. "I'm going outside for a while. This place is driving me fucking insane."

Luciana watched Sam walk with a little more ease than she had since before the explosion. Her balance was most definitely improving. As much as her heart burst with pride for Sam's recovery so far, Luciana still hated seeing her in pain. Unable to do much at all. She watched Sam take a seat at the unlit firepit, pulling her knees up to her chest.

Luciana glanced at Susan. "Should I go out to her?"

"That's entirely up to you, love," Susan said. "She may need some time alone."

"I feel as though she is constantly alone lately. And I know she's here with us, but it must feel lonely when you can't communicate."

"She's Sam. She'll never be alone."

Luciana appreciated Susan's comfort, but it didn't really help the situation. Sam was used to being so on the go, socially active, and now she was sitting alone by the lake with nobody around her.

"I think I'll go and sit with her for a while."

Luciana made Sam aware of her presence as she squeezed her shoulder. She sat down beside Sam, Luciana's hand instantly settling on her thigh.

"You really don't have to sit out here with me," Sam spoke quietly. "I really appreciate everything you've done for me, Luce, but you should head into the city and see friends. You'll only go insane sitting here, too."

Luciana wrapped her arm around Sam's shoulder, motioning for her to make herself comfortable. Sam could suggest leaving all she liked; it simply wasn't happening.

Sam nuzzled into Luciana's chest, holding her close. "I love you."

"I love you, too." Pressing a kiss to Sam's hair, Luciana was fully aware that Sam couldn't hear her own declaration of love. It didn't matter, though. Luciana would always hold Sam with pure love radiating from her. This morning wouldn't be any different.

Sam's phone buzzed in the pocket of her hoodie. She hadn't heard from anyone today—not even Lindsay—but she suspected her sister was still feeling the effects of their fight last week. And the one Sam, herself, instigated via text message. Right now, Sam couldn't care any less about what they'd fought about; it really didn't matter. Of course, she worried about Lindsay, she always would, but Luciana was right. Lindsay did choose to be with Janet and Sam had to accept that. She couldn't do any more than she had so far, and lately, she didn't want to. Lindsay had said what she needed to say. Sam would accept her opinion and move on.

Sam took her phone from her pocket, finding Cheryl's name on the screen. She'd briefly spoken to her yesterday with the help of Luciana, and her gut was telling her that this was about to be the backlash from her decision to cancel the build until further notice.

C: How are you feeling, boss?
S: I've certainly felt better. Enjoying your time off?
C: No. I'm still at the office.

Sam frowned. She'd told Cheryl to take some paid time off. It was useless being at the office if Sam wasn't there with her. After all, she was Sam's assistant.

S: Why are you at the office?
C: Dealing with the onslaught of abuse from your contractors.
S: What?

Sam's anger rose. How dare *any* of her contractors treat Cheryl that way. Sam knew it was because she wasn't around. None of them were usually this brave.

C: Paynter seems to think he can rule the entire thing because he has the most to lose in all of this. I don't think he realises that they never had the opportunity to ACTUALLY sign anything yet.
S: Paynter can do as he pleases. The build IS off.
C: And I told him as much.

S: Anything from anyone else?

C: Ruth from the accounts department of Gregson asked for your address. She wanted to send on some flowers to you. I told her to send them to the office and I'd make sure you got them.

S: That's sweet.

Sam smiled. It actually felt quite nice to hold a conversation with someone who wasn't in the house with her. It may be via text message, but she was taking what she could get right now.

C: Most of them have been. Some, not so much.

S: Let me contact them. I'll get back to you.

C: Sam, you have enough to deal with. Let me handle this. It's the least I can do.

S: I don't follow?

C: You told me I didn't need to be at the meeting on Monday. You effectively saved my life.

Sam hadn't thought about that. She hadn't had the time to think about it. It wasn't important, everything happens for a reason, but Cheryl's appreciation didn't go unnoticed by Sam.

S: Nonsense. I was just at the wrong place at the wrong time.

C: No. I ALWAYS go to meetings with you, Sam. I'm basically glued to your hip 90% of the day. You did save my life. So, thank you.

S: Wow.

C: Let me handle everything at the office. Call me when you can hear me, and I'll arrange to come over and visit you.

S: I'd like that.

Sam placed her phone down beside her on the couch, taking a moment to think about what Cheryl had just said. Had she saved her assistant's life? It didn't feel that way. Sam had simply told Cheryl to stay at the office, handling any calls that came in. Okay, Cheryl wouldn't usually be asked to take on that role, she was more than just a receptionist, but it was what Sam needed of her that morning.

Sam lifted her lukewarm coffee from the table in front of her, sipping it while she contemplated the strongly worded email she would soon send to Ben Paynter. Cheryl may *only* be an assistant to some people, but she had been with Sam for a long time. Cheryl had seen her through some of the toughest times of Sam's life; Lucia would appreciate everything she'd done.

And if it wasn't for Cheryl, I wouldn't have met Luciana.

That thought sunk in, shocking Sam. She had never thought about the fact that it was Cheryl who gave her the business card to Hush last year. Even though she felt embarrassed for taking it, for looking up escorts, Cheryl had, in fact, brought them together. *Oh, wow...*

Luciana stood at the kitchen island, swirling ice around in her glass. Sam had taken herself off to bed, Susan was *still* pottering around, and Luciana was about to pour one hell of a measure of scotch. She eyed the clock. 7:40 in the evening. The thought of climbing into bed appealed to her, but another sleepless night wasn't on the cards. No way. Sam could do without Luciana tossing and turning beside her; she really needed the uninterrupted hours to help her recover. So, Luciana grabbed her bottle of Macallan, took her glass, and headed for the couch.

The TV played low as she flicked through the channels. Spotting a football match that was about to kick off, she filled her glass, relaxed back, and lifted her feet onto the coffee table. This would take her mind off everything for a little while. So long as Sam was comfortable upstairs, and she was—Luciana had checked twenty minutes ago to find her snoring—she, herself, could relax.

"Luciana, love..."

"Yeah?" She looked back towards the kitchen, Susan was putting her coat on.

"I'm headed out, okay?"

"Okay." Luciana shot to her feet, seeing Sam's mum out of the door. She hoped she didn't look too enthusiastic, but she really had been waiting to wind down since around midday. "Sorry about today. Things haven't quite settled down yet."

Susan kissed Luciana's cheek. "Don't worry yourself about it. Sam will be okay soon."

"Hope so."

"If anyone can come back, it's my Sam. I'll be over tomorrow, okay?" Susan moved out onto the decking, her car keys jangling in her hand.

"Don't worry if you have things to do. We're okay here."

"I'll call you in the morning. Goodnight, love."

"Night, Susan."

Luciana closed the door, watching Susan back away from the house. She pressed a button to the side of the front door, alarming the house and lowering the shades on the floor-to-ceiling windows. Now that her and Sam were locked away, Luciana could truly unwind.

But then her phone started to ring.

"For the love of fucking God!" Luciana lifted it, accepting the call. "Hi, Linds. Everything okay?"

"Yeah. Just checking in with you. How's Sam?"

"Sleeping. Snoring. Still deaf."

Lindsay chuckled. "Mm. I always told her she snored. I even recorded her once and she told me it wasn't her."

"Mmhmm. She tells me she doesn't snore, too."

"So...I called because I think I ended things with Janet." Lindsay's voice held an element of relief. "She seems okay. I mean, she sounded upset when I called her and told her I needed some time with everything that's happened, but she hasn't shown up..."

"That's good."

"Should I be wondering if it's too good to be true?"

Luciana released a deep breath. "Honestly? I don't know." She was too tired for all of this. Sam was her priority, not fucking Janet Mason. But Lindsay meant a lot to her and while Sam couldn't defend her sister, Luciana would step in. "I think you should lock your door and if anyone calls, don't let them up."

"Well, that's filled me with hope."

"It's all I can offer you right now, Linds. If Sam was okay, I'd come and stay with you. But I really need to be here."

"No, I don't need you to stay with me. I'm perfectly fine here alone. I just wanted your opinion because I was under the impression that Janet would kick up a fuss."

There's still plenty of time for that. "She's probably looking for a new project since Sam cancelled everything at the office. Maybe you broke it off with her at the right time. She has something to distract her. You know, since she's a fucking child!"

"O-oh. She did?"

"She had to. She's in no fit state to work."

"No, I know." Lindsay fell silent for a moment. "I, uh, I was thinking about contacting Cheryl."

Luciana's lips turned upward. "Yeah?"

"But I don't know what to say to her."

"Just be honest. That's all you can do. If Cheryl wants to get involved with you again, she will."

"But what about Sam?"

"You really think Sam will fire Cheryl because she's dating her sister?" Luciana's brow creased. "I know you said Sam believes business should remain business, but you're not employed by her. You have no connection to the business whatsoever."

"I know. Just...worried for Cheryl."

"Trust me, Sam will be thrilled if you two get together."

"Maybe, I don't know." Lindsay cleared her throat. "Sounds like the match is about to start so I'll say goodnight and speak to you soon, okay?"

Luciana sensed that something was on Lindsay's mind. "Linds?"

"Y-yeah?"

"Is everything okay with you?" Lindsay fell silent. "Hello?"

"Has Sam mentioned me at all?" Lindsay's voice wavered. "About wanting to see me or needing me to come over?"

"She's been kinda moody today. She hasn't said much unless she was biting someone's head off. Usually mine. Occasionally your mum's."

"Right, yeah."

"Why don't you send her a text in the morning?" Luciana suggested.

"I already did that," Lindsay confessed. "Never mind."

Luciana's brows drew together. "And she didn't respond?"

"Oh, she did. Told me not to contact her. Something about how I should be happy she's hurt."

"Fucking hell." Luciana really needed to speak to Sam. None of this was healthy and something at the back of Luciana's mind told her that Lindsay was soon going to need the both of them. "She doesn't mean it, Linds."

"She won't even let me apologise. I've tried twice."

"I think once she's feeling better, she will want to see you."

"Hope so..."

"Call me if you need anything." Luciana really didn't want to play piggy in the middle, so Sam was going to have to get a grip of her attitude. This...it was all unnecessary.

"I will. Bye, Luce."

Luciana ended the call and threw her phone to the opposite end of the couch. Hearing footsteps descending the stairs, she glanced over her shoulder, finding a dishevelled Sam walking barefoot towards her.

Sam climbed onto the couch beside Luciana, pulling the thick fleece throw down from the back of the couch. Covering herself and Luciana's lap, Sam curled up against Luciana's body and held her tight. Luciana could only wrap her arm around Sam. It didn't appear that her girlfriend was in the mood for pointless conversation via notepad, so Luciana wouldn't bother. Sam was warm, snuggly against her. Sam was breathing…and that was what mattered.

CHAPTER THIRTEEN

Luciana rubbed her temples, willing the headache approaching to disappear. Sam's mum had been at the house for the last two hours, and Luciana's patience was beginning to wear thin. She appreciated that Susan was here to look after Sam—to help in many ways—but she hadn't stopped talking for the last hour. Luciana, in this moment, wished she was in Sam's position lying on the couch with no idea what was going on around her.

"So, as I said to Lindsay...I can stay with you two for as long as you need me to."

Huh? What? Luciana's heart stopped. Was Susan suggesting she stay over until Sam had recovered? No. That wouldn't work. Luciana didn't need it and Sam would deplore the idea.

"Then you can go to work as normal, love."

Luciana climbed down from the kitchen stool. She needed some time to herself. "Oh, that's okay. Work have given me as long as I need off, and I'm fine here looking after Sam."

"Then we will do it together." Susan beamed, catching Luciana by the wrist as she passed her by. "I'm glad she has you in her life."

"Yeah." Luciana didn't have the patience or energy to argue

with Susan. Five days had passed since the accident. Sam's overall health was improving, but Luciana wasn't sleeping. She hadn't since the first night at home with Sam. She was used to running on empty, but this was different. Every time she closed her eyes, she saw Sam lying lifeless on the floor. Luciana couldn't get to her, she couldn't fix her, but her body remained in a prone position...no signs of life. "I need some air."

"Okay, love. I'll see if our Sam needs anything."

"Right, yeah." Running her fingers through her hair, Luciana disappeared out onto the decking, slumping down in an over-sized chair.

She just needed a moment to herself. A moment when nobody was talking *at* her rather than *to* her. Susan belonged here, she was Sam's mother, but Luciana couldn't take much more. The headache medication she'd taken over an hour ago hadn't helped; her head felt as though it would explode before the afternoon was over.

Luciana glanced back through the window. Sam was still lying in the same position. Her tired eyes flickered open and closed as she focused on the TV; pointless daytime shows playing on repeat like a torture device. Sam was too sophisticated to watch daytime TV. She should be at the office working on her project. A project which had been cancelled until future notice. Luciana knew how upsetting it was for Sam to have to cancel; she knew how much deadlines meant to her girlfriend, but Sam was alive and that's what Luciana focused on.

Resting her head back, Luciana sighed, focusing on the sky above her. Cloudy. Grey. Miserable. Kinda like their life right now. Sam was still angry—short with Luciana whenever they woke beside one another—but it would pass. It had to.

As tiredness started to take over, Luciana revelled in that weightlessness she often felt as she was going to sleep. A weightlessness she hadn't experienced since before the explosion. She smiled and closed her eyes. *Just five minutes and I'll be good to go.*

THE CALL

"Where's Luce, Mum?" Sam stood at the kitchen island, grey yoga pants covering her legs, a white sweater hanging from her shoulders. "Mum?"

Susan turned around, pointing towards the staircase.

"Is she sleeping?"

Susan shrugged.

"Okay, well I'm going up for a few hours." Sam didn't wait for a response from her mum, turning and taking the spiral staircase slowly. She missed Luciana. She wanted to be in her arms while they snuggled in bed together. It didn't matter that the sun was shining outside; Sam was ready for cooler evenings. Luciana was avoiding her, Sam knew that, but she was feeling more positive this afternoon. Her late morning nap had been the best she'd had in a while.

As Sam approached the open bedroom door, she heard mumbling. It was clearer than what she'd been able to hear yesterday, but Luciana didn't know her hearing was improving. She wasn't keeping it from her for the sake of it, Sam simply didn't want Luciana to get her hopes up. Because that's the first thing that would happen. Luciana would be beside herself with happiness, while Sam wouldn't feel so much joy. She was thrilled to be able to hear—even if it was dulled—but she wasn't recovered yet. So, the party could wait a while. The last five days had been hard for them both, but as Sam moved closer to the door, hearing Luciana's voice settled her.

"No, I'll talk to her," Luciana said, Sam straining to hear. "You're okay?"

Who the hell was Luciana talking to?

"Okay, well if you need me just call. Leave Sam to me."

Sam's eyebrows rose, the cut to her head tight as she pushed the door open slowly. Luciana smiled fully, unaware that Sam had heard her conversation.

"I have to go. She just came in here."

Sam folded her arms across her chest, staring blankly at her girlfriend.

"God, I hate seeing her like this." Luciana continued to smile. "It's heartbreaking. I'll talk to you soon."

Sam moved towards the bedroom window, wrapping her arms around her body as she did. Luciana was hiding something from her, she had to be. The issue Sam faced right now was that she didn't want to get into another argument with her. She felt Luciana approach, her hand settling on Sam's shoulder.

"Who was on the phone?"

Nothing.

Silence.

Sam turned around to find Luciana scribbling on the notepad.

Lindsay. She was asking about you. She wondered if she could come over?

"We haven't really spoken about what happened..." Sam shrugged.

That could be because she knew you had more important stuff going on.

Sam shrugged, wishing Luciana would speak to her. Use her voice. *I should tell her.* Sam desperately wanted life to feel better. "We should talk. I was a complete bitch to her a couple of days ago when she texted me. She tried to apologise but I wouldn't listen. Well, I *couldn't* listen, but you know."

Luciana attempted to write something down, Sam's hand stopping her as she placed it on her wrist. "Don't."

"B-bu—" Luciana frowned.

"Talk to me. I need to hear your voice." Sam took the notepad from Luciana, throwing it to the bed. "Come closer and talk to me."

The confusion in Luciana's eyes was apparent. The little frown line between her eyebrows had always been cute to Sam, but she wanted to put her girlfriend out of her misery.

"Luce..."

"I-I..." Luciana narrowed her eyes, moving closer and dipping her head towards Sam's ear. "Marry me."

Sam's heart pounded. Had she heard Luciana right? She couldn't have. Surely not. Sam stepped back, focusing on Luciana's soft features. Her intense blue eyes. They had life back in them. "S-sorry, what?"

Luciana stepped forward, her fingers curling under Sam's chin. Tilting her head back, Luciana smiled into a kiss. "I said...marry me."

Sam's bottom lip trembled as Luciana's forehead pressed against her own. When Luciana looked at Sam how she was in this moment, Sam would give her the world. In a heartbeat. When everything else fell away and only Luciana remained in front of her, Sam could drop to her knees. "I-I."

"Please." Luciana's eyes begged Sam. "Please, be my wife."

Sam's forehead creased. Why was she even thinking about her answer? "Y-yes."

Luciana's eyes widened. "Yes? You actually mean that?"

"I mean it."

Luciana lifted Sam, forgetting momentarily that she was likely to still be in pain from the explosion. Sam didn't appear to care as she wrapped her legs around Luciana's waist, her arms around her neck. "Babe..." Luciana paused, kissing Sam hard. "God, I love you."

"I love you, too. And I'm sorry. For lashing out at you," Sam whispered against Luciana's lips.

"Don't ever be sorry. You've been through a lot. I'll always be here for you." Luciana lay Sam down on their bed, kicking the bedroom door shut before joining her. Her body screamed at her for sleep, but she was too hyped right now. Sam had just accepted her spontaneous proposal; there was no chance of coming by sleep any time soon. Luciana lay beside Sam, their fingers entwined as she took her hand. "You can hear me?"

"It's not great, but yes. I can hear you."

"Since when?"

"Yesterday afternoon, it started to come back," Sam explained. "I just didn't want to get your hopes up in case it didn't stay that way."

"I can't believe you can hear me." Luciana's voice broke. Every morning when she woke, she prayed Sam would feel better—that she would *be* better. She always believed Sam's hearing would one day return, but this soon? She hadn't expected it. "How are you feeling?"

Sam focused on the ceiling above her. "Tired...but so in love."

Luciana shifted closer, sharing Sam's pillow. "I'd do anything for you, babe. All I want is for us to be happy. I *need* you to be happy."

"I'm happy. And once I'm back to normal, life will be good again."

Luciana knew she needed to discuss Lindsay with Sam, but was this moment the right time to do so? The quicker it was out of the way, the more chance of Sam and Lindsay reconciling. "Should I call Lindsay?"

"Can you ask her to come over tonight?" Sam asked. "When Mum has gone?"

"Oh, uh..." Luciana chewed her bottom lip. "About that. Your mum thinks she's staying over until you're better."

Sam sat upright, shaking her head. "Nope. Not in a million fucking years."

"Babe. Relax." Luciana tugged her back down beside her. "She will still be here later. There is no rush to explain that we don't need help."

"I don't want her to get comfortable. And when you talk... could you talk a little louder, please?"

"Yes, darling." Luciana smirked, focusing on Sam's eyes as she turned on her side and faced Luciana fully. "Anything else you need right now? Meds?"

"Sleep," Sam said, aware that she'd only woken up a few hours ago. The more she slept, the sooner this nightmare would all be over. "And then when we wake up, you can tell me all about that phone call to Lindsay."

"W-what?"

"You asked her if she was okay. And the only reason I'm not worried right now is because you're lying here and not rushing out the door like a bat out of hell."

"I promise. I'll tell you everything she said to me. You don't need to worry." Luciana kissed Sam's nose. "Have I told you how beautiful you look today?"

Sam closed her eyes, smiling. "Mm. Have I told you how much of a liar you are today?"

"Rude."

"But true." Sam pulled Luciana closer, wrapping her arm around her waist. "Now, sleep. I know you haven't been getting any."

Luciana breathed slowly; her body relaxed as Sam lay beside her. The proposal a couple of hours ago really had been unexpected, but Luciana didn't regret it. A year on from meeting Sam, how could she possibly regret it? Sam was her entire universe. She would always come above everything else in life. Asking Sam to marry her may have come as a shock to them both, but Luciana was ready. She had been since the moment their eyes met at the tapas bar.

Luciana did have concerns as to whether Sam would still feel the same way once she woke, but she was trying not to dwell on it. Right now, Luciana was just thrilled to have her girlfriend—her fiancée—on the mend. And Sam could hear her voice once again. She hadn't anticipated Sam's hearing to come back so soon, but this had to be a positive step in her recovery. The days of worrying could now be forgotten; Luciana just had to find some sleep from this moment on. She couldn't fully function without it and that was becoming more apparent as the days passed. If Sam was healing, Luciana had to be on her *A* game. Her fiancée deserved someone fully present.

"What time is it?" Sam stretched, her body once again curling around Luciana.

Luciana glanced at the clock, her arm wrapped around Sam's body and pulling her closer. "Almost four."

"What time is Lindsay coming over?"

"I didn't confirm a time with her. I was a little busy planning to make you my wife."

Sam's eyes fluttered open, slightly brighter than they had been recently. "Mm. You were. I remember."

Luciana cleared her throat, shifting on the mattress.

"What is it?" Sam noted the apprehension in Luciana's eyes. She could read her like a book. "Baby?"

"I know I sprung it on you, but you do want this, don't you?"

"A proposal from you?" Sam's eyebrow rose. "Of course."

"I mean, I don't want you to think that you have to give me an answer right away. We've both had a shock recently—you more so —so I understand if you need to take some more time to think about it. I won't be offended."

"Have you quite finished?"

"Y-yes."

"To be honest, I never expected you to propose. I didn't think I could ever be that lucky. But you did and I'm so happy about that."

"But, Lucia—"

"Is my past." Sam lifted her hand, caressing Luciana's cheek. "She will always be a part of me, and I'm thankful that you acknowledge that. I'm thankful that you accept my past...but this is another stage of my life, Luce. You—you're my future."

"You're sure you want another wedding? Another marriage?"

Sam's eyes fluttered closed, her lips curling upward. "I am. I'm ready for anything with you."

"I feel like we've been a bit distant lately..."

"I'm sorry. None of this was supposed to happen. The explosion. Janet coming back. Working with her and then cancelling my project."

"But you're healing. You can get back to your project soon, can't you?"

"No, I can't," Sam said. "I just...I want to take some time off."

Luciana frowned. "Why? Is everything okay?"

"I need to make some decisions." Sam sat upright, leaning against the headboard. Her mind swam with thoughts, anxiety settling deep in her belly. An anxiety she wasn't sure she would shake any time soon. "I could have died on Monday."

"I know." Luciana's voice broke. Just thinking about this last week sent a shiver through her entire body. "But you didn't."

"Still. I want to take some time away from the business. To relax, you know?"

"I mean, if that's what you want to do..."

"I think it's for the best." Sam couldn't recall the last time she put an out-of-office on her email account, but the possibility sat well with her. "I've been so stressed lately. I've taken it all out on you, and you don't deserve that."

"Please don't do this because you think I want you to." Luciana mirrored Sam's position. "I understand how busy you are, babe. I support you fully in everything that you do."

Sam side-glanced at Luciana. "Then I'd like you to support me in this decision."

"Of course. Anything you want." Their hands found their way to one another, lacing together like a perfect fit.

"You and I both know that I could stop working tomorrow. We're set for life."

"You're thinking about leaving the business behind?" That idea shocked Luciana. Sam loved her work—her career—but

Luciana would stand by whatever decision she made. She had to. "Seriously?"

"When I was laying in that hospital bed the other day, I considered it," Sam confessed. "If I hadn't gone to that place earlier, I wouldn't be lying here with you now feeling like absolute shit."

"Babe, it's going to get better."

"I know, but this could have all ended differently." Sam searched the lake from the bedroom window. She had many decisions to make, but for the time being, a break from the office was good enough. "I don't know how I feel about that yet."

"Did you want to talk about it? You know I'm here if you're struggling."

"I'm struggling with the idea that I may not have seen you again." Sam lowered her eyes, a tear slipping down her face. Whenever she thought about leaving Luciana, her heart shattered all over again. "Because I wouldn't have been ready for that. To lose one another when we're only just truly getting to know each other. To love each other completely."

"I get that."

"And I don't even have funeral plans in place, you know?" Sam cleared the emotion from her throat. "I'd have left you completely in the dark. I mean, my business and everything else…I haven't even set up paperwork to state it belongs to you if I die."

"Babe."

"That stuff should be in place. I've been through it; I know exactly what should already be in place. Lucia and I had it all planned out, and even though I didn't think the time would come when I had to look into life insurance policies and the paperwork that comes with death, it did, but we were prepared. You and I, not so much."

"I just want you. I don't care about the rest."

"Well, you should." Sam faced Luciana fully. "If I die, I want you to have everything you could ever need. I want you to know that if you ever wanted to quit your career, you wouldn't ever have to work again. If you decided to travel the world, that would be more than possible for you."

"Sam..."

"I could have died this week and you would have had to fight the powers that be for this place."

"So long as I have you by my side, everything else is irrelevant."

"No, it's not." Sam climbed from their bed, moving towards the window. "I have to call my lawyer."

"F-for what?"

"To add you to everything I own," Sam said, nonchalantly. "If I ever leave you behind, I want everything I have to be yours."

Luciana's stomach lurched. Why was this even a discussion this afternoon? Sam was recovering and was going to be perfectly fine. On the other hand, she understood Sam's concerns. If she had already been in that restaurant when the explosion happened, Luciana *would* be preparing for Sam's funeral. That was pretty much set in stone.

Sam turned to face Luciana. "As it stands...with everything Lucia left me and my own accounts, I'm worth around seventeen million. When that time comes, it won't bring me back, but it'll certainly give you a good life."

Luciana felt her breath quicken. Her chest beginning to heave. "S-seventeen million?"

"Give or take, yes."

"Wow."

"It's mainly tied up within the business and whatever else I have in the works, but there will be a substantial amount for you."

"Sam, look..." Luciana climbed from the bed, only a black racerback and boy shorts covering her body. "I understand that all of this has freaked you out, but you're not going anywhere." She closed the distance between them, wrapping her arms around Sam's body from behind. "Trust me. You're never leaving me."

"Anything is possible, Luce."

"Agreed, but what happened on Monday was a freak accident."

"Perhaps." Sam sighed, her head falling back on Luciana's shoulder. "I'd still like to be sure that we have all of our things in order."

Luciana didn't know where to begin with anything Sam had said since she woke up. Seventeen million was an amount Luciana wasn't sure she'd ever spoken before, but it wasn't important to her. So long as she had Sam by her side and they were earth-shatteringly in love, she didn't care. She pressed a kiss to Sam's ear, smiling as Sam relaxed fully against her.

"Please don't let this eat you up. You're here and going to be okay."

"If you truly believe that, why have you spent the last four nights lying awake?"

Luciana stilled her movements, wishing Sam hadn't brought up her lack of sleep. Not only did it make Luciana feel as though she had failed to control her own issues, but Sam had other things to worry about. She knew Sam would lie awake with her and that wouldn't do.

"I'm getting plenty of sleep."

"No, you're not." Sam turned in Luciana's arms, smiling faintly. Luciana could argue all she wanted to; they both knew Sam was right. "You look terrible, Luce."

"Thanks."

"You have to look after yourself. While you're not at the station, you should try to catch up on as much sleep as possible."

"I need you to be okay first."

"I *am* okay. I've been sleeping right through."

"Yeah, I just like to be ready in case you wake up," Luciana lied. "In case you need anything."

"The medication they gave me is strong enough to knock out a horse. There is no chance I'm waking in the night."

Luciana closed her eyes, breathing slowly and deeply through her nose.

"Talk to me..."

"I'm just struggling at the minute," Luciana admitted. "But, it's nothing for you to worry about."

"Wrong answer, beautiful." Sam guided Luciana back towards the bed, sitting her down on the edge. "Please, sleep...for me."

"I've been asleep," Luciana continued to lie. "I've just been napping with you."

Sam snorted. "That's a lie."

"Please, just leave it. It's not important."

Sam simply nodded. She could see that Luciana had things on her mind, but it would be better discussed this evening when it was just the two of them. Susan had it in her mind that she would be staying over, but Sam didn't need that. Now that her hearing was improving, she wanted Luciana to herself.

"Okay. I'm going to take a shower and then I'll explain to Mum that she isn't needed here."

"She's going to insist that she stays."

"Don't worry about her." Sam leaned down, kissing Luciana. "And can you call Lindsay? Tell her tomorrow would be better for coming over."

"You're sure?"

"I just want to lie on the couch with you tonight...if that's okay?" Sam's lips lingered, pressing another kiss to Luciana's mouth. "Maybe we could rent a film?"

"That sounds like the perfect night, babe." Luciana hummed, her eyes closing. "But could you do me one favour?"

Sam nodded. "Anything..."

"Don't tell your mum I proposed just yet. I want to buy you a ring first."

Sam's eyes sparkled for the first time in a while. "You're too sweet. You and I will go shopping together. How does that sound?"

"Sounds great."

Sam reluctantly released Luciana's hand, backing up to the closed door. "Please, get just half an hour's sleep..."

"Okay."

The sound of laughter on the TV provided a barrier between Luciana and her thoughts. Today had thrown a whirlwind of emotions at her; she hadn't truly had the opportunity to sit back and dissect it all. But it didn't matter, not this second. Sam felt good against her body, Luciana's arms holding her safely as they relaxed into the soft leather couch together. Susan had thankfully left without much of a fuss—she too was just happy Sam was recovering—and Lindsay understood that Sam wasn't feeling like much visitation from people. Luciana did have to reassure Lindsay that it wasn't to do with their falling out, but she couldn't be certain Lindsay believed that. Understandable, but it could be dealt with tomorrow.

Luciana sighed, the intoxicating scent of Sam's shampoo creating a peaceful vibe around their home tonight. If Luciana closed her eyes, it felt as though nothing had happened this week. No injuries. No Janet to be concerned with. No heartbreak. If Luciana blocked out the mental images she'd been faced with lately, everything this evening was perfect. As it should be. The problem was, she couldn't block out the images. However hard she tried, they crept back to the front of her mind.

Without thinking, Luciana's mouth started to move. "I see you," she said. "Lying on the floor. Not breathing. Covered in blood."

Sam held her breath momentarily. What was she supposed to say to that? How was she supposed to comfort Luciana when her dreams could have been a reality?

"And I can't save you. I can't even get to you." Luciana breathed deeply through her nose. "When I do manage to fall asleep, I wake up in a cold sweat. And you're next to me, sleeping peacefully."

Sam turned in Luciana's arms, their face inches apart. "Hey. I'm here. Right beside you."

"I know that." Luciana smiled distantly. "But when I'm sleeping, you're not. You're dead, Sam. Gone. And then I freak. I don't know the kind of funeral you'd want. I don't even know the kind of casket I'd pick."

"And I went and said those things to you today. Talking about death and paperwork." Sam lowered her eyes, feeling guilty for adding to Luciana's stress. Of course, her fiancée hadn't shown any signs of discomfort during their previous conversation—she was a trooper like that—but Sam knew it had to hurt. "I'm sorry."

"I just...what if I'd lost you on Monday?"

"You didn't."

"But I could have, Sam. I could be sitting here now packing things into boxes and picking out an outfit to wear to your funeral."

Sam had nothing to offer. Luciana's face was a picture of complete heartbreak. In this moment, Luciana was a mirror image of Sam those years ago.

"I asked you to marry me earlier because I can't allow either one of us to ever leave this earth without being one another's wife. I can't ever say goodbye to you without having that connection between us."

"You won't ever have to." Sam caressed Luciana's cheek, her thumb ghosting across her lips gently. "I want nothing more than to be your wife, Luce. And I know this isn't ideal, what we've faced recently, but look at us. We're here together, in one another's arms."

"I know."

"Don't ever think I wouldn't fight to stay alive for you," Sam whispered. "You always tell me you will come home to me, that you'd fight to be with me, and I'd do the same. I'll *always* come home to you."

"Promise me?" Luciana's blue eyes shone, stealing Sam's breath. "I really need you to promise me."

Sam feathered her fingertips across Luciana's cheek, her eyes smiling. "I promise, baby."

"I could spend my life lying here with you. Just looking into your gorgeous eyes."

"That's the plan. That's always the plan."

As much as Luciana wished she could get comfortable for the night, she still had Lindsay's situation to explain. Sam would want to know what was going on. She also had every right to know the facts.

"Babe, I needed to talk to you..."

"About what?"

"Janet and Lindsay."

Sam groaned, shaking her head and nuzzling into Luciana's body. "Not tonight."

"Bu—"

Sam's eyes found Luciana's. "No. Please. Tonight is just about us. I don't want to hear *her* name, okay? And we can discuss Lindsay in the morning."

Luciana soothed Sam, running her fingers through her dark hair. "Okay. Tomorrow then."

CHAPTER FOURTEEN

Luciana continued to fold laundry into the correct piles on the dining room table, a light breeze flowing through the slightly ajar bi-folding doors. Sam was upstairs dressing for the day, but Luciana had been awake since the birds began to chirp. She was used to early mornings; being at the station on an early meant she was usually heading out the door around six-thirty. This was a welcome change, though. At almost eight a.m., she'd already gotten done what she would usually tackle after a lie-in.

Sam appeared to be sprightlier this morning, the colour coming back to her beautiful face, but Luciana still wanted her to take it easy. *Of course, she is taking it easy. She's basically walked away from her business for the foreseeable future.* Luciana wasn't sure how she felt about that. Sam without her business would be a huge adjustment to them both.

Luciana wouldn't broach the subject, only willing to discuss it if Sam brought it up in conversation. She meant it when she told Sam she would stand by her decision, but she wouldn't encourage her to step away from the office. Honestly, Luciana wasn't sure it was the right decision. She would be bored, irritable. Sam's empire kept her going from day to day. At one time, it had been all she lived for. To walk away from something like that, even if just for a short period of time, had to bring uncertainty. Luciana would be lying if she said she hadn't thought about spending more time with her fiancée, though. Of course it was what she wanted most. Being away from the station until Sam was back to full health—knowing Sam wouldn't be at the office—appeared to now be guaranteed.

A knock at the door pulled Luciana from her morning laundry duties. Nobody was due, not this early. She dropped the pair of shorts in her hands and moved towards the front door. When she opened it, she found Lindsay. Luciana had seen her looking better, a fear now settling in the pit of her stomach. Lindsay's eyes were tired, dark circles beginning to take hold. Her shoulders looked as though they had no more life in them. Lindsay appeared to have no energy left inside her.

Luciana dragged Lindsay inside. "What's happened? D-did she hurt you?"

"No. But she does keep calling me."

"Right, okay. Block her number." Luciana had to think on her feet. Janet would linger, there was no doubt about that, but if she couldn't contact Lindsay, perhaps she would let her be.

"I have. She just calls me from different numbers."

Luciana didn't like where this was going. Back when Janet was her client, she would continuously call, to the point where Luciana would answer just to appease the woman. If she was doing the same thing to Lindsay, it certainly had Luciana's back up. In that moment, Luciana knew Janet hadn't changed. She couldn't possibly.

"Just don't answer it," Luciana said, locking the bi-folding doors. "Did you come in the car?"

"No, I'm having trouble with it. I got a cab."

"Good. Okay."

Lindsay swallowed hard. "What do you mean good? S-should I be worried?"

Luciana leaned back against the wall, running her fingers through her hair. "Honestly? You should always be worried when Janet's around."

"Okay, I don't like this." Lindsay instinctively wrapped her arms around herself. "What the hell have I got myself into?"

"You'll be fine here," Luciana replied. "I promise you."

"Where's our Sam? I don't want her worrying about this. I should go…"

Luciana took Lindsay's hand. "No, you shouldn't. Come on. Have a seat and I'll get Sam. You can fill her in."

"I'm not explaining all of this through fucking pen and paper, Luce."

"She can hear you."

"Who can hear you?" Sam appeared from the staircase, moving into the open-plan living space. "Me?"

Lindsay gasped. "Oh, my God. Your hearing is back?"

"It is. Getting better by the day."

"More like by the hour, babe." Luciana smiled fully, taking a moment to forget about Janet and encourage her fiancée. "It's really improved."

"Mm." Sam nodded, sitting down and bringing her knees up to her chest. Her hand found the scabbed cut on her forehead. "Just need this to disappear now."

"You're still gorgeous." Luciana shrugged.

"She's right. You are," Lindsay agreed. "And I'm so happy you're feeling better, Sam."

"Thanks."

Lindsay cleared her throat. "Before we go any further…I wanted to apologise. For the things I said to you."

"Okay." Sam sat upright, nodding.

"I am, Sam. I'm so sorry for how I behaved." Lindsay lowered her head, focusing on her hands in her lap. "I never meant any of it. You must know that."

"I was shocked," Sam said. "I never thought you of all people would ever say something like that to me or Luciana."

"I was confused. Angry that Janet could do something like that."

"And I suddenly changed your mind?" Sam quirked an eyebrow. As much as she loved her sister, Sam wasn't sure she could simply forget about the things Lindsay had said. More pressing issues had occurred since that evening and Lindsay's slanging match, but Sam needed time to adjust to everything around her. "Why?"

"Babe," Luciana cut in, "Lindsay needs to talk to you. She needs both of us right now."

"She's hurt you." Sam shot to her feet, clasping her hands behind her neck as she paced in front of the window. "I'll fucking kill her. I warned her, Luciana. I warned her that night I met her. She knows what will happen, but I swear, I'll kill her with my bare fucking hands."

Luciana stopped Sam's pacing, placing her hands gently against her chest. "No, you won't. Please, sit down. You're still recovering."

Sam gritted her teeth. "I'm fine. I just need to find her."

"Sam," Lindsay started. "She hasn't hurt me. Not yet."

Sam frowned, taken aback by her sister's comment. "N-not yet? You mean, you believe what we told you?"

"I had a real conversation with Luciana the evening we brought you back from the hospital. I wanted to tell you, but you had no hearing and had just been blown halfway across the dock."

"Okay, I'm listening." Sam held up her hands, calming her breathing. Maybe she hadn't been the world's best sister lately, but Lindsay was also guilty of that.

"Janet hasn't hurt me, I promise you." Lindsay motioned for Sam to sit down beside her. Sam obliged, taking her sister's hand. "I explained to Luce the other night that Janet didn't like the idea of me around other women."

"What other women?"

"W-we went out to the bar." Lindsay cleared her throat. "While we were there, Cheryl showed up."

"Janet knows Cheryl. She's just a jealous bitch."

"Me and Cheryl..." Lindsay explained. "We had a thing a while back."

Sam shot Luciana a look. Instead of being angry that she didn't know, Sam simply smiled at her fiancée. Luciana had told her repeatedly that Cheryl and Lindsay had something between them, but Sam refused to listen.

"Sorry, babe." Luciana shrugged. "I did try to tell you."

"Did you know all along?" Sam's brow drew together.

"No, but I had an inkling. Linds only told me Monday night when we got home."

"Right, okay."

"Anyway, we're getting beyond the point here," Lindsay interjected. "Janet knew I'd dated Cheryl in the past. She freaked out and told me I wasn't to see her again. She got really controlling about it, and I didn't like it."

"You're not to see *her* again," Sam said with a tone that wouldn't be argued with. "I know you're old enough to make your own mistakes, Linds, but I'm taking this one into my own hands. I'm sorry."

"S-she knows."

"Knows what?"

"That I don't want to see her anymore," Lindsay said. "She won't stop calling me. I didn't know what to do so I came here. I'm sorry for showing up so early, but I think she's going to come to my apartment soon."

"She knows where you live?" Sam pinched the bridge of her nose, the thought of Janet Mason truly injecting herself back into their lives weighing heavy on her mind once again.

"Of course she does."

"Well, this is one fucking huge mess." Sam held her head in her hands. She didn't need a headache to go along with her already throbbing body. She could definitely do without a migraine today. "You're staying here until she fucks off back under her rock."

"Or, we could just call the police," Luciana suggested. "I know it's only going to bring trouble with it, but if it keeps Lindsay safe…it's our best bet."

"She hasn't actually done anything wrong, though." Lindsay sighed. "So, wouldn't that be a waste of time?"

"She did wrong the moment she stepped into my space, Linds. I have an injunction out on her for a reason. It's also part of the terms of her suspended sentence."

"Suspended for how long?"

"Two years." Luciana moved into the kitchen, preparing a pot of fresh coffee. "Right, let's sit down and figure this out together. If we come up blank, I'll call the police."

"She's going to come after you if you do that, Luce." Sam followed Luciana, taking her hand as it trembled against the marble kitchen counter. "And I know you want to do the right thing, but I'm not at full health so I don't know how much use I'll be." Sam's pulse picked up, tension building in her shoulders. She was no use to anyone in this condition.

"I don't want you to worry about a single thing, Sam." Luciana pulled her close, wrapping her arms around Sam's body as she pressed a kiss to her hair. "This isn't your fight. Let me handle it."

"You're the woman I love," Sam said, her voice firm. "It's *always* my fight."

Luciana rocked Sam as they held one another, soothing her worries momentarily. "Not this time, babe. Lindsay will be safe here with us. Janet wouldn't dare show up here again."

"She's been here?" Lindsay asked. She appeared anxious, twisting her watch around her wrist repeatedly. "When?"

"Before the explosion. She basically came to ask for Sam's blessing to date you."

Sam snorted. "That woman will do as she pleases. She had no intention of following anything I said."

"She also came to tell Sam that she wouldn't cause any trouble while they worked together on the new build."

Lindsay's eyes widened. "Y-you were going to work with her. Why? I thought you wouldn't agree to it."

"Because while I kept her busy, she couldn't hurt you."

A sudden anger rose within Luciana. "I wish she'd been the one going into that restaurant. I wish she'd been the one left injured."

Sam smiled, kissing Luciana softly. "You don't mean that. You're so much better than wishing someone ill."

"No, I do mean it." Luciana's tone harsh, she exhaled a deep breath and stepped back. "Then I wouldn't be sitting here worrying about you. I wouldn't have sleepless nights and—"

"Hey. We talked about that last night. I'm not going anywhere."

"I know." Luciana nodded. "I know."

"So, you make the coffee and I'll check the CCTV is running as it should be. If she shows up here, we're going to need all the proof we can get. The moment her tyres hit that gravel, I'm calling the police."

Luciana grinned. "God, I love you. My little detective."

"I love you both." Lindsay rounded the island, pulling Sam and Luciana into a group hug. "And I'm so sorry I doubted anything either of you told me."

"It's forgotten about," Sam said. "But in future, listen to your sister. I've been around long enough to know things you don't."

"I promise."

Sam watched Lindsay fidget with the cuff of her shirt. Neither knew where to begin with conversation, but Sam really was tired of sitting around in silence. Her hearing was back, much improved, so why did she feel as though it wasn't?

Was Lindsay too worried to talk to her? Probably. After all, Lindsay had reached out twice since Sam's accident, but Sam shrugged her off. Now that life was slowly improving, they both owed it to one another to try and work through their differences.

Sam chose to break the silence first. "So, you and Janet are over?"

"Yeah."

"And this thing with Cheryl?"

Lindsay slowly found Sam's eyes. Sam couldn't quite gauge the reaction to her question, but it had clearly provoked some kind of emotion inside Lindsay.

Lindsay shrugged. "It was nothing."

"If it was nothing, why did you tell Janet about it?"

"It just slipped out in conversation. She wanted to know why Cheryl was dancing with me."

"So, it was just a fling?"

"I'm sorry." Lindsay shook her head, a tear escaping her eye as she did so.

"For what?"

Lindsay exhaled a long, deep breath. "Getting involved with Cheryl."

Sam frowned. Was Lindsay honestly worried about what Sam would think? "You think I care if you and Cheryl were together?"

"She's your assistant. It's unprofessional, I know. I should have come clean sooner."

"Unprofessional..." Sam allowed her reply to linger in the air for a moment. Lindsay wasn't on Sam's payroll. She wasn't employed by the business. Even if she was, Sam wouldn't have asked her to end it. She was her sister; Sam wanted her to find happiness. If that was Cheryl, then so be it.

"Yeah. Unprofessional."

"For who exactly?"

"Just for everyone concerned." Lindsay's shoulders sagged. "I didn't want Cheryl to get into any trouble, so we ended it. It was going really well, too." Lindsay's lips curled into a small, sad smile. "She was really great. Nothing like Janet."

Sam's heart broke for her sister. "Linds..."

"But we moved on. Cheryl is off and on with the woman she was dating last year. If she's happy, I'm happy for her."

Something in Lindsay's tone led Sam to believe that she was talking complete rubbish. Lindsay's eyes always gave away the truth and as she looked into them, nothing about Lindsay looked happy for Cheryl. If anything, Sam saw devastation.

"I didn't want Cheryl to lose her job."

"She could have been my business partner and I wouldn't have asked you to call things off with her."

"W-what?" Lindsay sat forward on the couch, focusing fully on Sam.

"Lindsay, I know how hard it is to find someone who you love and trust completely. I know that at any given moment...life can be taken away from you. Do you really believe I would ever stop you from dating someone you really had a connection with?" Sam may have been contradicting herself, but Janet and Cheryl were two completely different people. "Do you?"

"I-I don't know."

"Wow." Sam seriously needed to change her ways if that's what Lindsay believed. She wrinkled her nose. "Really?"

"I see how stressed you are at work. How much you want to be anywhere other than at the office. I just thought that if you knew Cheryl and I were dating, you wouldn't like it. You need her to be fully there. Her mind focused on work."

"That's why you stopped coming to the office last year..."

"I just thought it was best for everyone," Lindsay confessed. "Every time I walked through those doors to see Cheryl sitting at her desk, I questioned if I'd made the right decision. I couldn't even look at her without wanting to kiss her."

"Call her."

Lindsay offered her sister a pathetic smile. "No."

"Please, Linds? Call her."

"Sam, she wouldn't want to be with me now. I'm the one who broke it off. I'm the one who slept with her one final time and then asked her to leave my apartment the next morning. She's spoken to me once since that day…at the club when I was with Janet. So I'm pretty sure she hates me."

"I don't think anyone could ever hate you."

Lindsay sneered. "*You* hate me."

"No, I don't." Sam took Lindsay's hands in her own, pulling her closer. "Listen to me, okay? If you want to be with Cheryl, you call her. Show up at her place. Do something to show her you're interested."

"I think it's best left in the past." Lindsay climbed to her feet, clearly no longer willing to discuss what could have been. "Did you want me to make myself useful while I'm here?"

"You could take me to the office while Luce has a bit of downtime if you wanted to?" Sam hesitated as soon as she asked. Was it the wisest idea in the world to leave the house? Surely Janet didn't have the balls to show up here. As far as Janet was aware, she'd caused a rift between Sam and Lindsay. "What do you think?" Sam asked. "How pissed off is Janet?"

"Convenient how you want to go to the office now that you know about Cheryl…" Lindsay rolled her eyes. "And Janet? I don't know that she *is* pissed off. The last time I spoke to her, I told her I needed some time alone. That I'd called her once I was feeling up to things again. I kinda may have used your accident to get her off my back.

"She wouldn't stop calling and it was all I could think of, I'm sorry. I'd originally told her I wanted to see less of her, that it was too much too soon, but I think she believed me the second time around. You *had* just been blown up. It wasn't like I was lying."

Sam smiled. "Whatever works to keep her away from you. So, the office?"

"It's just...Cheryl, you know?"

"She won't be there. The place is shut down for the foreseeable."

"O-oh." Sam noted the disappointment in Lindsay's eyes. It was unmistakable. "Okay then."

"But for the final time...call her."

Luciana watched from the other side of the room as Sam and Lindsay got caught up on life. Seeing this pleased her—they were sisters and never should have fallen out—but she did have that slight panic at the back of her mind.

Janet *would* come looking for Lindsay. It was inevitable. Luciana could only hope that she didn't show up here. Sam needed peace and calm, not Janet all guns blazing at the front door. While she felt a familiar worry that always came with Janet Mason's name, Luciana also felt strong. Certainly stronger than the last time around. Janet had always brought out a weakness in Luciana, but this time, she had a true reason to fight. For family. This no longer *only* involved Luciana; it was now so much bigger.

Luciana toyed with her phone, twirling it through her fingers. She should call the police. As she pondered that thought, her eyes focused on an invisible spot on the floor, a barefoot Sam approached.

"Lindsay is going to drive me to the office for some things."

Luciana got to her feet. "No, let me go for you. I could do with some fresh air."

"So, go and sit on the terrace. I'm okay. I'm feeling good today."

"Are you sure it's a good idea for Lindsay to be out while Janet's trying to contact her?"

"We can't hide away. And Lindsay isn't sure Janet quite knows what's going on yet."

Luciana's forehead creased. "What do you mean?"

"She told Janet she needed some space after my accident. You think she bought that?"

"Possibly. I don't know." Luciana couldn't be sure of anything that involved Janet.

"We won't be long. If Janet knew Lindsay was lying and that she was here, she may have shown up by now. But I don't know if she has the audacity to after everything that's happened this year."

"You're probably right." Luciana was satisfied that everyone would be okay. Sam was only going to the office; Janet wouldn't cause a showdown in public. And Luciana could lock herself away in the house if she didn't feel safe. Then, there was also the opportunity to call the police. "If you're sure? About the office?"

"I'll be an hour, maximum."

Luciana accepted defeat. "Okay, but you'll call me if anything happens? Or if you don't feel too good?"

"I'll come straight home if I don't feel good." Sam beckoned Luciana closer, planting a firm kiss on her lips. "You don't mind Lindsay staying over?"

"Of course not."

Sam reached the front door, sliding a pair of Converse on as she threw her keys to Lindsay. "Ready?"

Lindsay smiled. "Always."

"See you both later." Luciana waved Sam and Lindsay out, closing the door only when they were safely inside Sam's car and backing away from the house.

She lifted her phone, dialled a number, and waited for the call to connect. Janet's time was up. It should have been weeks ago.

"Hi, I'd like to report breaches of an injunction."

THE CALL

The sun warmed Luciana's face as she reclined on a slouch chair, not a soul in sight. These kinds of days were what she lived for. If only Sam were here, too. She'd called her fiancée twenty minutes ago, but Sam and Lindsay had gotten waylaid on the way home. Explaining that she wouldn't be much longer, Luciana was satisfied that they were both safe.

It shouldn't be like this, Luciana was well aware of that, but Janet Mason would soon be out of their lives for good. Luciana had contacted the detective on her case around thirty minutes ago and was content that they would look into her accusations. The Lindsay situation couldn't be monitored—nothing untoward had happened—but Janet *had* breached the conditions of her suspended sentence. Luciana didn't need the police to explain that to her, but it still left her feeling marginally positive about the outcome. She couldn't be sure they would find her any time soon as Janet always had a knack for knowing when to lay low, but the moment she surfaced, they would be on her back.

Luciana crossed her legs at the ankles, clasping her hands as she rested them behind her head. This truly was the life, especially after the week she and Sam had been subjected to. If she was being honest with herself, she didn't imagine for a moment that Sam would be out with Lindsay just short of a week after her ordeal, but Luciana should have known better. Sam was the strongest woman she'd ever met. No explosion was ever going to keep her down for long. Just satisfied that they could talk to one another again, Luciana relaxed her body, praying she could drift off to sleep without any interruptions from her mind creating worst-case scenarios.

The sound of a car approaching further relaxed Luciana. Sam was home, but the sun on the skin of Luciana's face felt too good. She would remain here a while longer; Sam would call her inside when she needed to. Luciana hummed along to a made-up tune, her lips curling upward as the engine cut out and gravel crunched beneath shoes.

"Where is she?"

Luciana froze, her entire world falling away around her. That wasn't Sam's voice. It also wasn't Lindsay's.

"Don't fucking ignore me!" The scent of Janet's familiar perfume drifted towards Luciana, her throat drying as the seconds passed. Nope. Not happening. Janet was mistaken if she thought for one moment that Luciana would take this attitude. This woman seriously had to go.

Luciana sat upright, breathing through the fear that tore through her. Janet was nothing to her. She never would be again. The moment Luciana showed her fear, Janet would play on it. In this moment, she had to remain strong. She had to be the woman she should have been last year.

"Can I help you?" Luciana glanced up at Janet, her raven hair longer than usual but her eyes as black as ever. "You shouldn't be here."

"Where is she?"

Luciana's forehead creased. "Who? Sam? Didn't you know she's delayed the build?"

"I'm not here looking for Sam and you know that." Janet crossed her arms, a lame attempt to insert her dominance over Luciana. She was failing miserably.

Luciana got to her feet, no longer feeling fear. As she looked into Janet's dull eyes, she actually felt embarrassed for ever allowing this woman to treat her the way she had. "Am I supposed to be a fucking mind reader, Janet?"

"Excuse me?"

"You're asking where *she* is, but I don't know *who* she is..."

"You really ought to lose that tone, sweetheart." Janet stepped closer, her eyes scanning every inch of Luciana's body. "I don't think you realise who you're talking to."

Luciana laughed sarcastically. "Ah... Big Bad Janet Mode. I see."

"Where the fuck is Lindsay?" Janet clenched her jaw.

"No idea."

"Don't bullshit me!" Janet lunged forward but Luciana moved out of her way, sending Janet onto the chair.

"Oops."

"You're really beginning to push your fucking luck!"

"Oh, I think that would be you," Luciana said. "You forget that you're *not* supposed to be here."

"You think some silly piece of paper is going to keep me away from you?"

"I thought you were looking for Lindsay?" Luciana knew she was riling Janet up, but it was more fun than she'd anticipated. "Make your mind up."

Janet cleared her throat, climbing to her feet and brushing her suit jacket down. "Do you honestly think Lindsay is my type?" Janet smirked, her mouth barely moving for the amount of Botox it held. "Why would I want her when I can have you? You know how much I enjoyed my time with you…"

"Mm. Because you could beat the shit out of me."

"I wish you wouldn't say that," Janet breathed out, inching closer to Luciana. "You know I care about you. I always will."

"Care? Someone like you could never *care* about another human being."

"First you ruin my life. Then you turn my girlfriend against me. And now insults?" Janet's eyebrows rose, the vein in her neck pulsing like it often did when she was angry.

"You deserve more than insults," Luciana spat. This woman was incredible. Not only did she have the nerve to show up here, but she honestly believed she hadn't done anything wrong. "Have you thought that maybe Lindsay left you because she just doesn't like you?"

"You told her about my past. You had no right to do that."

"I have every right. Do you really think I'd sit back and watch you ruin her? Like you tried with me?"

"I *loved* you."

Luciana shook her head. "No. That wasn't love, Janet. That was destruction. Pain. Abuse."

"Oh, and what you have with Sam is better than what I could give you?"

"Better?" Luciana's brows rose with surprise. Could it be considered better? No. What she had with Sam was life changing. "It's worlds apart from what I had with you. You disgust me; you always will."

Janet smirked, stepping painfully close to Luciana. "Is that so? Because I can ruin you all over again if you want this to play out that way." Janet suddenly lifted her hands, gripping Luciana by the neck. "Don't fucking test me. You're still the whore you once were, and I'll show you that."

"Fuck. Off." Luciana struggled to breathe, Janet's thumb pressing against her windpipe. "Get your fucking h-hands off me!"

Janet leaned in closer, smirking as her breath washed over Luciana's lips. "I'm going to fuck you in the bed you share with your girlfriend. Over and over and over…"

Luciana saw red, unbridled rage taking over. Without a second thought, she whipped her head back and then forced it forward, connecting with Janet's face. Janet hit the floor, holding her nose as blood dripped between her fingers.

"I don't think you understand." Luciana stood over her, ignoring her throbbing forehead. "I'm not here for you to fuck around with anymore. I'm also not your sex toy." She shoved Janet out of her way with her foot, laughing. "Touch me again and I'll do more than break your fucking nose. Your legs will be next."

Janet scoffed, gingerly rising to her feet. "Assault. You've just assaulted me."

"You're lucky to still be breathing." Luciana backed away. "And Sam isn't my girlfriend. She's my *fiancée*."

"S-she…what?"

"If you could leave our property, that would be fucking fantastic." Luciana continued to back up the decking. Her heart racing as adrenaline coursed through her, she wasn't sure if she was about to collapse with exhaustion. "Oh, and smile for the camera on your way out." Luciana offered Janet a wink, coupled with her middle finger. "The police will be in touch."

"It's your word against mine," Janet spat.

"You were the one stupid enough to come here." Luciana chose to rile Janet up just a little more. She was certain she wouldn't ever see this woman again, so why not make this meeting worth her while? "I thought you were smarter than that. Seems you're beginning to lose your touch."

"Fuck you!"

"Oh, no." Luciana's smile beamed, the image of blood dripping down Janet's face strangely *and* worryingly satisfying. "Fuck *you*."

CHAPTER FIFTEEN

Lindsay pulled up outside Sam's place, cutting the engine and handing the keys back over to her sister. Offering Lindsay a genuine smile, Sam climbed from her Range Rover, feeling settled as the day wore on. Settled, but tired.

Today had to be the first time she'd done anything remotely taxing on the body; just a simple walk through town knocking the wind out of her sails. Things would improve—life would get better—but she wasn't used to this. Lounging around every minute of the day, exhaustion setting in before mid-afternoon. Sam was used to being on the go twenty-four-seven. This was a huge adjustment. One that she was willing to take slowly.

"So, are you sure about putting the business on hold for the time being?" Lindsay asked as she rounded the car, linking her arm through Sam's. "I mean, what will you do with yourself?"

"Nothing at the moment. Get myself back to one hundred percent."

"You were nervous walking around town today, weren't you?"

"I was that obvious?" Sam rolled her eyes, shaking her head. "Don't tell Luciana."

"Don't you think she should know?" Lindsay asked. "If you have anxiety about it, she really should."

"Why?"

"Because what happens the next time she offers to take you out to lunch and you pass on it? If you tell her you don't feel good about being out in crowds or around town, I'm sure she will understand."

"Luce has her own stuff going on at the moment."

"Like what?"

Sam stopped at the decking. "She's not sleeping. I think last night was a little better, but she still tossed and turned for most of it."

"Sorry to hear that." Lindsay's eyes lowered to the decking beneath her feet. She frowned, crouching down. "What's that? Blood?"

"What?" Sam's heart rate shot up, her chest tightening. "Is it? Are you sure it's blood?"

"It looks like it. I don't really want to touch it…"

Sam tugged her keys from her pocket, rushing towards the door. When she opened it, the place was silent. No whoosh from the dishwasher, no sound from the TV. No sign of life or Luciana. Everything remained as it was a few hours ago, the laundry piles still on the dining table. It didn't bother Sam, but it wasn't how Luciana would usually leave the place. She always tidied things away before she went out anywhere. Sam glanced back at Lindsay.

"What is it?"

"Luce's car is on the drive, right?"

"Certainly is." Lindsay closed the door, following Sam.

"So, she didn't go out," Sam said, setting her keys down on the kitchen island. "Luce? You home?"

Sam heard a groan coming from the couch. "Mm? Sam?"

"Baby, what are you doing face-down on the couch? You should have gone up and lay on the bed."

"My head is pounding." Luciana cracked one eye open, rolling over and falling to the floor. "Ow, shit!"

"Oh, shit." Sam rushed around the couch. "Come on. Let me help you up."

"Sorry." Luciana clambered back onto the couch. Though she may be thrilled about Janet and standing up to her, Luciana couldn't get rid of the headache it had caused. *That's what happens when you headbutt someone, Luce.* "Babe?"

Sam gasped. "What happened to your face? And why is there blood on the decking?"

"Oh, I'll hose that away in a bit." Luciana winced. "And what's wrong with my face?"

"Well, you have a little bruising coming up above your eyebrow." Sam's eyes landed lower, focusing on Luciana's neck. "L-Luce..."

Luciana rubbed at her forehead. "Mm?"

"S-she's been here, hasn't she?" Sam's voice trembled. The thought of Luciana being alone with Janet here terrified her. "Luciana?"

"She's gone now."

"What happened?" Tears fell freely from Sam's eyes. "Did she hurt you?"

"Kinda," Luciana answered. "But I gave just as good as she did."

"Huh?" Lindsay appeared, taking the other side of the couch.

"Hey, Linds."

"Luce, what happened?" Lindsay's face was a picture of confusion. "Why do you have bruises on your neck?" She narrowed her eyes. "Oh. They're...handprints."

Luciana took her fiancée's hand. "Sam. I, uh...I broke her nose."

Sam's heart swelled. She shouldn't feel good about someone hurting another woman, but God, she did. She suddenly felt better than she had all week. Her only wish was that she could have been here to witness it. Sam couldn't hold back the smile curling on her lips.

"She just...she wouldn't leave. She went back to her old ways. You know, threatening me and telling me things I didn't need to hear."

"Mmhmm." Sam tried to contain her happiness. Luciana was clearly struggling with what she'd done. The least Sam could do was pretend she wasn't happy.

Luciana rolled her eyes. "Then she choked me. Original as ever. I just couldn't let her get away with it again. I'd already called the police when you two left earlier. I didn't expect her to show up here, though."

"Baby, I'm so proud of you." Sam pulled Luciana against her, massaging her scalp as she relaxed against Sam. "So proud."

"I warned her, Sam. I told her not to touch me again. The anger I felt. I could have happily beaten her to death."

"But you didn't. Instead, you defended yourself."

"Still. That anger didn't feel good." Luciana sat up, pulling her hair up on the top of her head. "It didn't feel good at all."

"Did you call the police again? Update them?"

"Yes. I've left the CCTV disk on the unit by the door. They said they'd need a copy. I've also emailed a digital version over."

"What does this mean for Janet?" Sam asked. "Not only did she breach the conditions of her sentence, but she assaulted you, too."

"It's looking like prison time for her." Luciana climbed to her feet, straightening herself out. She needed to wash the day off her, even if it could only just be considered the afternoon. "Do you mind if I go and shower?"

"Of course not." Sam stood, taking Luciana's hand and guiding her towards the stairs. "Hey," Sam spoke quietly. "Are you okay? Do you need to see someone?"

"No, I'm okay."

Luciana disappeared up the stairs leaving Sam at the bottom, watching her. Lindsay remained seated on the couch. Sam assumed she was taking all of this information in. Lindsay may have believed the things they'd told her, but that didn't mean she was expecting this. Sam had hoped that Janet had changed, but as with everything in life, her gut had never let her down before. This time wasn't any different.

Sam sat on a stool at the kitchen island, her head in her hands. Since Luciana had taken herself upstairs, a million and one thoughts had whirred around in Sam's head. How could she have been so stupid, leaving Luciana here alone when Janet was on the prowl? How could Sam have ever thought that Luciana would be safe? Yes, she had defended herself when the time came, but it never should have happened. Janet shouldn't have ever had the opportunity to get inside the grounds of their home.

The more Sam thought about it, the stronger she felt about the fact that this was her fault. While she was protecting Lindsay, she had opened Luciana up to more hurt. A hurt she was never supposed to be subjected to.

She felt tears approaching, unsure if she could genuinely hold them back. Sam felt as though she needed to cry. Everything appeared to be overwhelming of late, nothing ever going right when Sam thought life could be returning to normal. Would this set everything back with her and Luciana? Would Luciana choose to go back on her proposal? As much as Sam would understand if that did happen, she wasn't sure she could take the rejection. Luciana asking Sam to be her wife meant more than she could have anticipated, but now it was potentially ruined. Sam had vowed to protect Luciana. Now, she had failed monumentally.

"You look like you could use a hug." Lindsay gently placed her hand on Sam's shoulder, encouraging her sister to meet her eyes.

"Everything is falling apart, Linds..."

"What? How?"

"Luciana. Us. I feel like everything is going to turn to shit."

"You and Luciana are fine. The same goes for us, too." Lindsay pulled a stool closer to Sam, taking a seat beside her.

"I wasn't here to protect her, Lindsay. After everything that happened last time, I promised her Janet wouldn't ever hurt her again."

"How could you know that Janet would show up here?"

"Because I should have known. I know exactly what that woman is capable of. Instead of being here, I was in the office collecting pointless shit from my cabinet."

"You really shouldn't blame yourself, Sam." Lindsay's thumb softly stroked Sam's knuckles. Soothing, but not quite making everything better.

"You didn't see the state she was in last time." Sam lowered her eyes, the image of Luciana bruised and beaten flashing through her mind. "You didn't hear the terror in her voice when I got to her apartment. Linds, I didn't know what to do. I didn't know how I was ever supposed to help her. She looked like a frightened child."

"Sam…"

"And when I tried to touch her, hold her…it was heart-breaking." Sam whimpered, her tears falling freely down her face. She could never forget that day, no matter how hard she tried. "I didn't know it was possible to see so much pain in someone's eyes, especially not someone like Luce, but God! Lindsay, you have no idea."

"I wish I could have been there for you both."

"It just wasn't something Luce wanted people to know. I'm sure you can understand that."

Lindsay squeezed Sam's hand. "Of course."

"You remember telling Mum that you thought something was going on? When she showed up worried?"

"Y-yeah." Sam knew Lindsay still felt guilty about that day, they rarely spoke about it.

"That was the reason I'd been so distant. It was the same time as everything happened with Janet."

"I'm so sorry." Lindsay's voice cracked.

"I'm not telling you that to make you feel guilty, but now that you know about Janet, perhaps you can understand why. Maybe now you can see why I wasn't around much. I needed to be sure Luce was okay. She wouldn't even go to the police. Or the hospital."

"I understand completely."

Luciana's phone started to ring on the island, buzzing against the cool marble.

"It's the detective who originally worked the case."

Lindsay climbed down from her stool. "You should answer it. I'll give you some privacy."

"H-hello?" Sam's heart plummeted into the pit of her stomach.

"Miss Foster?"

"No, Detective Clarke, it's Sam. Luciana is taking a shower. Is everything okay?"

"Janet has been arrested," Detective Clarke said. "We found her at the hospital. Luciana really did fight back."

"Luciana won't be arrested, will she?"

"Miss Mason did try to suggest that she had been assaulted. We have to pass it on to the CPS, but it looks cut and dried from our side. Luciana was simply protecting herself. Given Janet's background with Luciana, we don't see any reason for her to be brought in for questioning. It looks like self-defence from the CCTV footage I've seen, too. Luckily, that will help matters."

"Okay." Sam breathed a sigh of relief. "So, what now?"

"Miss Mason will likely see out the rest of her sentence behind bars. We will be pushing for additional time for the breach of injunction and recent assault. Her anger management self-referral clearly didn't do much for her."

"Thank you."

"Luciana really should have called us when Janet first showed up at the club."

"I-I know." Sam felt partially to blame for that, too. She should have pushed Luciana to call it in. Hell, she could have done it herself. "Hindsight, huh?"

"If we require anything else, I'll be in touch."

"Thanks, Detective Clarke." Sam felt a weight lift from her shoulders. "I'll pass on everything you've told me. I think Luciana just needs some time to herself for now."

"Understandable. Take care, Sam. Goodbye."

"Yeah. Bye."

Sam slowly placed Luciana's phone down on the island, focusing on the screen as it dimmed before locking. Janet was in custody. That had to mean something. As much as Sam wanted to climb the stairs and hold Luciana—tell her everything would be okay—that phone call didn't quell the fear in her belly that Luciana may walk away.

To Sam, this was entirely her fault. *I should have called the police the second Janet showed up.*

Luciana sat on the edge of the bed, popping two paracetamols into her mouth. Sam had given her space, but now she was ready to move forward with her life. Janet wasn't a part of it—she was never supposed to be—so now they could forget about her once and for all.

Luciana would be lying if she said she hadn't shocked herself earlier today. Her reaction to Janet. How she willingly hurt another woman. It went against everything Luciana believed, but was needed at the same time. The last time Janet attacked her, Luciana ended up in bed with her, but now? That behaviour wouldn't work anymore. It simply couldn't. Luciana had Sam and an entire future ahead of her. If Janet Mason thought for one moment that she could disrupt that, she was sadly mistaken.

Luciana heard footsteps approaching and set the glass of water in her hand down on the bedside table. She looked up at the open door, smiling when Sam appeared with damp hair that had been pulled up atop her head.

"Hey."

"How are you feeling?" Sam asked.

Luciana stood up. "I've been better, I won't lie."

"I thought maybe we could order in tonight? I don't have the energy to cook and Lindsay is going home to Mum's now that Janet has been arrested."

"Lindsay should stay here a while longer. The detective I spoke to earlier didn't know how long it would take them to track Janet down. It's...just for the best, Sam."

"Didn't you hear what I said? Detective Clarke called your phone a little while ago," Sam explained with a small smile. "They have her, Luce. She's in custody now."

"O-oh." Luciana was taken aback by that knowledge. Janet really was losing her touch if she'd been caught up with so soon. "Well, okay then."

"You seem unsure about today..." Sam didn't want to get into this, but she should. If Luciana was about to take her proposal back, Sam needed to prepare herself for losing her.

"I broke her nose, Sam." Luciana looked pointedly. "Of course I'm going to have mixed feelings about it."

"And that's all it is?"

"I don't know what you mean."

"I just...I feel like this is all my fault, Luce. You've been busy looking after me; perhaps you let your guard down. I shouldn't have taken Janet on for the project. I also should have just called the police the moment you told me Janet had been at the club. That in itself was one hell of a warning sign."

"I also chose not to call the police, Sam. I could have, but I didn't."

"Why didn't you?"

"Once I knew she was around Lindsay, I didn't want to come across as meddling. She has an injunction from me, Sam, not anybody else. As much as I hated her and as much as I didn't want her around, Lindsay means a lot to me. She's your sister and I didn't want to interfere with her relationship."

Sam blinked and shook her head slowly. "You put yourself in danger for Lindsay."

"And I'd do it again if it meant she was happy."

"I tried to encourage Lindsay to contact Cheryl. She won't do it."

"Funny. I told her to contact her, too."

"Great minds, huh?" Sam relaxed against Luciana, enveloped by her arms.

Luciana pressed her lips to the tip of Sam's nose, smiling. "The greatest."

"Come on. Let's go downstairs and relax before we order the world's biggest Indian banquet."

"That actually sounds really good." Luciana's stomach growled in agreement, Sam rolling her eyes as she guided her fiancée out of the room. "How are *you* feeling, babe?"

Sam yawned, taking the stairs slowly. "Tired."

"You had quite the day. You should probably relax for a few days. I don't want you doing too much and burning yourself out."

"I'm feeling relaxed," Sam said. "I'm more concerned about you at the minute."

"Oh, don't be. I'll be fine."

"You know, I really hate it when you say that." Sam followed Luciana into the kitchen, taking a glass from the cupboard and filling it with water. "I know you like to be the strong one, but it's not necessary around me."

"I don't follow."

"This. Pretending that everything is fine. I know it's not, Luce. Just be honest with me."

Luciana frowned. "I don't know what you want me to say. I mean, you saw the CCTV. There really isn't much for me to explain. Unless you had something specific in mind."

"You want the truth?" Sam pulled herself up onto a stool, facing Luciana fully. "I think you feel bad. I think you feel guilty for hurting Janet, when, really, you were defending yourself. There is a reason you haven't been arrested, Luce."

"I know, but it doesn't make how I feel any easier. I've never hurt another person, Sam."

Sam scoffed. "We both know Janet deserved it."

"That may be true, but it doesn't mean I have to like what I did." Luciana glanced at the clock, realising she had somewhere to be. "Would you mind if I went out for a couple of hours? While Lindsay is still here?"

Sam studied Luciana's face. "If you must."

"Just...I had something I needed to do. I won't be long and then we can order that Indian you mentioned."

"Sure, yeah. Take your time." Sam climbed down from her stool, choosing to allow Luciana whatever space she needed. Sam didn't particularly like the idea of Luciana leaving right now, but she also wouldn't keep her here. Not if Luciana would prefer to be elsewhere. "See you whenever you're back."

Luciana appeared behind Sam as she flopped down on the couch. "Hey, I'm not avoiding you. I just really do have something I needed to do."

"What?"

"Nothing for you to worry about."

"Secrecy?" Sam glanced back, her brow arched.

"No, not at all." Luciana really didn't want to explain right now. If she had any hope of her plans actually *going* to plan, she really needed to leave soon. "Look, I'll be back soon. Nothing is going on and I'm fine. But, thank you for caring."

"I love you. Of course I care."

Luciana squeezed Sam's shoulder. "A couple of hours, okay?"

"Okay."

Luciana lifted her phone from the console between herself and the passenger seat. She had a call to make, and then she would get to the real reason why she was sitting alone at a graveyard. She hadn't wanted to leave Sam alone earlier but knowing Lindsay would hang around a while longer meant that Luciana didn't have to worry. It meant she could sit here—alone—contemplating this last week. A week which had brought about a brush with death, hearing loss, a sudden proposal...and Janet Mason.

It felt like too much for one couple to handle, but they were. Luciana and Sam were more than handling it. At least, Luciana could lie to herself and pretend she was handling everything life seemed to be throwing at her lately. Truth be told, Luciana wasn't sure how much more she could actually take. It was a lot to bear.

She pressed the call button sitting below a familiar number, bringing the handset to her ear and waiting for the call to connect.

"Luce?"

"Hey, I got it." Luciana relaxed back in her seat, lowering the volume on her radio.

"Is it the right one?" Shannon asked. "The woman in the store said you'd called up at short notice. She was kinda bitchy but whatever."

Luciana closed her eyes, her heart no longer hurting for the pain she inflicted on Janet earlier. "Oh, yeah. It's definitely the right one. Thanks for dropping into the store for me earlier. They wouldn't hold it without a cash deposit. I'll transfer it back to you when I get home."

"Any time. I hope it all goes well for you. Call me if you need anything, okay?"

THE CALL

Luciana couldn't repay Shannon for the help she'd given her today; it really did mean the world. They may not see each other as often as Luciana would like, but Shannon was always there.

"Thanks, Shan. I should go. I have something to do before I head home to Sam."

"Everything okay?"

"It will be, yeah." Luciana reached for the handle on the door, pulling it and exiting her car. She wouldn't stay here too long—it wasn't her place to do so—but she felt compelled to come here. She had for a few days now. "Shan, I have to go. I'll speak to you soon. And, thanks again for today. I really appreciate it."

"Anytime. Bye, Luce."

Luciana crossed the short grass-verge, passing by a bench as she approached Lucia's grave. She'd thought about coming here alone once or twice in the past, but something always got in the way of it. Luciana wasn't sure how Sam would feel about her visiting her wife's grave, but Sam didn't seem to mind whenever they spoke about Lucia. And Luciana made it a habit to ask about her. She didn't ever want Sam to think that she couldn't talk about her deceased wife.

Luciana crouched down, brushing the freshly cut grass from Lucia's marble gravestone. It was in impeccable condition, Sam always made sure of that, but Luciana would keep it as clean as possible for her own sanity. If she did her bit while she was here, she would feel marginally better about showing up to Sam's wife's grave without permission.

A wave of sadness coursed through Luciana, her eyes welling with tears.

She blew out a deep breath. "Hey, so you don't know me. I'm, uh...Sam's partner. Girlfriend, whatever." Luciana may be talking to a gravestone, but she still wasn't sure how to address who she was. "I've never been here alone before. I didn't think it was appropriate, but I'm hoping Sam won't mind. She's great like that." Luciana got to her knees, fixing the arrangement of flowers in front of Lucia's full name and her birth and death details. "I guess I wanted to thank you for bringing Sam into my life, f-for allowing me to love her. I probably should have thanked you long before now.

"It wasn't easy in the beginning; she couldn't see past her heartbreak. But in time, things got better. I promised I'd look after her, and to an extent, I did. Just…the last week has been pretty hard. Sam…she was in an accident."

Luciana cleared her throat, squeezing her eyes shut in an attempt to stem the flow of tears. Would she forever be reminded of the call? The thought and the image that played in her mind of Sam, dead?

"I thought I'd lost her, Lucia. When I received the call, I truly believed that I wouldn't see her again. And I don't know what I would have done." Luciana couldn't believe she was kneeling here, talking to a gravestone, but she was. "So, I asked her to marry me. She lost her hearing and I panicked. I want to marry Sam, of course I do, but I need her to know that I don't ever expect her to forget who you are. I don't want her to think less about you. I'm not trying to replace you. You were her wife…and one day I hope I can make Sam as happy as *you* made her.

"I know you were her one true love, but if I can just have a tiny slice of what you both had…that's enough for me. Just the ability to love her is enough for me. I mean, I didn't even give her a ring when I proposed so I'm already failing, but I have it here. Safely in my pocket. It may never mean to her what yours did, but I'm going to try to make her happy, Lucia. I have to."

Luciana climbed to her feet, aware that she likely looked odd talking to nothing and nobody. "If you could just give me a sign…a blessing…it would mean the world to me." Luciana moved towards Lucia's gravestone, placing a kiss to the flat top of it. "Thanks for listening. I can see why Sam enjoys coming here."

She backed away, her hands in her jacket pockets. Startled

when her phone rang, Luciana took it out and answered the call. "Hi, babe."

Sam sighed. "Is everything okay? I'm worried about you."

"Everything is fine. I'm coming home now."

"Okay, because I kinda did something." The line remained silent, only Sam's light breathing telling Luciana she was still on the line. "Just...did you call the station and tell them you could go back to work?"

"No, why?"

"I thought perhaps we could go away for a few days."

"That sounds great, babe. I'll have a look online at some places when I get home." Luciana reached her car, unlocking it with her fob. "Anywhere you have in mind?"

"Actually, yes," Sam said. "Lucia's parents have a cottage in The Dales. I've just spoken to her dad. He said it would be fine for us to go."

Luciana glanced back at Lucia's grave, smiling. "Yeah?"

"I thought with everything that's happened lately, especially today, we could use some time alone. Just you and me..."

Luciana closed her eyes, relief washing over her. "I'd love that, Sam. I'd really love it."

"Okay, well I've already started packing. You can grab whatever else you need once you get back and we will leave in the morning. It's only a couple of hours away."

"I love you, you know." Luciana always told Sam how much she loved her, daily, but she wasn't sure Sam could begin to conceive just how much. This love...it was everything.

"I know. I love you, too."

CHAPTER SIXTEEN

Sam fumbled through the set of keys in her hand, stopping when she came across the one with a purple top. She hadn't been to the cottage in about two years, but it felt good to be back. It appeared completely different this time around. Luciana was apprehensive, of course, but Sam didn't have any connection to Lucia here. She never had. This place meant as much to Sam as it did to Luciana and that was very little. Sam had merely used it as a getaway when the city became too much. The surroundings were tranquil, absolute beauty. With nothing around other than rolling green hills, masses of lavender in places, Sam felt content here. Given half the chance, if she didn't have the home she already did, she would move to The Dales in a heartbeat.

Sam pushed the front door open, offering a thankful smile when Luciana took care of their luggage. They didn't have a date when they would be leaving the cottage, so Sam had simply packed everything and anything they may need. Luciana didn't appear to mind; she'd been wanting to go away for a while now. Okay, it wasn't sun, sea and sand, but it was still a million miles away from what they'd faced this week.

Sam couldn't actually believe that it had only been a week since the explosion. She felt wary at times, especially when she'd gone into the city with Lindsay, but she knew she was safe here. She didn't have to worry about being thrown across a pavement. This cottage was her safety.

"Wow, gorgeous place." Luciana moved further inside, wheeling the rest of their bags in. She had an idea that the cottage would be gorgeous, everything involving Sam usually was, but the rustic feel to the place was ideal. Autumn was approaching, the fields around them ready for rain following a scorching summer, and the trees Luciana had spotted on the drive up to the cottage were already beginning to change colour. Some still green, quite a few yellowing, and a handful with that burnt orange look. "It's very homely."

Sam approached the patio doors and sighed. "Isn't it?"

"Why didn't you and Lucia live here?"

"Lucia never came here," Sam said. "Her parents bought it after she died."

"Oh."

"It wouldn't have been her kinda thing anyway. She preferred the modern look. Not all this oak and open fireplaces. Rugs and worn leather couches."

"I really love it." Luciana took it upon herself to get better acquainted with the cottage, moving around freely. The kitchen was huge, potentially housing the country's biggest island with a gigantic range cooker freestanding against the outside wall. "Mm, I can't wait to spoil you with dinner."

"Oh, and what exactly are you cooking?" Sam asked. "You didn't bring last night's left-over takeaway, did you?"

"Ew. No, I did not. I also took the liberty of throwing it away before we left. God knows why you kept it." Luciana wrinkled her nose, shaking her head as she took the bags of shopping from beside her luggage. They'd stopped off at a supermarket on the way, Luciana choosing to bring everything they could possibly need. Cinnamon rolls, she had them. Fresh vegetables, those too.

Wine, beer, chocolate. She had everything Sam could ever possibly want during this stay. The reason for her coming out with two carts of shopping? Luciana didn't want to leave the confines of this cottage until they had to. If she could leave her job and become a recluse here, she would. Without a shadow of a doubt.

"So, you're really going to cook for me?" Sam perused the ingredients Luciana was setting out on the island, impressed with the array of choices.

Luciana feigned offense, placing her hand against her chest. "You make it sound like I've never cooked for you before."

"No, I didn't…I didn't mean it like that." Sam rounded the counter, pulling Luciana against her. Being here alone and away from the world was already beginning to feel like the ideal way to spend their time. "I'm looking forward to this, okay?"

Luciana pressed a kiss to the tip of Sam's nose, running her fingers through long, dark hair. "I know. I am, too."

"So, what did you feel like doing?"

"Honestly…nothing."

"So, that's a no to the hot tub outside?" Sam quirked an eyebrow.

"What? There's a hot tub?" Luciana's blue eyes brightened, her smile widening as she pulled Sam away from the island and towards the patio doors. "Holy shit! There is."

"Mmhmm."

"Let me put all this stuff away and then that baby is ours."

Luciana sunk down into the water of the hot tub, bubbles soothing her immediately. Sam relaxed beside her, handing a glass of red wine to Luciana. With nothing but silence surrounding them, sheep in the distance, Luciana sighed, content with how the rest of this evening would unfold. They both had things to talk about and people to discuss, but for just five more minutes,

Luciana would revel in this feeling. With her phone turned off and Sam's set to silent, nobody could disturb them. Janet was in custody, and Lindsay was safe. Tonight, it would all be about Sam and Luciana. The rest of the world could take a backseat.

Sam glanced to her left, sipping her wine as she watched Luciana over the rim of her glass. She appeared to be relaxed, the gentle sigh falling from her lips confirming Sam's suspicions, but Sam needed to be sure. Only yesterday, Luciana had been once again subjected to Janet and her cruel ways. Sam wasn't entirely sure what had been said or how it unfolded, but seeing Luciana once again bruised by Janet's hands sent a wave of anger through her. An anger that could easily consume her if she wasn't careful. Sam already felt on edge, wary of everything around her. Perhaps it was good that she wasn't there when Janet arrived. If she had, she might be sitting in a police cell right now, waiting to be charged with Janet's murder.

Sam took Luciana's hand beneath the water, their fingers entwining as Luciana relaxed her head back. Luciana's lips turned upward as Sam's thumb caressed her skin, her eyes flickering closed as Sam continued her movements. "I like seeing you relaxed."

"I like feeling relaxed," Luciana countered.

"I'm sorry about everything you've been through lately, Luce."

"Don't ever apologise. None of this was your fault."

Sam nodded. "I know, but it's just been one thing after another."

"That's life, babe." Luciana squeezed Sam's hand, turning her head and meeting deep, concerned eyes. "We're good and that's what matters most."

"Did you want to talk about it?"

"Janet?" Luciana could have pretended she didn't know what Sam was talking about, but there was no use lying. Sam would always see through it. "If we really have to."

"We don't *have* to do anything. But I think you should talk about it. Whether either of us like it or not, she did hurt you yesterday."

"Sam, this is supposed to be our time together."

Sam knew this was coming. Luciana would forever hold in her feelings if it made life easier. Whether it was her own personal issues, or work related, Sam would always have to force it out of Luciana one way or another. As much as Sam wanted to truly unwind at the cottage, she couldn't do so until she knew Luciana was okay. The only way she could be sure of that was to encourage Luciana to talk about what happened. Holding it in would never put their minds at ease.

"And it will be our time together. Every single second of it."

"So, why don't we just bypass the whole Janet conversation and do absolutely nothing?" Luciana eyed Sam, certain her suggestion wouldn't wash. "Doesn't that sound perfect?"

Sam shifted closer to Luciana. "You know, it does sound perfect. But discussing this sounds even better."

"I beg to differ, but okay."

"I just need to know that you're okay, Luce." Sam couldn't bear the thought of Luciana worrying about Janet. Of course, she would always be at the back of her mind, but Sam wanted Luciana to be fully present during this trip. If there was so much of a hint that Luciana was hurting, Sam wanted to fix it. "Please?"

"I'm okay. I promise."

Sam rolled her eyes. "Well, that was easy."

"Babe," Luciana started, "I know you worry and I appreciate it, but I don't want to give her another moment of headspace. She's not worth it."

"I understand that," Sam said, lowering her eyes. "But she laid her fucking hands on you once again and I don't know how to feel about it."

Luciana set her glass down on the edge of the hot tub, pulling Sam into her lap. "You're angry."

"Damn fucking right I am," Sam spat. "I told her, Luce. I told her I'd kill her if she touched you again."

Luciana cleared her throat. She hated knowing Sam felt this way. Anger didn't suit her; she was too beautiful for something so consuming. "I, uh...I think Janet was bluffing. About Lindsay. About her reasons for being around. I just...I don't want Lindsay to feel as though she's been played."

Sam frowned. "But she has. If Janet was using her to get closer to you, Lindsay has well and truly been played."

"I don't think Lindsay ever loved her, if that means anything to you."

"Makes me feel tonnes better."

Luciana knew Sam was being sarcastic, her tone of voice told her everything. Luciana also knew that Sam didn't blame her, but Luciana did feel partially to blame. How could she not when *she* was the one who brought Janet into their lives in the first place? As much as Luciana believed she was free from Janet now, she'd been fooled. Just like everybody else.

Luciana fought back tears, wondering if she would ever break free from Janet Mason. "Sam, I am sorry that I ever got involved with her. If I'd known the type of person she was—"

"No." Sam held up her hand. She wouldn't listen to Luciana try to defend her reasons *or* lay the blame on herself. "We're not doing this. I just want you to tell me how you're feeling. I don't ever want you to feel as though any of this is your fault."

Luciana's eyebrows drew together. "Isn't it? Because it certainly feels like it is."

"No, baby." Sam adjusted the setting on the jets, kneeling between Luciana's legs in the tub. "You were doing your job."

"Mm. Escorting."

"So?"

"Y-you said something a few days ago," Luciana said. "About how you wouldn't sit at home with two escorts. When I invited Shannon over."

Sam dropped her head on her shoulders. "Shit."

"Is that still the way you see me? As your escort?"

Sam's eyes flew open, tears welling. It hadn't ever been Sam's intention to make Luciana feel this way. She also hadn't meant to call her by her old profession. "You know I don't. Please, Luce. Don't ever think that."

"I just didn't expect you to say that is all."

"I was angry," Sam confessed. "Not with you, but with the situation. I couldn't hear your sweet voice, I looked a mess, and I couldn't understand why you wanted Shannon to come over."

"I understand that, and I don't want to even get into this...but I just needed someone to talk to." Luciana couldn't understand why this was the topic of conversation. If she was being completely honest, she didn't know why they were talking at all when they could be doing so much more. "I thought I'd lost you when I heard about the explosion. Then you couldn't hear me. I couldn't hold a conversation with you. I was hurting for you while I watched you struggle."

"I shouldn't have said what I did."

Luciana brushed Sam's hair from her face, the gash to her forehead beginning to scar. Sam's hair covered it most days, but even when it didn't, she was still incredibly beautiful.

"Luce, I love you. You know I do."

Luciana smiled. "I know, babe."

"And you promise you'll talk to me if you're feeling *anything* about Janet?"

"I promise." Luciana drew Sam into a kiss, smiling as she moaned against her lips. "Until we leave here, it's just you and me."

CHAPTER SEVENTEEN

Luciana fumbled with the string tie on her sweatpants, her hands trembling as she attempted the bow for a third time. Sam was sitting by the fire, wrapped up in a mountain of throws, the flames flickering in her deep, brown eyes. Luciana could watch the moment forever. With Sam content and Luciana finally feeling as though life was settling back down, she could freeze frame this moment, savouring the image of Sam wrapped up in blankets, a sweet smile on her mouth. Sam sighed, reaching for her gigantic glass of red wine on the oak coffee table they'd pushed to one side of the room. Luciana realised she was never going to master the bow on her sweats any time soon—her nerves getting the better of her—so she shoved the string inside the waistband of her pants and dropped to her knees beside Sam.

"This is so perfect," Sam said, pulling back the blanket covering her and motioning for Luciana to climb inside. Tonight, as with every night, Sam's heart held a monumental amount of love for Luciana. "Being with you. Just us. God, I never want to leave this place."

"I'm so happy you're feeling more like yourself again."

"Me too. About, um...the things I said at home."

Luciana frowned. "What things?"

"How it would be okay if you wanted to leave."

"Oh, those things." Luciana nodded, lowering her eyes. She had tried to push Sam's comments to the back of her mind since Sam hadn't been in the right frame of mind, but the suggestion Luciana could leave did hurt.

"I never meant it. I just...I couldn't bear the thought of you being stuck with me if things hadn't improved. You know?"

Luciana took Sam's soft hand, the bruising barely noticeable anymore. "I'm not here until something goes wrong, Sam. I'm here to love you forever. No matter what happens, I'll always be by your side."

"I know." Sam had always known.

"And if things *hadn't* improved...I still would have loved you unconditionally."

"I panicked," Sam confessed. "And I know it was foolish—stupid—but I am sorry."

"I need you to listen to me, okay?" She pulled Sam into her lap, Luciana's back resting against the couch.

Sam nodded, chewing on her bottom lip.

"The day I met you...you absolutely blew me away. I'd never known what it felt like to be in love—I didn't care, either—but I truly fell in love with you the moment I met you." Luciana took a breath. She had never felt so nervous. "Sam, I know you've already had the magical, white wedding. I know you've lived with the love of your life. But if I can even come close to that love—that inability to live without one another—I'll be forever happy. I don't expect to ever compare, and I don't expect you to feel for me what you did for Lucia, but I do love you. More than I thought was possible."

Sam stared, her cheeks wet with tears. Luciana may not know it, but she meant just as much as Lucia. Luciana meant everything to her, and before this was over tonight, Sam would tell her exactly that. The words spoken from Luciana, in this moment, rendered Sam speechless.

"I still feel like I'm dreaming when I wake up each morning with you. You have truly given me everything I could ever need by loving me." Luciana took Sam's engagement ring from beneath the blanket next to her, opening the ivory-coloured box. "I don't know what this means to you, or if it could ever mean the world, but *I* meant it when I told you I wanted you to marry me, Sam. I almost lost you last week. There was that possibility that I would never see your face again. I cannot bear the thought of losing you and never having the opportunity to call you my wife. That thought alone cuts deeper than any pain I've ever felt."

Luciana took Sam's hand, kissing her knuckles. "So...Sam Phillips, the most beautiful woman in the world, will you be my wife?"

Sam sobbed, her arms wrapping around Luciana's neck. "I would love nothing more than to be your wife."

Luciana turned her face, nuzzling Sam's neck. "I promise to make you happy."

"You already do," Sam said. "You mean just as much. I hope you know that."

"As much?"

Sam pulled back, her hand settling on the side of Luciana's face. "As Lucia."

"Sam, I—"

"Don't ever think that I don't love you fully, Luce. I love you so much that *you* kept me alive while I lay waiting for someone to rescue me."

"You thought about me?" Luciana's voice broke. "It was really me you thought about?"

"Every second I lay on that concrete." Sam cupped Luciana's face with both hands, her engagement ring sparkling in the light of the fire. "You really don't understand just how much I love you, do you?"

"I know you love me." Luciana cocked her head, smiling faintly. There was no denying that Sam loved her, Luciana felt it bursting from her, but would it be the same a second time around for Sam? "I just...you know how I feel about your past."

"And you know how I feel about you."

"I-I went there," Luciana confessed. "Yesterday."

"Where?"

"Lucia's grave."

"Oh." Sam lowered her eyes. "Why?"

"To ask for her blessing. To apologise for not protecting you. To tell her that I was going to try to love you as much as she loved you."

A steady flow of tears fell from Sam's eyes. Luciana had visited Lucia's grave. Sam didn't know how to feel about that. She wasn't angry or upset; she was overwhelmed with love. Complete, heart-stopping love.

"I just felt like we needed a moment alone. Me and Lucia."

"Yeah?" Sam leaned into Luciana's touch as she wiped the tears from her face. This woman wrapped around her had to be the sweetest.

"A lot has happened over the last few weeks. Whether it was our fight, Lindsay's fight, Janet, or the explosion...we've just had a lot on. I knew it would be peaceful at Lucia's grave and I just, I don't know. I drove there."

"She's good to talk to." Sam closed her eyes momentarily, allowing herself a second to breathe. "But I let her go, Luce. She will always be there, I couldn't ever forget her, but I let her go."

Luciana frowned. "I-I don't want you to do that."

"I had to," Sam explained, her heart bursting with both joy and sadness. "You may never understand it, and I hope you never find yourself in a position where you feel how I once did, but I had to let her go."

"Why?"

"Because you have my heart now. You have me completely. Everything I am...belongs to you."

Luciana blew out a deep breath, holding back her own tears. "I won't let her down, Sam. I promised her I would do my best for you."

"You don't have to promise anyone anything. I see you. I know exactly who you are. Your love for me is all encompassing, and I couldn't ask for anything more."

Luciana toyed with the ring on Sam's finger. "Looks beautiful."

"When it was given by you...I didn't expect anything less."

Luciana narrowed her eyes. "You know, I think we should take this to the bedroom. If you're feeling up to it."

"Thought you'd never ask." Sam rushed out of Luciana's lap, smirking as she pulled her up to her feet. For the first time since the explosion, Sam felt settled in every sense of the word. Yes, she ached when she woke up in the morning, but right now? Right now, she was feeling more than happy to take this to the bedroom. "Come on. We have some making up to do."

Luciana could barely contain her excitement. When it came to Sam and her body, she often found herself rendered speechless, but tonight was going to mean more than any other night they'd spent together. Now that Sam had a ring on her finger, Luciana could only imagine how different everything would feel. If her heart felt it, her body would, too. Before she'd joined Sam by the fire, Luciana had taken a shower and prepared the bedroom how she wanted it. Candles which let off a soft glow flickered—away from anything that may catch fire— and warmed oil waited to be drizzled all over Sam's skin.

Luciana pushed the bedroom door open, the scent of lavender

enveloping her as she pulled Sam in behind her. "So, I thought maybe I could offer you a massage."

"A massage?"

Luciana shrugged. "Yeah. You've been tense lately. You deserve to be pampered."

"Well, I'm not going to turn down a massage." Sam lifted her T-shirt from her body. "So, where do you want me?"

Sam had that sparkle in her eyes. That look. A look that could turn Luciana to jelly at any given moment.

"I, uh..." Luciana shook her head, removing the aroused thoughts from her mind. This night wouldn't end with *just* a massage, but Luciana would like to remain composed long enough to actually give Sam what she was offering. "O-on the bed."

"Completely naked, or...?"

"Probably best if you take everything off, yeah."

Luciana watched Sam slip her sweats from her legs, her underwear swiftly following. Sam's eyes didn't once leave Luciana's, a craving within them Luciana knew they both felt. A craving that only Sam could ever cause so deep inside Luciana.

Everything was laid out as it should be, fresh, fluffy towels covering the huge bed and the comforter topping it. As much as Luciana wanted to get down to business with her fiancée, Sam deserved to be worshipped. Relaxed. Cared for.

Luciana remained silent as Sam climbed onto the bed, lying down on her front. She truly had no words for this moment. Sam was a masterpiece.

Luciana took the jug of warm oil from the nightstand, smiling as Sam made herself comfortable on her stomach. With her naked body fully on display, her bronzed skin sending Luciana wild, she tilted the jug and dripped oil between Sam's shoulder blades. Watching in delight as it rolled down her spine, a moan spilled from Sam's lips, breaking Luciana from her thoughts.

She removed her sweats, straddling Sam's ass and shifting until they were both comfortable. Starting at the base of Sam's spine,

Luciana worked her thumbs up Sam's back until she reached her neck. Her fingertips caressed the skin beneath them, and with Sam's hair pulled up into a high bun, it provided Luciana with the most delicious view of her neck and shoulders. Repeating the movement, Luciana felt Sam's entire body relax under her touch.

"Oh, God," Sam mumbled, her face buried in the pillow beneath her head. "T-that feels amazing." Sam wasn't sure she had ever felt such incredible hands on her body, igniting her skin with each move. Luciana continued to work the muscles in Sam's back, every fibre of Sam's being bursting with unimaginable pleasure.

Luciana climbed off Sam, once again taking the jug of oil from the nightstand. This time moving lower, Luciana drizzled the oil over Sam's ass cheeks and thighs. Thrilled when Sam's hips moved of their own accord, her body arched on the bed from the sensation. Luciana now had a flawless view of Sam's glistening sex. The oil slid down her swollen lips, a guttural moan falling from Sam's mouth.

"Feel okay?" Luciana smirked but her voice gave nothing away. As far as Sam was concerned, this was just a massage.

"Mm. Yes."

"Good. Just relax, babe."

Luciana's hands glided over Sam's ass cheeks, kneading the strong muscles as she alternated with her thighs. Luciana's hands ached to touch Sam in *other* places...but not yet. She continued to work Sam's thighs with her thumbs, moving higher and kneading her ass once again. With every movement, Luciana opened Sam up to her, engorged lips now slick with not only oil, but arousal, too.

"S-shit, Luce," Sam gasped, forcing herself down against the bed. She needed more. Her body had missed Luciana. "Baby..."

Luciana removed her boy shorts and tank top, climbing back on top of Sam. Adding a little oil to the front of her own body, Luciana leaned down over Sam, her nipples brushing Sam's ass and lower back.

Sam groaned as Luciana moved higher, taking her earlobe

between her teeth, nipping and sucking. Teasing. Not only was Luciana creating some of the most powerful sensations Sam had ever felt, her body was covering Sam's. Slipping up and down, grinding, God, it was almost too much.

Sam lifted her head, turning it and capturing Luciana's lips. Luciana immediately noticed the hunger in Sam's eyes—black with desire—but that only spurred her on. It only encouraged Luciana to give Sam exactly what she wanted. What they *both* needed.

Sam sat up on her elbows, moaning when Luciana slid her hand around her stomach, inching higher and rolling her fingertips over Sam's painfully hard nipples. Tugging, pinching, gasp after gasp continued to catch in Sam's throat.

Both slick, Luciana ground against Sam, fresh arousal coating her own thighs when Sam pulled and sucked on Luciana's bottom lip. Nothing had ever felt so good. Sam slid her tongue into Luciana's mouth, her breath catching when Luciana's hand returned to her chest, caressing Sam's skin and teasing her breasts.

Luciana lifted up off Sam, rolling her over onto her back. She positioned her body against Sam's, their legs tangling together.

"Baby..." Sam gripped Luciana's face, her eyes begging, desperate for more.

Luciana braced herself on her forearm, her freehand gliding down Sam's taut stomach. Stopping above the small strip of dark hair, Luciana's lips worked Sam's neck. Every touch was passionate. Every kiss held the potential to shatter their world. Fervent. Craving. Sensual. As Luciana lifted her head, smiling into a kiss, her fingertips pressed firmly against Sam's clit. Sam shook, lifting her hips.

"You feel," Luciana said against Sam's lips, smirking, "so fucking good."

Sam lifted her hand—Luciana's working her clit—and slipped her thumb into Luciana's mouth. Luciana sucked gently, Sam's mouth falling open with a moan as her eyes fluttered closed momentarily. This intensity felt new; perhaps it was the official proposal earlier this evening.

As Luciana's hand worked Sam harder, their eyes locked. Foreheads pressed together, Luciana suddenly slid two fingers inside Sam, deep. Sam's world almost shattered, her walls pulsing and throbbing around Luciana's slender fingers. This moment was something else.

Sam revelled in Luciana's touch, her soft mouth roaming down her chest, those full lips enveloping her nipple. Luciana suddenly slipped out of Sam, her hand ghosting up Sam's stomach, her chest, her neck, until Sam found Luciana's fingers—wet with her arousal—pushing past her lips. Sam tasted herself, Luciana hurtling her towards the edge when those same fingers landed in Luciana's mouth, her tongue lapping up Sam's juices.

Luciana moaned. "Fucking beautiful."

When Luciana's hand returned to Sam's arousal, her fingers pushing back inside, Sam almost lost her mind. Luciana really was driving her insane. As her fingers pushed deep and slow, the sound of sex filling the room, Sam ran her own hand down her stomach, touching herself with a perfect pressure. Her cries grew louder, Luciana's crystal blue eyes trained on her hand. Sam knew how much Luciana loved it when she touched herself. After this evening, it was the least Sam could do.

Luciana became breathless. There was something incredibly satisfying about watching herself fuck Sam, her fiancée writhing and moaning, begging for the opportunity to come undone. Luciana curled her fingers, lowering her mouth to Sam's clit and taking over from Sam's hand.

A strangled cry ripped from Sam's throat, her aching clit being sucked while Luciana hit that spot inside her. "O-oh," Sam whimpered, forcing her head back into the pillow, her fingers tangling in Luciana's long, blonde hair. "S-shit! Fuck!"

Sam shuddered, her thighs clamping around Luciana's hand. She rocked, trembled, as shockwaves coursed through her. Sam's heels dug into the bed and her ass lifted, convulsing when Luciana brought her to another orgasm. Sam's world turned dark and her breathing grew laboured, but God she felt good. Luciana had just erased the entire past week, the pain and horror. Luciana had just given Sam the absolute time of her life. Potentially the orgasm of her life, too.

"Babe?" Luciana's sweet voice brought Sam back to reality. "You okay?"

"In your hands...always."

CHAPTER EIGHTEEN

Sam crept out of the bedroom, the wood flooring beneath her bare feet warming with the help of the log-burning fire. Luciana was in the kitchen, the blaring music and the clanging of utensils giving her away. Sam appreciated the lie-in Luciana had offered her this morning; her body ached from head to toe. Last night had been beautiful, their connection unquestionable, but she did need some pain meds. She wasn't fully healed, but she couldn't have turned down last night even if she'd thought it was a good idea to do so. If Luciana wanted to roll around in bed, Sam would oblige. Every time. Without Luciana, Sam wasn't sure she could have gotten through the last week or so. While everything felt muddled in her head—Luciana taking the brunt of whatever Sam threw out—she still fully supported Sam. Day and night, Luciana was there for whatever she needed. Last night, intense lovemaking was the least Sam could offer.

She rounded the corner and into the expansive open space, her lips twitching upward at the sight before her: Luciana, in boy-shorts and a T-shirt. Her choice of clothing this morning wasn't the only thing to take all of Sam's attention. No, it was the singing and dancing vision in front of her. Luciana gripped a wooden spoon, bringing it up to her mouth as she threw her head back and forth, dancing to the pop song playing loud on the radio. Her ass shook, her blonde hair flew in every direction, and her voice grew hoarse as she tried to hit the high notes.

Sam could only watch on, enchanted by everything her fiancée was. Those nights when she lay in bed alone around the time she met Luciana—worried as to whether the relationship would fizzle out—were all a distant memory. She recalled the evening she told Luciana they couldn't be together; Sam could truly kick herself repeatedly for ever saying such a thing to a beautiful woman. This...this was her life now. One hell of an incredible life.

Luciana spun around, her arms in the air, smiling when her eyes landed on a dishevelled-looking Sam. "Good morning, pretty lady."

"Mm, it certainly is." Sam slipped closer, wrapping her arms around Luciana's waist. She would never tire of mornings with this woman. Soft and safe arms enveloped her. Strong, supportive, but gentle. "I could watch you dancing around this kitchen all day long."

"I'm so out of shape." Luciana blew out a deep breath, her chest heaving.

"Nonsense. You're completely in shape."

Luciana shook her head. "Babe, I'm really not. If I go back to work in this state, the chief will kick my arse."

"And when the chief does that, he will have me to deal with." Sam captured Luciana's lips, swallowing the moan that she released as their tongues slid against one another's.

"And if you keep doing that, I'm going to burn breakfast." Luciana pulled back, her forehead pressing against Sam's as she took her bottom lip between her teeth.

Sam quirked an eyebrow. "Perhaps I need to work up your appetite a little more?"

Luciana turned Sam in her arms, pulling her back against her body while Luciana's tongue worked Sam's neck. "Or," her voice dropped an octave or two, "I could fuck you against the counter while I cook breakfast."

Sam's body throbbed. And not necessarily in a good way. "Baby..."

"Mm?"

"We have to stop," Sam groaned, aware that stopping Luciana wasn't the greatest idea she'd ever had. Was she completely out of her mind to put a halt to all of this? Yes. Yes, she was.

"Just...I'm a little sore this morning."

"I'm so sorry," Luciana whispered. "Did I hurt you last night?"

Sam spun around in Luciana's arms. "No, not at all. I just thought I was healing better than I appear to be. Everything is achy, but I'll be okay as the day wears on."

"You should have said something." Luciana dropped her head. "If I'd known, last night wouldn't have happened."

"Hey, I didn't know I'd be in pain this morning. Neither did you. Last night was amazing and I'd do it all over again whatever the outcome today."

"I hate seeing you in pain." Luciana's jaw clenched, her eyes not quite as soft as they had been moments ago.

"You wanna talk about this anger, or...?"

"I'm not angry. Well, I am." Luciana released Sam, running her fingers through her hair as she backed away. She was angry with everything life had thrown at them. It wasn't enough that Sam's wife was taken from her...now she had to be blown up, too? "Not with you, though."

"We should still talk about it."

Luciana appreciated Sam's concern, but she was good. Great, even.

"You know..." Sam cleared her throat, following Luciana into the kitchen. "We should talk more often."

Luciana frowned. "Talk?"

"Mmhmm."

"About what?" Luciana asked.

"Life. Work. Whatever."

Luciana focused on the French toast on the hob. Work truly had been the last thing on her mind recently, Sam taking number one priority above all else. "I'll call the station once we get back home. When I know you're okay, I'll go back."

"That's not what I'm talking about, Luce..."

"Then I've no idea where you're going with this, babe." Sam noted the slump in Luciana's shoulders. Usually, Sam would read Luciana's body language and take it from there, but not this time. Luciana bottled things up far too much. It had to stop. "Breakfast will be a few minutes. There's fresh coffee ready if you want it. I'll bring it over to the dining table in a minute."

"Okay, thanks." Sam smiled when Luciana glanced over her shoulder at her. She would let this conversation lie until they were both seated and sharing breakfast. Sam could only hope that Luciana didn't decide to forgo breakfast with her for that reason alone.

Luciana wasn't stupid. She knew full well that Sam would be waiting to continue this discussion. She'd given up too easily otherwise.

Sam took a seat at the oak dining table, pulling her feet up onto an empty chair and taking her pain medication from the centre of the table. Once they kicked in, she would feel drastically better. She watched Luciana move around the kitchen, plating up breakfast with a tension in her shoulders. Sam didn't want it to be this way, but if Luciana was going to continue running towards fire and away from how she felt, they would have to figure out a way to communicate about it. This time away would be the perfect opportunity to lay everything out. Their relationship had changed significantly; it was time to discuss what was expected of one another.

"Okay..." Luciana set down everything they could need. A mountain of bacon, maple syrup, a stack of French toast. Fresh fruit already sat on the table waiting for them to dig in, organic sausages now sitting beside the other various plates of food. "Enjoy." Luciana disappeared again, returning moments later with a pot of coffee. "I think I have everything we need."

Sam dug her fork into the French toast, her mouth salivating. "Looks delicious."

"Not overly healthy but I'm starving, sorry."

"Me too."

"So, you've taken your meds?" Luciana helped herself to a little of everything, tipping the jug of maple syrup over her French toast before her eyes finally found Sam's. "I am sorry if I hurt you."

Sam's hand instinctively found Luciana's on the tabletop. "You didn't."

"Okay, well if you're feeling up to it later, I thought we could take a walk around the hills."

Sam smiled. "Sounds like a beautiful day. But I wanted to talk to you about something."

"O...kay."

"Your health means a lot to me, Luce. Your mental health, too. You can't expect me to brush it all under the carpet like you do. When you're angry, if you're sad...Just..."

Luciana looked incredulously at Sam. What the hell was she trying to say? "My mental health is *fine*."

Sam couldn't believe how blasé Luciana was about it all. Yes, she had to block out elements of her job; she wouldn't go to work otherwise. But to be so nonchalant about everything was worrying. And then there was Janet. Another conversation Sam had to drag out of Luciana.

"That doesn't mean you're just supposed to shut up and get on with it."

"It's easier that way."

"Do you really believe that it's healthy to maintain this, Luce?"

"Maintain what?"

"Hiding your emotions." Sam offered Luciana a slight smile. "I know you're angry about everything; I am, too. But you don't speak to me unless I beg you to give me something, anything. I don't want it to be that way. I want you to know that you can come home from work and have a cry if you need to. That I won't judge you or see you as weak, as you've put it once before. I *want* you to get mad about Janet; let's face it, that woman is fucking infuriating."

"I'm sorry. It's just how I've always dealt with stuff."

"Well, *now* we deal together, okay?"

"I'm just trying to keep our little bubble perfect."

Sam snorted. "Perfect? Baby, it's been far from perfect...but it doesn't need to be."

"But it *should* be." Perhaps this was Luciana's downfall. She'd never been in a real relationship before Sam. She was trying too hard, and Sam really didn't need that. She just needed honesty and commitment. If she had those things, life *was* perfect.

"Look." Sam sighed, running her hand through her hair. "What I'm saying is...I want to know everything, okay? If you're upset or angry, come to me. I can't be there for you if you walk around daily telling me you're fine. Our future just became concrete. I'm going to be your wife, Luce. If we can't talk about what's bothering us or if we're mad at one another, how is it ever supposed to work?"

"I'm not mad at you." Luciana's brows drew together.

"I know you're not, but when you are...it's okay to be."

Luciana was shocked. She didn't know where Sam's little speech had come from, but it had clearly been affecting her to come up now. She exhaled. "Okay."

"Promise me?"

"Yeah. I promise you." Luciana squeezed Sam's hand. "But I am okay. If something was troubling me, I'd talk to you."

"Okay, I believe you."

"Now, we should eat up so we can spend the day outside together. You'll let me know if you're not feeling up to it, though?"

"I'll be fine. And while we're out, I'd like to discuss something else with you."

"Oh, God. What have I done now?" Luciana's fork clanged on her plate.

"Nothing, except for be amazing." Sam winked in Luciana's direction. "This is about Lindsay and Cheryl."

Luciana threw her hands in the air. "Finally. I thought you'd never have anything to say about it."

"Trust me, I have *a lot* to say about it."

Luciana got up from the table; she needed more bacon. Sam suddenly placed her hand on her wrist. "Hey, seriously. Stop being so strong around me. You're putting me to shame."

"You're the strongest person I know, babe. You have nothing to worry about."

Luciana shoved her hands in her pockets, taking the incline up the hill with ease. She followed behind Sam, worried that she was in some discomfort, her heart in her mouth as Sam stumbled towards the top of the hill. She caught her, reaching out swiftly to prevent Sam from falling face first into the soft ground. Things were certainly getting better, but not soon enough. Sam released a frustrated groan, offering Luciana a thankful squeeze of the hand as they reached the top of the peak they'd spent twenty minutes walking up.

"You good?"

"Yeah." Sam straightened herself out, squinting as the sun caught her eyes.

"Maybe we walked too far," Luciana said. "I know you like to do as much as you can, but this is supposed to be a relaxing break. You don't look very relaxed to me."

Sam ushered Luciana towards a rock, taking a seat on it as she looked out over the Yorkshire Dales. Deep green rolling hills calmed Sam, only the sound of the whoosh of the breeze around them. This really was the picture of a peaceful life, even if Sam didn't feel peaceful inside.

What was changing about her? She'd always been used to running around—stressed—so why did she no longer want to feel that way? Why did she dread the thought of going home?

"Babe?"

"Mm?" Sam's eyes fluttered open and closed as she turned her head.

"Are you okay?"

Sam chose to refrain from going deeper into how she felt. It may be hypocritical of her since just this morning she'd insisted that Luciana be more open about her own struggles, but Sam's own issues could wait. She felt too anxious to discuss it right now. "Lindsay and Cheryl."

"What about them?"

"We need to figure out how to get them back together, Luce."

Luciana grimaced. "Do we?"

"I do, at least."

"And why do you feel as though you have to do that?" Luciana lifted the hood on her jacket, preventing the chill that was about to roll down her spine. The sun was deceiving today. "I mean, don't you think we've done enough meddling in Lindsay's life lately?"

Sam wrinkled her nose. "Is that what you think?"

Luciana exhaled slowly. "Honestly, I don't know. I'm just worried that Lindsay doesn't want us to get involved. I would also understand completely if she felt that way."

"She broke things off with Cheryl because of me, Luce. The least I can do is try to get them back together."

"I still can't believe you didn't believe me the other month when I told you something was going on between them."

Sam's shoulders slumped. "I've been busy."

"Hey, that wasn't a criticism." Luciana wrapped her arm around Sam's shoulder, pulling her closer. Sam appeared to be off today; she clearly had things on her mind. "Is everything okay with you?"

"Of course, why?"

"You seem...different. Distant."

Sam suddenly felt light-headed, an unease rising from deep within her. "Sorry."

Luciana's heart suddenly sunk. Last night had been emotionally taxing before they took things to the bedroom. In the cold light of day, was Sam having second thoughts? Surely not. Luciana also didn't quite know how Sam felt about her going to Lucia's grave. Sam hadn't really spoken much about it at all, but Luciana had noted the look on Sam's face when she told her. One of uncertainty. Had she completely stepped out of line?

"Sam?"

"Yeah?" Sam rubbed her hands up and down her thighs, breathing through the tingle that coursed through her body.

"About last night," Luciana started. "The proposal."

Sam's lips twitched upward, relaxing Luciana momentarily.

"Did I overstep? You know, going to visit Lucia's grave. Saying the things I did?"

"No, beautiful." Sam lay her head against Luciana's chest. "No, you didn't."

"So, what's on your mind?"

"Just everything."

Luciana's phone pinged. As she removed it from the inside pocket of her jacket, she found a voicemail waiting. "That's odd."

"What?"

"I have a voicemail, but I don't remember my phone ringing."

"Poor reception in some parts..."

Luciana listened to her mailbox. She had one new message.

Sam studied Luciana's face, an apparent relief washing over her features. Something in her eyes had changed; something had happened. Luciana appeared to be smiling on the inside, her intense blue eyes shining against the bright sunlight, but Sam had no idea what was going on.

Luciana released a deep breath as she ended the message.

"It's over."

Sam swallowed hard. "What is?"

"Janet. She will be serving *at least* the remainder of her sentence behind bars."

"Thank God." Sam hadn't expected to feel such a weight lift from her. It wasn't exactly her story. But it had; it had lifted and now she felt as though life could settle down. Janet wouldn't be around for the foreseeable and Luciana was safe. So was Lindsay.

But then Sam's chest suddenly began to heave, her breathing compromised.

"Babe?"

"O-oh, God." Sam's chest tightened, her hand clutching at her zipper. She needed her coat off. She needed everything off. "L-Luce."

"Babe, it's okay." Luciana got down on her knees in front of Sam, helping her lower the zipper. Sam was having a panic attack —one Luciana hadn't expected. She took Sam's hand, placing it against her own chest, directly over her heart. "Concentrate."

"I-I can't." Sam gasped for breath.

"You can." Luciana had Sam focus on her eyes, the sensation of her heart beating beneath the palm of Sam's hand. "Feel that? Breathe slowly, Sam. Feel my heartbeat and focus on that."

Sam closed her eyes, her entire body shaking. This was new for her. She couldn't say she'd ever had a panic attack before, and she definitely didn't want to experience one ever again.

"Breathe." Luciana's soft voice was helping. Sam didn't know why, or how this had happened, but having Luciana here was helping. "I've got you, Sam. Just breathe."

Sam felt her body relaxing slightly, the sudden coolness in the air causing her to shake excessively. Whatever was currently going on with her body, Sam wasn't here for it.

Luciana moved closer when Sam's body started to slump against her. Her fiancée was worn out, mentally *and* physically. This had been too much for her today, even if it was just a quiet walk with some fresh air thrown in for good measure.

Sam sobbed into the side of Luciana's neck, uncontrollably. She didn't want to be out in the countryside any longer; she needed to be locked away. Until when she didn't know, but she had an overwhelming sense of anxiety rushing through her. "W-we have to go."

"Okay. Just give yourself another couple of minutes to calm down. Then we will leave."

"Okay." Sam spoke barely above a whisper, Luciana's body almost taking her full weight. "Another minute and then we'll go."

CHAPTER NINETEEN

Luciana draped a thick blanket over Sam, the sound playing low on the TV in front of them. She should prepare dinner, clean up their mess from this morning, but she struggled to leave Sam's side. Today had worried Luciana, truly frightened her, but she couldn't show Sam that. She couldn't confess that she was worried about her.

Sam was proud, strong. Sam was usually everything that she didn't appear to be today. Instead of leaving her alone, Luciana sunk to her knees at the side of the couch, placing a kiss to Sam's temple. She was sleeping, her breathing even and sound, but it didn't quash the worry inside Luciana. In this moment, she wasn't sure anything could.

She lifted her phone from the coffee table, a message from Lindsay displayed on the screen.

L: You two enjoying your break together?

Luciana chose to ignore it for the time being. She should speak directly to Lindsay, not via text message, but doing so would likely wake Sam. As they'd walked back this afternoon, Luciana felt the heaviness inside Sam. She also felt it in the way she carried herself. Tired. Shattered. Lifeless, in some way. Luciana didn't know why

Sam had reacted the way she did to the news of Janet, but she had been under a lot of stress lately. In some way, it was foolish to even consider that a break away would solve everything. After the last couple of weeks, it would take a lot more than a cottage in the countryside to fix anything.

"I don't think you realise how much it means to me having you by my side." Sam's voice was barely audible, her eyes closed. "But it does. It means the world."

"Try to sleep, babe." Luciana fixed the blanket over Sam's feet, covering her hands and bringing it up to her neck. "You don't need to explain anything right now. I just want you to rest."

"I thought I was over the worry of being outside."

"Sam..."

"When I was out with Lindsay at the office, we went into town."

"I know."

"But we didn't stay long. I couldn't bear to be outside any longer. I started to panic, but nothing like what I experienced today."

Luciana sighed. "Why didn't you tell me this sooner?"

"You had stuff going on. Janet had just been to the house. You didn't need to know."

"I did need to know."

"I shouldn't have reacted like that. I was in the middle of nowhere. Nothing was going to hurt me."

Luciana watched Sam's eyes flutter open, a little more life in them than earlier. "Maybe it had nothing to do with being outside."

"I don't understand."

"You had that attack when I got off my voicemail," Luciana explained. "Maybe it was something to do with everything that's been going on lately, I don't know."

"I didn't feel so good before you took that call."

"Oh."

"It wasn't anything I thought I needed to worry about. Clearly, I was wrong."

"We shouldn't have gone out today. I just thought some fresh air would do you good. You've been cooped up for a while and I know that's not you. I'm sorry; I thought it would help."

"Hey..." Sam lifted up, resting on her elbow as she drew Luciana closer, their lips caressing. "I *wanted* to go out with you today. I'll always want to be with you."

"Okay, but no more until you're feeling better."

"Yes, darling." Sam's fingers curled beneath Luciana's chin, smiling against her lips. Her episode today had truly worn her out but being back in the comfort and safety of the cottage had lessened that anxiety. "Why don't we call Lindsay and Cheryl? Invite them here."

"Mm, I don't know if that will work."

"Cheryl is my assistant. If I ask her to join me, she will."

Luciana raised an eyebrow. "And Lindsay?"

"You can call her. Invite her over. I'm sure she could use something like this to take her mind off Janet."

"Crafty."

"But a good idea, wouldn't you agree?" Sam smirked.

"Of course. Anything you say."

Luciana monitored Sam for a moment. Was she truly feeling better now that they were back here? Luciana couldn't be sure of that but having company could only keep Sam's mind occupied. That in itself was good enough to settle Luciana's own mind.

"So..."

Sam's voice shocked Luciana from her thoughts.

"What?"

"Are you going to call Lindsay?"

"Whatever you desire." Luciana exhaled, climbing from the floor beside the couch and taking Sam's phone from the kitchen counter. "You should call Cheryl first. If she's not available at short notice, it's a waste of time."

"She's here." Luciana pulled back the curtain and watched Cheryl's car slow to a stop on the driveway. "I can't believe she just agreed to drive up here."

"I pay her a good wage. Cheryl would show up in the middle of the night if I asked her to."

"I still can't get over the fact that her and Lindsay thought you would fire her. Do they really think you would do something like that?"

Sam sighed. "Clearly, they did. But I'm going to put that right. Would you mind if I had five minutes alone with her? You can keep an eye out for Lindsay."

"Can do. She texted me a while ago. She should be here soon."

A loud knock on the thick oak door startled Sam, alerting her to Cheryl's presence. Cheryl believed she was here to update Sam on the comings and goings of the business, but Sam couldn't care any less about the office lately. If she pushed the place from her mind, she felt better for it.

Sam opened the door, instantly enveloped by Cheryl's arms. "Oh, my God. It's so good to see you, Sam."

"Whoa." Sam laughed, wrapping her own arms around Cheryl. This wasn't their usual relationship, but it was nice seeing her assistant. "Come in. It's getting a bit chilly out there this evening."

"How are you? Feeling better?" Cheryl asked, moving into the living room. Her eyes scanned the space, landing on Luciana who was curled up on the brown, leather couch. "Hi, Luciana."

"Hey. How was the drive?"

Cheryl slung her satchel to the floor, dropping down into a seat. "Quiet."

"We got stuck behind an accident on the way up here. Didn't look too serious when we drove past."

"That's the M6 for you."

"Hate it. Nothing but trouble on that stretch of motorway." Luciana eyed Sam; she was chewing her bottom lip. "Everything okay, babe?"

"Yep. Perfect." Sam rubbed at her forearm, a crooked smile on her mouth. "Cheryl, should we go through into the kitchen?"

"Whatever works for you, boss."

Sam shook her head, laughing. Cheryl always was overenthusiastic when she believed she needed to be. "Did you want coffee or something stronger?"

"Oh, I'm driving."

"We have plenty of space here if it turns into a drinking session. Unless you had somewhere to be?" Sam studied Cheryl as she pulled herself up onto a stool. She was trying to place the name of the woman she usually dated, but it escaped her. "You and thingy still dating?"

"Bex?"

"That's the one." Sam uncorked a bottle of red wine, setting it on the island and allowing it to breathe. Cheryl didn't appear to care for Bex at the mention of her name; that could only work in Lindsay's favour.

"No. It was just a casual thing anyway, but she's been seeing someone else. They're exclusive now."

"Oh, I'm sorry to hear that."

"Honestly, it was always going to happen. I wasn't all in with her...I had other things on my mind."

"Other things, or other people?"

"Well, the business more so than anything else." Cheryl toyed with a stack of Post-it notes on the counter, lifting her head and finding Sam's eyes. "How are you?"

"Feeling much better. Still aching when I wake up but compared to last week, I'm feeling like myself again."

"It must be nice having Luciana by your side. Losing your hearing can't have been pleasant."

"My anger was what bothered me more than anything. God, I was a bitch."

"Sam Phillips, a bitch?" Cheryl smirked, quirking an eyebrow. "I've never heard the two in the same sentence."

"I'm perfectly happy tearing people a new one within the business, but when it comes to family and the people I love, not so much."

"It's really good to see you." Cheryl reached her hand across the counter, settling it over Sam's. "When I heard the news, I thought the worst."

"Mm, we all did."

"But then I remembered who my boss was, and I knew you would get through it. Nothing keeps you down."

Sam exhaled. "Oh, I don't know. I did lie there wondering if I'd been beaten one final time."

"Well, you're here and I'm thrilled."

"Our Lindsay should be here soon." Sam narrowed her eyes, gauging Cheryl's reaction to that news. Honestly, she couldn't read the look on her face. Terror? Heartbreak? The need to run out the door?

Cheryl took the wine from the counter, helping herself to a large measure. "Right. I'll just have this one and then I'll leave you all to it."

"Or, you could hang around."

"You're spending time with family, Sam. I'm sure you don't want business mixing with that. I can always update you on everything another time."

"If I've ever given you the impression that I would end your career based on what you do outside the office, I'm sorry." Sam sat beside Cheryl, confusion in her assistant's eyes. "You've been there for me over the years, at times more than anyone else has, and all I want is for *you* to be happy, too. I found my happy ending, and in many ways, I have you to thank for that. I still wonder how it happened…Luciana is just something else, but it did."

"I-I—"

"Are you in love with my sister, Cheryl?"

Cheryl's face fell, discomfort visible in the way she shifted on her stool.

"You really thought I would fire you?" Sam cocked her head, smiling faintly. "If I found out about you and Lindsay?"

"She's your sister, Sam. It was inappropriate. You were always so strongly against workplace relationships."

Sam nodded. "And I still am."

"So, this conversation is a waste of time." Cheryl took a long, slow sip from her wine glass, tears welling in her eyes. "Lindsay is dating Janet Mason. Even if it was perfectly okay, I couldn't compete with that."

"First of all, Lindsay doesn't work for me. She just insists on being at the office so she can get on my nerves ninety percent of the time. Secondly, Janet Mason is *not* welcome in my family *or* my life. You, on the other hand, are more than welcome."

"I-I don't understand."

"I'll let Lindsay explain everything when she gets here." Sam winked, climbing down from her stool as another knock sounded against the door. "And it looks like it won't be much longer that you have to wait."

"Sam, I don't think I can do this." Cheryl's voice trembled. "Lindsay is the one who broke it off with me. I...if I try to patch things up with her and she turns me down, I just...I don't want the rejection."

"Breaking things off with you was a huge mistake. Hear her out, okay?"

Cheryl chose not to respond, instead focusing on the countertop in front of her.

Sam rounded the wall separating the kitchen and living area, finding her sister hugging Luciana. They were having a moment, that much was clear, but it was a moment Sam could watch over and over again. Things were certainly beginning to look up for the three of them; Sam just hoped Lindsay and Cheryl could now get back on the right track. One that didn't include meaningless dates or psycho interior designers. At least the latter was certainly out of the picture.

"Sam." Lindsay pulled out of Luciana's embrace, instead enveloping her sister. "Luce said you needed me to come over. Is everything okay?"

"Someone is waiting for you in the kitchen." Sam cocked her head.

"W-who?"

"Why don't you go and find out for yourself?"

Before Lindsay had the chance to do exactly that, Cheryl appeared behind Sam, the slightest of smiles curling on her mouth. "Wanna talk?"

"Y-yeah." Sam noted how Lindsay's eyes lit up at the mere sight of Cheryl. How had she missed this all along? Sam was the first to admit that she usually had her head up her ass, but this? It was now *so* obvious. Lindsay turned to Sam and breathed, "Thank you."

"Just make things right with one another. You've got nothing but support from me, Linds."

Luciana sidled up next to Sam, wrapping her arm around her fiancée's waist. "And me."

"They've been out there for hours." Sam bounced her leg up and down, her hands clasped in her lap. She knew things couldn't be too bad between Lindsay and Cheryl since nobody had run out crying yet, but she thought they'd have cleared the air by now. Sam and Luciana had watched an entire film in the time they'd spent talking. Now they were outside, sitting close to the hot tub.

"Stop worrying. Nothing is being hurled through the air. I think they're good."

Sam knew her nerves weren't only based on her sister. No, she had other reasons to be nervous.

"You feelin' okay, babe?"

Luciana scooted closer to Sam, taking her in her arms and pulling her back on the couch. Their day may have started off filled with anxiety and Sam's concern with being outside, but she was safe here in Luciana's arms. Luciana would always be sure of that.

"Luce..."

Luciana's brow furrowed. "What is it?"

"I just..." Sam shook her head, clearing her throat as a nervous smile worked its way to her lips. "I had something I wanted to give you."

"Not the lawyer papers."

"No. I haven't had the chance to have them finalised yet, but I will."

"Babe. I've told you, I have you and that's all I need."

"We're getting off track and the way I'm feeling right now, I don't want to do that." Sam exhaled a deep, long breath. She removed a box from her pocket and placed it in Luciana's hand, closing her fingers over it. "I want you to have this."

"W-what is it?"

Luciana slowly opened the box, her breath catching when her eyes landed on a platinum, blue sapphire diamond ring. This piece of jewellery had to be worth a fortune. "B-babe, I can't take this. It's too much."

"It was Lucia's," Sam explained. "We'd gone to Italy, and I had it made for her there. When it was handed back to me with the rest of her things, I had it cleaned and locked it away. I swore I would take it to the grave with me, that nobody would ever be worthy enough in my eyes to touch it, let alone wear it."

Luciana bit back a sob, but Sam? Sam was the picture of complete calm. On the outside, at least.

"This isn't me giving you a second-hand ring because I couldn't be bothered to try harder. This is me giving you every piece of me, Luciana. I told myself I'd never fall in love again. I promised myself that Lucia would be the only woman to ever call me her wife. But here you are." A tear escaped Sam's eye, gliding down her cheek and falling to the couch between them. "You fill me with so much love every morning and I can truthfully say that this, what's happening between us, is one of the most beautiful experiences of my life. You allow me to be myself. You give me the opportunity to grieve when I need to, to remember, and you do it with such love and respect that I don't know how to ever thank you for that.

"You saw me. When I didn't want to be noticed, you had your eyes firmly on me...and God, I will always be thankful for that moment I met you. However fleeting it all may seem given the last year, I will always remember seeing your eyes for the first time. They reminded me of the sapphire sitting in your hand right now. They told me that it was okay to fall in love again. They told me I could be happy again. And you, Luciana, you have picked up my heart and shown me what it is to be loved again. I love you so much. The pride I have for you...my heart could burst."

Sam moved closer, taking the ring from the box and slipping it on Luciana's engagement ring finger. Her eyes glazed ever so slightly, but it wasn't sorrow. It wasn't pain. It was love. Sam lifted Luciana's hand, placing a kiss to the ring, and smiled. "Perfect."

"B-babe." Luciana sobbed as Sam's eyes found hers. "I just..."

"Oh, my God." Lindsay rushed into the room, her face wet with tears. "That was the most beautiful thing I've ever heard."

Sam smiled weakly as she turned to face Lindsay. "Thanks, Linds."

"What's happening here? Do you two have something you need to tell me?" Lindsay propped her hand on her hip, looking expectantly at Sam.

"A few days ago, Luciana asked me to be her wife."

Those words hit Sam square in the chest. Actually confirming it to someone other than herself, Sam's entire body buzzed with a love she wasn't sure she'd felt before. Everything with Luciana seemed so different to when she was with Lucia. Neither could compare, they never would, but this was an entirely different stage of Sam's life. A year ago, she was happy just to be in Luciana's company...but now, she couldn't imagine ever not being called her wife. Wasn't it funny how life played out?

"T-this is huge." Tears fell steadily down Lindsay's face, Cheryl's arm wrapping around her waist in support. "S-Sam, this is..."

"I know." Sam got to her feet, dragging Luciana up with her. "And if it wasn't for you two, I wouldn't be in this position. I wouldn't be standing here now with such an incredible woman beside me."

Lindsay shook her head, crying. "Sam."

"No, it's true. You pushed me to find myself again, to love again. I continuously denied everything you were telling me, but in the end...you were right. And Cheryl," Sam continued, "you are the one who got this entire thing going. I know neither of us expected anything to come of it, but if you hadn't given me that business card, I'd still be living in the city and miserable."

Cheryl smiled. "You mean a lot to me, Sam. I watched you live a beautiful life with Lucia. I watched you grow into a person who didn't take crap from anyone—me included—and then I watched it all fall apart around you. I felt so helpless and I couldn't possibly comprehend what you were going through, but you never once made me feel like I didn't belong in your office. Through the hardest times, you still had a massive respect for me. Nobody expected that, your world had just fell away, but you still held that strength, and I, for one, admire *that* more than anything else."

Sam held out her arms, pulling Cheryl and Lindsay into a hug. She'd had her moment, her second shot at love. Now it was their time. "I really hope you can both make up for lost time. I'm sorry you thought I wouldn't support you."

"Sam, it's okay."

"No, it's not." Sam returned to Luciana's side, her fiancée still speechless but no longer standing on shaky legs. "Once you leave here, whenever that is, I want you to pack up some things and get your passports together."

"W-why?" Lindsay frowned.

"Well, Cheryl isn't needed at the office for a while yet. Don't worry, I'll still pay you—"

"Sam, that's not necessary."

Sam held up her hand. She appreciated that Cheryl understood her desire to not be at the office, but this was Sam's issue and nobody else would suffer the consequences by not receiving their wage. "It is. And you won't argue with me about it."

"Okay."

"I'm sending you both away. Somewhere sunny. Take your pick and send me the details."

"Really?" Lindsay's eyes lit up.

"Well, I'm assuming you're both willing to give this another go since you haven't run out on one another?"

"Yeah, we uh…" Lindsay cleared her throat, her cheeks reddening. "We've just booked into a hotel a few miles down the road."

Sam quirked an eyebrow. "Oh?"

"Get it, girl." Luciana grinned, suddenly snapped from her emotional daze.

"Can you not encourage my little sister to have hotel sex, baby?" Sam nudged Luciana in the ribs, smirking as her eyes found the deepest of blues.

Luciana snorted. "Why? Hotel sex is the best kinda sex."

"Then I will keep that in mind."

"As much as we would love to stay and celebrate with you, I think you need this evening alone." Lindsay lifted her bag from the coffee table and grabbed Cheryl's satchel from the floor. "But we do want to celebrate with you at some point."

"We'd love that," Luciana said, wrapping her arms around Sam's waist from behind. "Right, babe?"

"We would."

The four of them walked slowly to the front door, Luciana never separating from Sam's body. Those things Sam had said before Lindsay interrupted them had been like nothing Luciana had ever heard before, nor did she expect them. And the ring... God, the ring had only tipped everything over the edge. Luciana didn't know where to begin with anything she wanted to say, but Sam knew how she felt and that was what mattered more than anything else. They had an unspoken love and understanding when words were hard to come by.

Lindsay turned around as she stepped out onto the drive. "I'm so happy for you, Sam."

"And I'm happy for you." Just a few days ago, Sam and Lindsay didn't have the best form between them. Hostility and harsh words had never been how they'd grown up with one another, but life had simply gotten in the way. Now, it was time for all of them to settle down and be happy. It was the least they deserved. "Text me when you get to the hotel."

Lindsay nodded, her eyes switching to Luciana. "Bye, Luce."

"See you soon, Linds."

Sam relaxed back against Luciana, sighing as her hand settled over the sapphire occupying Luciana's finger. Lindsay and Cheryl disappeared down the drive in their own cars, beeping as they drove away into the country lanes. Sam suddenly felt herself being pulled backwards, the door slamming shut as her body was pushed up against it.

"I have so much that I need to say to you, Sam. So many reasons to thank you...but not right now." Luciana's lips feathered across Sam's, both smiling into a soft, sensual kiss. "I love you so much. Don't ever forget that."

"I couldn't if I tried..."

Luciana's hands trailed Sam's soft, recovering body. She was still impressed by how far Sam had come in such a short span of time. They had a hospital appointment next week, but Luciana knew it would be a good outcome. Sam had excelled with her recovery.

"Come on, I want to *show* you exactly what you mean to me," Luciana purred in Sam's ear. "And I'm going to take the entire night to do that."

CHAPTER TWENTY

6 *months later...*
Luciana studied the garlands and the sheer, ivory voiles surrounding her as she spun in circles slowly. Today had been breathtaking in many ways, but the decoration and the effort executed in all of this...incredible. Sam certainly had an eye for detail and beauty. Luciana knew this day had been in safe hands for that reason alone, but the outcome and the finished product still stunned her to the core. A platform had been built out on the lake—distressed oak—which led back to the decking at the front of the house.

A huge marquee stood to the side of the driveway. Twinkly lights weaved through every tree, every bush, down to the trunks. The lawn had been treated for months leading up to this day, the intensity of the green quite impressive. Sam, she had truly gone to town with their plans. Each gold chair was individually tied with an ivory bow, and silk ruched drapes pulled from the roof of the marquee and gathered along the sides gave it that elegant feel, but just having Sam here made the entire day elegant. It radiated from her. As it always had.

Luciana's eyes scanned the marquee, Sam was standing in the

far corner talking to someone she recognised but couldn't quite place. The woman was covered head to toe in tattoos. Luciana weaved through the tables, joining Sam.

"Luce, I've been looking for you." Sam held her champagne flute delicately, her free hand pulling Luciana closer to her. Sam looked like an absolute vision today. Her caramel highlights were back in her hair, pulled up on the right side to expose her neckline with a double milkmaid braid gathering her luscious dark locks around the back of her head. The style was finished with a crystal pin, everything about the design typical Sam.

"How do I know you?" Luciana focused on the tattooed woman standing to the side of Sam. She definitely knew this woman.

"I don't know but I do recognise you, too." The woman spoke with a strong Liverpool accent, her tattoos impressive as they caught Luciana's attention.

Oh, God. Sam's stomach dropped. Was this escort-related? Sam wasn't sure she could cope with other clients coming out of the woodwork. Not when they were related to her. She continued to watch their interaction, praying one or both realised who the other was…and it *not* involving sex for payment.

"I love your sleeve," Luciana said, pointing her champagne glass towards the woman's right arm. "I recognise the work. It looks like something I have…"

"It's my own work."

"Wait!" Luciana appeared to have a lightbulb moment. "The tattoo place in town. Off Victoria Street. Uh…"

"Dark Angel?"

"That's the place."

Sam exhaled a deep breath. That was close.

"I had some work done there about four years ago. You were my artist."

"Ryann Harris." The woman held out her hand. "Sam's cousin."

"O-oh." Luciana switched her gaze between them both. Sam hadn't mentioned she had a cousin who was into tattoos. "You should have said, babe. I'm thinking about getting more work done."

"You are?" Sam quirked an eyebrow.

"Sure, yeah." Sam appeared to be taken aback by Luciana's decision, so why not play around a little. "You know the picture I have of you on my bedside?"

"The portrait thing?"

"Yeah. I was thinking of having that tattooed on my back. You any good with portraits, Ryann?"

"No way!" Sam held up her hand, finishing her glass of champagne. "Not a chance."

Luciana winked at Ryann, both of them smirking as Sam almost choked on the liquid in her mouth. Sam was easy to fool around with; this could be fun.

"Actually, it's one thing I specialise in," Ryann said. "You should get a picture over to me when you're ready. I'd love to be involved."

"You're both out of your fucking minds. *You* are not tattooing my wife." Sam looked pointedly at Ryann before giving Luciana a death glare. "And *you* are not having me tattooed on your body."

"Oh, we'll see about that." Luciana's hand slid to the base of Sam's spine, slowly smoothing over the curve of her ass as she brought her lips to Sam's ear, her voice painfully low. "Wouldn't you want to look at yourself while you have me on my knees, babe?"

"Canapes!" Sam slid out between Luciana and Ryann. "We need more canapes. Where the hell are the waiters?"

Ryann laughed as Sam disappeared, her attention turning to Luciana. "It's nice to see our Sam happy again."

"Do you not live around here, or...?" Luciana asked. "I thought we may have met before now."

"I've been travelling for a year. Australia. Came home when I met the woman of my dreams and she was leaving, too."

"That's some story to tell the kids."

"Oh, I'm not even thinking about that yet." Ryann moved through the marquee with Luciana, the evening air refreshing. "Gorgeous wedding."

"Sam did a great job. I didn't expect anything less."

"She's a talented woman," Ryann agreed, catching the attention of Susan. "Look, it was great meeting you. I should catch up with Auntie Sue. She'll chase me around later if I don't get it out of the way now."

"Oh, be my guest. While she's talking to you, she's leaving me alone."

Ryann's tall frame disappeared, her undercut now apparent as she walked away from Luciana. She was certainly an attractive woman, androgynous and stylish. She did have a look similar to Sam, though. It was the eyes. They definitely had similar eyes.

"So..." Sam stepped up behind Luciana, lowering her lips to her wife's ear. "About that tattoo."

"What about it?"

"You're not serious, are you?"

"Maybe I am."

"Baby, as much as I love the thought of forever being on your body, there are other ways to go about that." Sam turned Luciana in her arms, fresh champagne waiting for both of them. "Like, mind-numbing sex for the rest of our lives."

"That was already a given."

"Mm. So, Ryann was your artist." It was more of a statement than a question. Luciana wondered where Sam was going with this. "I had a moment of panic when you two met. I thought for a second she may have seen you naked for *other* reasons."

"Babe, I haven't banged every woman in the city. Most came from out of town. I promise, you have nothing to worry about. I haven't slept with *any* of your family. I can put my life on that."

"I'm not concerned."

Luciana cocked her head. "Ryann *is* a bit of a looker, though. You have the same eyes."

"Worried you chose the wrong cousin?" Sam's eyes flickered with a hint of jealousy. "I mean, it's not too late for you to rip up the paper we signed today. I'm sure the minister is still here somewhere."

"Now, now, honey." Luciana stepped closer, pressing her body against Sam's. "She's got nothing on you. Don't worry." Without another word, Luciana's lips found Sam's, the desperate need to taste her wife becoming more apparent. "Her eyes don't turn into pools of honey when the sun catches them like yours do. That would be the deciding factor for me."

Sam exhaled a long, slow breath, her forehead pressing against Luciana's. Today had been beautiful, Luciana's dress too, but Sam really needed her out of it. "How much longer do we have to entertain the guests for?"

"Mm, quite some time yet." Luciana had plans before this evening was over, and if Sam didn't stop looking at her the way she was, those plans would be happening right now. Guests or no guests.

"I've been thinking about you all day," Sam said. "Being away from you last night was hard. All I wanted was your hands on me. Your lips. Calling my name over and over and over…"

"Allow me to make it up to you tonight?"

"Mm. The first night as my wife. God, I can hardly wait."

A clearing of the throat behind them separated Sam and Luciana. As they turned, they found Jackie standing in front of them in a typical mother of the bride outfit. A huge blush hat covered half of her face, a matching fitted knee-length dress accompanying it.

"Hi, Mum." Luciana instinctively leaned in and hugged her mother. "You enjoying the evening?"

"Oh, it's gorgeous, girls. Really beautiful." Jackie's eyes held tears, worrying Luciana.

"Mum, is everything okay?"

"Of course, yeah." Jackie waved off her daughter's concerns, dabbing under her eyes with a tissue. "It's just been so lovely seeing you two today. God, you're so in love."

Sam tilted her head, offering Jackie a small smile. She knew exactly how Luciana's mum felt. Sam felt it, too. Something about today had truly tied everything up for them. The future...it was theirs for the taking.

"And Dad? Is he enjoying himself?"

"He's off discussing the layout of the garden with Sam's dad."

Sam smiled. "Should have known."

"I just...I wanted to give this to you both." Jackie handed an envelope over to Luciana. "It's not much, but it's just a little gift from us."

"Mum, you didn't have to do that. You've done enough preparing all of this with us."

"No, it's just a little something. Go away or buy something together for the house, I don't know. A piece of art or whatever it is you ladies are into these days."

"Thank you, Jackie." Sam pulled her mother-in-law into a strong embrace, appreciative of the gesture. It meant a lot. Sam knew Luciana's parents had struggled for cash over the last year, but she wouldn't offer it back. Sam knew how insulting that could be. After all, she'd been in the business long enough. "We will put it to good use."

"Maybe a little break away," Luciana chimed in, aware that her mum felt awkward for offering money. Neither of them needed it, but it really was thoughtful, and Luciana appreciated it. "I'm thinking a spa weekend."

Sam's smile beamed, mirrored by Jackie's. "And I think that is the *exact* reason I married you."

"Well, so long as you enjoy yourselves."

"We will. While you're here, can I get you another drink?"

"That's okay. I have one at the table I'm at with Marian."

"Marian?" Luciana was puzzled. She didn't know anyone called Marian.

"Ryann's mum. My mum's sister," Sam offered.

"Oh, right. Well, you know where I am if you need anything, Mum. And please enjoy yourself." Luciana gave her mum another hug, releasing her from her grip as she watched her walk away.

Jackie threw a wave over her shoulder. "I'll catch up with you girls later."

"Did I ever tell you how much I love your mum?" Sam sighed, wrapping her arm around Luciana's waist.

"She loves you, too."

"The night I met her," Sam started. "The night I came home from working away when she was at your flat…"

"Yeah?"

"We had a good talk. A much-needed talk. It was actually the reason I told you I loved you that night. She encouraged me to be honest with you. About how I felt."

"She's never told me that…"

"Because you didn't need to know." It was true. That conversation between Sam and Jackie had been exactly what Sam needed at the time. It wasn't anything Luciana needed to concern herself with, and as it happened, Sam wondered if Luciana had intentionally left her mother and girlfriend alone. "It all ended how it should have."

"Yeah?"

"Well, I've just married her daughter so I'm going to assume so."

Luciana watched from the decking as their guests slowly started to fade away. The night was wearing on, Luciana's feet throbbed, but Sam appeared to be having the time of her life. As she slowly resumed normality in the months following her accident, Sam slipped back into her usual self as the woman Luciana loved more than anything. Strong. Sexy. Empowering. Tonight, she exuded exactly that. The more Luciana watched her wife, the sooner she wanted this night to be over. It had been beautiful, magical, but it was time for her to steal Sam away…and lock them both inside the bedroom until further notice.

Lindsay and Cheryl sat out by the lake, wrapped up in one another's arms. Luciana smiled. How had everything worked out so well for the four of them? Fate. A blessing from above. Sheer determination and hard work. It could have been any of those things, or all three. Luciana was just happy to see Lindsay content for once. Lindsay's eyes held something different when she spoke about Cheryl. Nothing like they held for Janet when her name was unfortunately the topic of conversation.

Just three months after they got back together, Cheryl moved in with Lindsay. Sam's old apartment had never seen so much love, or so much colour. Cheryl had taken it upon herself to redecorate the place, explaining she didn't wish to live in what resembled a hospital theatre. Sam agreed; she'd always hated it. Luciana, on the other hand, couldn't hate the apartment. After all, it was where she'd shared her first kiss with Sam. The place where they first made love. During the nights when she was escorting, it was her sanctuary. That apartment would forever hold a place in Luciana's heart, but home was here by the lake.

"Luciana?"

Luciana turned her head; Ryann was standing beside her.

"Hey. I didn't know you were still here."

"I'm leaving now with Mum," Ryann said. "I just wanted to thank you for a great day. And for making our Sam the happiest woman in the world."

"It's been nice getting to know you. Small world though, huh?"

"Isn't that always the way?" Ryann smiled.

"I'll definitely be in touch to have some more work done, if you're up for that?"

"Always willing to feel the buzz of a tattoo gun in my hand." Ryann embraced Luciana. "I'll keep in touch with you both. Now that I'm home, we could hang out if Sam's ever out of town. Or even if she's not, whatever."

"Sounds great. You could always keep her company when I'm on shift..."

"You've got it."

Ryann disappeared out onto the lawn, saying her goodbyes to Sam. Her mum, Marian, followed closely behind. Too much champagne in such a short woman hadn't been the best idea in the world. Luciana suspected Marian would feel the effects of it in the morning. She, herself, had stopped drinking several hours ago; she wanted to remember her wedding night with Sam.

Lindsay and Cheryl moved towards Luciana, throws wrapped around them as a chill set in the air. Lindsay's eyes glistened against the twinkly lights surrounding them, Cheryl's face a picture of love. "We're headed home, Luce."

"Thank you for everything you've both done today. You know Sam and I appreciate it."

"Well, when you asked us both to be bridesmaids, I knew how hard I would have to work."

"You've been great, really."

"Our cab will be here in a few minutes. We should go and say goodnight to Sam."

"Yes, you should," Luciana agreed. "Come on, I'll head over with you."

Sam sunk down into a seat, kicking her heels off and groaning as the cool air hit her feet. She spent her life in heels, so why did they insist on retaliating today? Right now, she could do with a long, hot soak in the tub, but something in Luciana's eyes told her she had other ideas. Sam could hazard a guess as to what those ideas may entail, but the rest of this evening would surely lose the element of surprise. *Mm, I know exactly what she has planned. Sex. Lots and lots of sex.* Sam smirked as she watched her wife approach, her sister and assistant in tow. "Ladies..."

"Sam, we're leaving."

"You're the last two here. Just as I expected." Sam forced herself from her chair, embracing Lindsay and Cheryl. This night really was over now. As much as that saddened Sam, this was just the beginning of the rest of their lives together. "Be safe getting home, okay?"

"We will." Lindsay yawned, the night now taking its toll on everyone here. "You looked gorgeous today, Sis."

"As did you." Sam kissed Lindsay's cheek, the rumble of an engine up the drive catching her attention. "Cab's here."

"Thank God. It's been a long day."

"But a beautiful one," Cheryl chimed in. "I'll see you when you're back from your honeymoon, okay?"

"I trust you to keep the office standing while I'm gone."

"Yes, ma'am."

Sam held Luciana close to her, waving as Lindsay and Cheryl climbed into a cab. She had thought about offering them a spare room for the night, but she wasn't sure her sister would be overly enthused listening to them all night long. And that was exactly how this night would go...on and on until dawn broke.

"So, Mrs Foster," Luciana whispered, thrilled that Sam had chosen to take her surname, "can I tempt you with joining me in the bedroom?"

"Mm, I thought you'd never ask."

"In that case...meet me upstairs in five minutes."

"We're not going up together?" Sam's eyebrow rose. "No fireman's lift?"

"Not tonight, babe. I need a moment to prepare."

Sam sighed, her eyes beaming. "I can hardly wait."

Luciana heard footsteps in their bedroom as she approached the closed bathroom door. She'd snuck upstairs a few minutes ago to prepare for their first night of married life together; her only hope now that Sam wouldn't turn down her suggestion. This night...she wanted it to be perfect.

She gripped the handle, opening the door to find Sam leaning against the window frame. Her long, white gown trailed across the floor behind her, a vision against the moonlight pouring through the window into the darkened room. Luciana was rendered speechless. She could only watch on in silence and stillness as her wife took a moment to allow the day to end. Sam, tonight, could take as long as she needed. No rush. No urgency. No pressure to do anything other than just be.

This is what their lives had become lately. Calmer. Less stressful. Sam had handed off her last project to a team she set up and knew she could trust, and life moved along just fine. She didn't spend as much time as she used to at the office, only choosing to be there when Luciana worked a day shift. If Luciana was free, so was Sam. And it worked perfectly. Less pressure meant that Sam could manage her time *and* her life better. As the days wore on, she decided that pleasure was significantly more appealing than business.

Once they'd returned from the cottage in Yorkshire, Luciana helped Sam through her anxiety surrounding public spaces, affording her whatever time she needed. Sometimes they made it as far as the office, other times to the end of the garden path. It was all trial, error, patience, and occasionally sheer luck, but Luciana didn't push Sam. She simply stood by her side, encouraging her to do whatever she felt comfortable with. Now, the explosion was a distant memory. One they both chose not to discuss. That time represented hell on earth for Luciana—everything appearing to go wrong—and it didn't need to be rehashed. Ever.

Sam pulled the pin holding her hair in place, silky, dark locks falling down her naked back. Her dress plunged to the base of her spine, sending Luciana's heart rate through the roof when she saw her wife for the first time today. Luciana now knew what it felt like to have her breath stolen. Of all the moments she'd thought it true in the past, nothing compared to their wedding. Today, as she met Sam out on the lake, only family and close friends witnessing their marriage, Luciana would have given everything up to the gods. Sam, in all her beauty, stole Luciana's heart for the final time. There was no backing out anymore. Luciana was cemented in Sam's life, and she couldn't imagine being anywhere else.

Luciana slowly crossed the room, reaching out her hand and taking Sam's as it hung at her side. Their fingers laced, Luciana pressing her body against Sam's back, removing Sam's hair from her shoulder.

"This day..." Sam's voice held an array of emotions.

Luciana slid her free hand around her wife's waist, pulling Sam back against her as she whispered, "Has been beautiful."

"You made me the happiest woman in the world this afternoon." Sam wanted to say so much to Luciana. She was also struggling with the idea of keeping her hands to herself for much longer. Her fingertips ached to touch Luciana's skin.

"Thank you," Luciana said against the skin of Sam's neck, her perfume comforting. Home. "For giving me a chance to love you. For trusting that I could be the one you spend your life with. For loving *me*."

"I never imagined this for one moment, Luce. How could I? I had tunnel vision and all I saw when I woke up was work. It was a miserable existence but look at what I gained. You." Sam would spend forever making Luciana happy. It was the least she could do after the difference Luciana had made to Sam's life. "This, what we have, is all down to you. How I feel every morning when I wake up, the happiness, is *all* down to you. So, thank *you*."

Luciana turned Sam in her arms, brushing a few strands of hair from her face. "God, you're so beautiful."

"Do I really get to wake up beside you for the rest of my life?"

Sam's eyes filled with tears; her heart thrumming hard when she leaned into Luciana's touch. "Do I...really?"

"You do, babe."

"Oh, God." Sam's tears fell, caught by the pad of Luciana's thumb.

"Hey, come on." Luciana wrapped her arms around Sam, soothing her until her tears subsided. "You good?"

"I'm so good." Sam smiled as she moved towards the bed and dropped down with a thud. Sam kicked off her heels, her feet thankful for the opportunity to breathe now that the evening was over. Luciana stood in front of her, staring, watching her every move. "Why are you looking at me like that?" Sam couldn't quite place the look Luciana was giving her—a sexy squint laced with an animalistic urge to fuck Sam against the nearest wall was the closest she could describe it.

"Stand up," Luciana whispered, prowling towards Sam as her heart beat out of her chest. "I want to see you one last time in this dress before I take it off your delicious body and make love to you as my wife."

Sam's body reacted instantly. She did exactly as Luciana asked, brushing her hair from her shoulder and standing, meeting Luciana's eyes.

"Look at that," Luciana exhaled, taken aback by the incredible beauty Sam possessed. "Just as breathtaking as you've looked all day. Flawless. Stunning." Luciana reached out, touching Sam's face lightly. "Nobody in this world looks as beautiful as you do, Sam. *Nobody.*"

"Thank you."

Luciana turned Sam around, loosening the back of her wedding gown with ease. She watched the silk material fall down Sam's back, her breath catching when it pooled at Sam's feet. "O-oh, sweet Jesus."

Sam turned back around, a white lace strapless bra covering her full breasts, complete with a matching garter belt and suspenders.

Sam's hands instinctively found her own stomach, wrapping her arms around herself. Why did she feel nervous? "Does it look okay?"

"O-okay?" Luciana was losing the ability to speak. "You did this for me?"

"Y-yes."

Luciana took her bottom lip between her teeth, closing her eyes briefly. She just needed a second. One moment to compose herself. The throbbing between her legs was making it painfully hard to do so. "I-I need you to help me out of my dress." It was all Luciana could offer. Her communication skills suddenly lacking.

"Turn around, baby." Sam placed a kiss to the back of Luciana's neck, lowering the hidden zip on her dress. Sliding the pin out that was holding Luciana's hair in place, long blonde locks cascaded down her back, sitting above the base of her spine. Luciana's back muscles flexed as the cool air reached her skin, arousal tearing through Sam the longer her teasing continued.

Sam traced her fingertips down the side of Luciana's toned stomach, stopping abruptly when they reached her waist. Something was preventing her from moving further, but it wasn't underwear. No, it was a harness. Sam's want skyrocketed. They'd discussed the use of a strap-on once in the eighteen months they'd been together, the conversation coming to nothing.

"Babe?" Luciana spoke quietly. She wouldn't be upset if Sam chose to remove the harness she was wearing, but she would be angry with herself for overstepping. Right now, she wasn't sure which way it would swing. With any luck, it would be in her favour.

Sam didn't respond. Instead, she pressed her body against Luciana's back, her fingers dipping between strong thighs. Her wife was soaked.

"O-oh, Sam..." Luciana's thighs closed around Sam's hand. She needed to stave off the release she already felt building. "S-shit!"

"Turn around, Luciana."

Her name fell from Sam's lips like honey. When Luciana turned, Sam's eyes told her she had *nothing* to worry about. Black. Aroused. Desperate for more. Sam trusted her; that's exactly what her eyes said.

"D-do you?" Luciana asked, Sam's breathing laboured. "Do you want this?"

Sam stepped away, climbing onto the bed and positioning herself in the middle. Luciana remained still a moment longer, Sam's eyes focused on the toy hanging between her legs before they trailed the expanse of Luciana's body. Realising that her wife truly did want this, Luciana placed her knee at the foot of the bed, climbing up and between Sam's legs. Her sex was completely exposed, just waiting for Luciana to sink deep.

Nervous anticipation travelled through Sam's body, her skin on fire as Luciana's fingers ghosted her thigh, ultimately dipping between her legs. They moaned in unison, Sam's due to Luciana's featherlight touch, Luciana's caused by Sam's wetness on the tips of her fingers.

Luciana braced herself on her left forearm, her right hand still working her wife up. She wanted Sam to be fully ready for her, even though it appeared she already was. Luciana wanted Sam begging for more, desperate for the intensity Luciana was currently feeling.

"Luce." Sam's voice dropped low, her desire heightening when she looked down between their bodies. "Fuck, I need you inside me."

Luciana gave her exactly that, pushing two fingers inside. "You feel amazing." Luciana dipped her head, taking Sam's lips softly. Her blonde hair fell over them like a veil, protected from the world outside. Luciana drew back, her eyes focused on Sam's. "Do you trust me?"

Sam's heart burst. She cupped Luciana's face as she whispered, "With my life."

Luciana gathered Sam's arousal, coating the silicone between her legs with it. Sitting back on her knees, she took a moment to take in the vision of Sam lay before her, open and ready for one hell of an experience. She saw the nervous element in her eyes, but that was overpowered by the want and love shining from them. Luciana guided the strap-on between Sam's lips, running the shaft up and down her slit—swollen and slick.

Sam gripped Luciana's wrist. "Have you done this before?"

"Yes." Luciana noted the flicker of hesitation in Sam's eyes. "But feeling how I do right now...*never*."

Sam released her grip, offering Luciana a slight nod. She wasn't jealous of those before her, Luciana had a past, but so long as this moment felt new for them both...that was what Sam would focus on.

Luciana pushed the head inside Sam, their eyes never leaving one another's. This moment was something beautiful. Sam was a vision. She slid deeper, giving Sam a moment to adjust.

Sam nodded, silently begging Luciana for more. This intensity was new, interesting, but extremely satisfying. Nothing and nobody had ever been so deep. "M-more." Sam beckoned Luciana closer, thrilled when her wife's body weighed her own down. Nothing was as pleasurable as Luciana's skin on her. Their hearts beating in rhythm. Slick and sweaty.

Luciana popped the clasp on the front of Sam's bra, instantly taking a nipple into her mouth while her hips rolled, filling Sam so perfectly. "Babe," Luciana moaned against Sam's breast. "God, you're so fucking tight."

With those words, Sam's walls squeezed. Sam would always love the raw honesty in Luciana's voice as she drove her towards the edge. Her laboured breathing, those intense deep blue eyes, her lips. Sam weaved her fingers through Luciana's hair, bringing their lips together.

When Luciana's mouth fell open, the base of the strap-on pushing against her clit, a guttural moan rumbled in her throat.

Sam's hips matched every thrust, hitting that sweet spot inside her. She gripped Luciana's ass, forcing her deeper and harder as her release approached.

Luciana felt it coming; she could barely move inside Sam. "Together," Luciana breathed, her eyes on Sam. Her hand slid between them, pressing her fingertips to Sam's swollen clit, grinding herself against her hand, anything she could. "Babe, I'm so close."

Sam guided her hand around the back of Luciana's thigh, sinking two fingers inside her from behind. Luciana clenched, the sound of sex filling the room as the bed strained, slamming against the wall. "O-oh, fuck." Sam's head buried deeper into the pillow as she arched into Luciana. Every muscle in her body screamed for release, white hot heat burning low in her belly. Sam thought she would explode. "I-I—" A strangled cry ripped from Sam's throat, Luciana's name quickly following before her mouth fell open.

Luciana fell forward, short sharp thrusts all she could manage as her own orgasm rolled through her like a steam train. Sam gripped her back, her sweet moans reaching Luciana's ear as her breath washed over the side of her face. "Oh, babe..."

"Shush." Sam turned her face into Luciana's neck, inhaling her intoxicating scent.

Luciana refrained from trying to find the words to describe what had just happened. In her eyes, monumental. Her body, it would never be the same again. Her thighs damp with arousal, she slowly pulled out of Sam, her bottom lip firmly between her teeth. "You're so wet..."

"Mm." Sam had nothing else to give.

"I should probably get you cleaned up."

"I wouldn't disagree." Sam watched Luciana move lower down her body, Sam's hand pushing on her head and helping Luciana find her way. As her wife's skilled tongue reached her sensitive clit, Sam arched off the bed, her hands fisting in the sheets, and gasped, "Fuck! I married the woman of my dreams today."

EPILOGUE

One year later...
Luciana pushed through the front door, an array of takeout bags in both hands. Sam wanted curry, so curry was what she would have. The wait had been tedious, Luciana almost falling asleep in the car outside the local Indian curry house, but Sam wouldn't sleep tonight without it. Luciana knew that as she drove home from her shift at the station, her eyes requiring matchsticks in order to stay open.

"Sam?"

"Coming!" Sam trudged down the stairs, her footsteps heavy and requiring more effort than usual. She could happily eat dinner in bed, but the thought of Indian spices attacking her nostrils first thing in the morning had her stomach lurching. "Did you get everything we usually have?"

"Yes, Your Majesty."

"You're amazing." Sam exhaled, kissing Luciana's cheek as she disappeared into the kitchen.

"You're sure you wanted the extra hot?"

Sam was already ripping the brown paper bags open on the

counter, grabbing a spoon from the marble as she forced the lid of a container open. "Mm. Extra hot."

"You're insane." Luciana plated up their dishes, taking another container from Sam. "Babe, you can have a pakora in the next ten seconds. Just give me one moment to dish it all out." Luciana looked up to find a pakora hanging from Sam's mouth. "Or not."

"Sorry."

"Have you eaten at all today?"

"Yeah. Lindsay came over this afternoon with food from the new deli."

Luciana frowned. "But you're starving."

"Can't help it." Sam swiped a plate from the counter, rushing into the living room as fast as she could. Luciana had been working a lot lately, Sam not so much. Tonight was the start of three days off for her wife. Three days that couldn't have come soon enough. "How was work?"

"Pretty quiet."

Luciana joined Sam in the living room, getting down to her knees at the coffee table. Sam relaxed back on the couch, her legs uncomfortably crossed beneath her body. "You said on the phone earlier that you had good news..."

"Craig's wife. She's in remission."

Sam dropped her fork to her plate. "What? That's amazing. I'm so happy for them both."

"Craig was crying when he called us. I'm just so glad they can relax now. I mean, we all know it isn't necessarily the end of their journey but God, I really hope it is."

"Me, too." Sam reached out, squeezing Luciana's shoulder. "Join me up here?"

Luciana obliged, dropping down beside Sam with her own mountain of samosas, jasmine rice, and beef Balti. "You feelin' okay, babe?"

"I think so, yeah." Sam blew out a deep breath, resting her dinner on her stomach. "Just can't do much now."

"I know. I'm sorry. Everything will be over before we know it."

"This could go on for a couple more weeks. I don't think I have the strength to carry myself *and* a child around with me. Not in here, anyway." Sam smoothed her hand over her baby bump, the size of it surprising them both as the months wore on. Sam didn't know it was possible to become so huge during pregnancy, and Luciana often wondered how Sam coped carrying such a weight around with her. "I noticed you'd rearranged my bag again."

"Sorry. I'm getting impatient. It gives me something to do when I'm trying to pass time." Luciana's head fell to Sam's shoulder as she sighed. In the coming weeks, they would be parents. In a few weeks, everything around the house would change. Sam had already lessened her load at the office in the last year or so, but Luciana still felt as though she didn't see her as often as she would like. Work was getting harder with government cutbacks, and since Sam's accident—two years on—Luciana's desire to be at the station was becoming less and less. Throw in a pregnancy and she never wanted to leave Sam's side again.

She had thought about it—quitting her job—but it wasn't that simple. She couldn't just leave a career behind that she'd worked so hard for. A career which was extremely fulfilling in every way. The difference between now and a few years ago though was that Luciana had other priorities. They both did. It was no longer going to be just the two of them. Luciana seriously had to consider her options.

Sam had thrown out a suggestion several months ago regarding the need for a new fire officer for her company, but Luciana hadn't discussed it with her wife yet. Sam hadn't *actually* offered Luciana the job, but she knew that was where Sam was going with the conversation. Since Sam had begun struggling to do everyday tasks, her feet swollen and her back aching, Luciana had started to ponder it. Working within Sam's company wasn't anything she had ever thought about, but she would be lying if she said she hadn't toyed with the idea this afternoon as she sat around with the lads. She would still be doing what she loved—protecting the public, just in a different way.

Given the circumstances around Lucia's death, Luciana knew how important fire safety was to Sam. Of course, it *should* be important whether there is a past with fire or not, but Luciana saw the dedication and determination in Sam's beautiful brown eyes whenever she discussed concerns with her properties. She was also shocked to learn of the lengths other property developers would go to in order to save a little extra money, corner cutting and using cheap materials. Nothing like that would *ever* clad Sam's buildings.

"Hand." Sam tugged at Luciana's wrist, settling her hand on her belly.

Luciana smiled, her eyes closing momentarily as their baby kicked. She would never tire of experiencing the sensation of an unborn baby making its presence known. Luciana often lay awake at night smoothing her hand across the tight skin of Sam's stomach; she would spend forever in that position given half the chance.

"Baby is thanking mummy for dinner." Sam's own hand rested on top of Luciana's, the room falling silent once again.

Luciana set her plate down on the coffee table. "Baby can have *anything* they want."

"You know..." Sam watched on as Luciana pushed her T-shirt up her stomach, her lips caressing every inch of skin. She should just enjoy these moments, but pregnancy made her one hell of an emotional wreck and she had so much she needed to say. "I never thought this would be my dream. Lying here, *heavily* pregnant. I mean, it was always supposed to be this way, I know that, but after my life fell apart...it was just something I couldn't envisage. I thought my chance had come and gone. That it was some kind of punishment when Lucia died because I hadn't taken the time to step away from work. To create the life we both wanted."

Luciana understood Sam completely. They'd discussed Sam and her desire to have children not long after they'd become exclusive, but Luciana, too, didn't imagine this moment would arrive. To say this all felt surreal was the understatement of the century.

"I never thought I would find someone who I love so much that I cannot bear to be away from them. I certainly didn't imagine you, Luce. And I know, we've been over this before, more than once, but I really need you to know that I couldn't see myself doing this with anyone other than you. You made me your wife, and now I'm going to be the mother of your child. This has to be the greatest achievement of my life, and I have *you* by my side for that. To cheer me on. To support me. To love me, fully." Sam closed her eyes, breathing through the ache that settled in her lower abdomen. "Sorry, but I think I need to pee."

"Okay. Let me help you up." Luciana wanted to assure Sam that everything was good, that her words meant the world to her, but Sam *did* look like she needed to use the bathroom.

Luciana gripped both of Sam's hands, helping her up from the couch. She appeared to be in mild discomfort, but Sam had been experiencing some aches and pains in the last few days. Nothing worrying. Luciana believed it was Sam's body telling her it'd had enough. She could hardly blame it for feeling that way. "You good?"

Sam wrinkled her nose. "Mm."

"You're sure?"

"I just..." Sam shook her head, exhaling a deep breath. Before she could explain to Luciana how she was feeling, water started to trickle down her thighs, seeping through her grey, yoga-style maternity pants. *Well, that's flattering.* "Um."

Luciana's brow furrowed. She had no idea what was going on with Sam, but she was growing increasingly concerned. "Babe? You okay?"

Sam looked down between them, Luciana still holding her hands tight.

"What's going on? Tell me how you're feeling. Do you need to lie down?"

"I-I think it's happening," Sam said, a wave of anxiety tearing through her, followed by a stronger lower back pain. "Yep. It's happening."

"W-what?" Luciana's eyes widened as she visibly swallowed hard.

"The baby. It's ready to get this show on the road."

"O-oh, fuck! Shit. Uh..."

"Calm down." Sam breathed deeply through her nose, Luciana's face becoming paler as the seconds passed. They had this. It couldn't be that hard. Sam was really praying that the mind-numbing anti-natal classes would pay off. It was time to find out.

"Calm down?" Luciana repeated. "How can I calm down when you're about to give birth and I've got no idea what to do. I mean, are you sure this is happening? I know you're overdue, but really? You're sure? You haven't just peed yourself?"

Sam laughed, cocking her head to the side. "Did you honestly just ask your wife if she's peed herself?"

"Well, yeah. I mean, it's nothing to be embarrassed about. The baby is pressing on probably everything in there. If you have, it's okay. I still love you."

The dull ache in Sam's back became stronger, sending her upper body forward and bent as she gripped Luciana's hands tighter.

"Nope. You didn't pee yourself. This is happening."

Luciana was panicking. An overwhelming sense of uncertainty rolled through her, sending her blood pressure through the roof. She was almost certain she was sweating profusely—that was never a good look. Everything she had read and everything she had learned at the classes she'd taken with Sam had gone right out of the window. Everything Luciana *thought* she knew...gone.

"Right. Okay. Let's do this." Luciana remained frozen in her spot with Sam still keeled over in front of her. *Get a fucking grip, woman.* She internally chastised herself, closing her eyes momentarily and breathing with Sam. It was all she could do. She was lost. "Um, what do we do again?"

"You know t-the bag you've been rearranging s-since we found out we were pregnant?"

"Yeah."

"Well, we kinda n-need it now, Luce."

"Oh, yeah. Bag. Got it." Luciana attempted to move towards the staircase but stopped. "Wait, I can't leave you. You could fall or give birth and I wouldn't be here."

"Baby, I'm not going to give birth in the next thirty seconds. And I won't fall. I'm okay."

This side of Luciana—terrified to within an inch of her life—had to be the most adorable thing Sam had ever witnessed. If she wasn't already busy trying not to push out their child, Sam would surely pick up her phone and start recording. The seriousness of Luciana fell away and all that remained was a woman who didn't know which way was up. Yes, it was hilarious.

Luciana came flying back down the stairs, her feet barely touching the floor. "Right, um..."

"You should call the hospital. Tell them we're on our way up. Even just to check if I need to be there or not."

"Okay. Maybe we could get you into some fresh clothes before we leave? I'm sure you'd be more comfortable in some clean pants at least."

And there she was. The woman who Sam needed by her side. "That would be great."

"Sit down for a second. I'll be right back."

Luciana paced the floor outside the entrance to the hospital, her phone in her hand as she tried to reach her mum. She needed some words of encouragement—someone who would tell her everything was going to be perfectly fine and go according to plan. In her heart, it couldn't be any more perfect, but Luciana was slowly losing the plot the longer she sat around in Sam's hospital room. Lindsay was with her, the second birthing partner, and she would call Luciana immediately if there were any signs that their child was about to enter the world. By the time they'd reached the hospital, Sam was four centimetres dilated. The midwife chose to keep Sam in, explaining that things were moving along exactly how they should be, and quicker than Sam or Luciana had anticipated.

"Luce, love..."

"Hi, Mum. Just calling with an update."

"You only texted me ten minutes ago." Jackie's voice held an element of amusement; she knew her daughter too well. "If something is on your mind, come out and say it."

"I can be a good mum, can't I?" Luciana hadn't thought about it before now, but what if this all fell apart once their baby arrived? "I mean, I'll know what to do, won't I?"

"It all comes naturally, love. And I know better than anyone just how loved yours and Sam's baby will be."

Luciana's smile widened. "Yeah?"

"You're both wonderful people. The love you have for Sam will only spill over into your child. That baby will be *so* loved."

"I hate seeing Sam in pain," Luciana confessed. "You know, I just want it all to be over."

"And I'm sure Sam does, too, but this is all a part of the process, Luciana. When the time is right, your baby will come into the world and nothing will ever be the same again. You'll wonder how either of you ever survived without your son or daughter. Life before won't make any sense."

"Thanks, Mum." Luciana could have done with having her mum around at a time like this, but it was too short notice and Jackie would only panic, rushing from Manchester to be by her daughter's side. "I'll call you again if I have any news, okay?"

"When my grandchild arrives, I want you to embrace every

second of it. I'll *know* when they're born. Mother's instinct that her daughter's life has come full circle."

Luciana held back the tears in her eyes, smiling. "Mum?"

"Yes, love?"

"I'm leaving the brigade."

"Does Sam know?" Jackie asked.

"Not yet. I've just been thinking about it."

"And what made you decide?"

"This moment. Knowing I have a child who is going to rely on me being there. I don't think I can run towards burning buildings anymore, Mum."

"O...kay."

"And I know I've spent years telling you that nothing is going to happen to me. That I'm perfectly safe doing what I love. But I love my wife and kid more than my career. I'm not willing to risk anything that could take me away from them."

"Only you know what's best for you, my love. And I know Sam will stand by any decision you make. You're a good partnership. Just...enjoy this moment. It'll be over like a flash, and *then* you can think about the next step of your life."

"Thanks, Mum. I knew I could rely on you."

"Always, sweetheart. Now, go and be with your wife. If that child pops out and you're not there, that'll be on your mind for the rest of your life."

"Oh, I'm pretty sure I'd be divorced by the end of the week if I wasn't there with her." Luciana laughed, feeling dramatically calmer than she did before her call connected with her mum. "Well, I should go. It's almost time to become a mum."

"The two most beautiful mums in this world, love. Give Sam a kiss for me."

"I will. Love you. Bye."

"Goodbye, Luce."

Sam rocked back and forth on her heels, her body bent forward over the bed. The sooner this was all over, the sooner she wouldn't feel as though her insides were being torn out. This pain wasn't *anything* like she had anticipated, assuming they would be similar to her cramps every month. This? This was nothing like that. A couple of paracetamol wouldn't subdue any of this; the internet was a liar. "Luce..."

"What do you need, babe?"

"C-can you rub my back again for me?" Sam braced her arms in front of her, balling her hands into fists and resting her forehead on them. Luciana had been an angel from the moment they arrived at the hospital, doing anything and everything Sam needed. It wasn't lost on Sam that her wife had recently finished a twelve-hour shift at the station, but she was here being incredibly supportive and very much awake. Possibly more awake than Sam.

Within a second, Luciana was at Sam's side. The palm of her hand rubbed slowly but firmly against Sam's lower back, directly above her ass cheeks. She knew that the harder she pressed, the more relief Sam felt. The more attention to detail she could give, the calmer Luciana felt. She didn't know how they'd made it through this night so far, it was coming up to two in the morning, but Luciana felt more awake and more alive than she ever had. Knowing that they would soon hold a bundle of joy in their arms —one that probably looked strikingly like Sam since she held the dominant features—sleep was the last thing on Luciana's mind.

During the choosing of the sperm donor stage, Sam made it clear that she wanted their choice to have elements of Luciana's features. Of course, being dark-haired with deep brown eyes, Sam would always dominate, but Luciana appreciated her wife thinking about the little things.

Sam would carry this child because of her age, but they had no plans to stop at one. If Sam wanted ten kids, Luciana would do everything she could to make that happen. The next would be cooked up by Luciana. Both had been through fertility testing, and thankfully, Luciana would be able to take it from here when the time came for them to decide to try again.

"I-I feel like I need to push." Sam's voice held an element of pain, but frustration more than anything. With the nurse in the room monitoring Sam's and the baby's vitals, Luciana glanced her way.

"Okay, Sam. Maybe we could get you onto the bed..."

"I don't know if I can."

"Well, we will give it a go," Jenny, their nurse, said. "We want you to be as comfortable as possible, but I would really like to examine you before we go any further in terms of pushing."

"Okay. Yeah." A tired and weary Sam forced herself onto the bed with the help of Luciana. Lindsay was at her other side, throwing out some words of encouragement whenever she thought she should. So far, Sam had been the epitome of calm, but that could change at any moment. Luciana *and* Lindsay knew that. Given the condition her sister was in, Lindsay really didn't want to push any of Sam's buttons tonight. Not a single one.

"L-Linds," Sam started, getting herself into the correct position as her nurse gloved up. "Have you called Mum since we got here?"

"I have. She said she would make her way over whenever I gave her the go-ahead."

"Okay, good." Sam half-smiled, resting her head back as Jenny's hand roamed about between her thighs. "Luce, did you call your mum?"

"I did, babe."

"Is she okay? Does she want to be here?"

"I had thought about asking her to travel down, but you know what she's like. She'll panic."

"No, I know." Sam squeezed Luciana's hand, lifting it and pressing her lips to her skin. "How are you? Do you want to sleep for a bit?"

"Sorry, ladies." Jenny cleared her throat. "No signs of sleeping any time soon. You're ten centimetres, Sam. If you feel like you need to push...be my guest."

With those words, Luciana started to second guess herself. Time felt as though it was slowing, so why was her heart rate increasing? Luciana's face suddenly drained of colour as the realisation hit her. They were about to become parents. She took a seat in the mottled blue, high-back leather chair beside Sam, she had to remain calm. "Y-you're sure it's time?"

"Baby's head came to greet me. It's time." Jenny changed her gloves, gowning herself ready for the delivery of their baby.

"Sam..." Luciana exhaled a deep breath, closing her eyes. "T-this is happening, babe. Right now, this is happening."

"Thank God."

Lindsay sat quietly in the corner of the room, her eyes trained on the floor as Jenny allowed Sam to get into a more comfortable position. As much as she loved being here, she had no intentions of checking out Sam's most intimate areas. They were close, but nobody needed to be *that* close.

"Okay, I r-really need t-to push," Sam panted, aware that Luciana's hand was trembling in her own. "Baby, I need you with me, o-okay?"

"I'm here. I'm not leaving." Luciana climbed to her feet, removed her jacket and pressed a kiss to Sam's forehead. Once again taking her wife's hand, Luciana squared her shoulders and looked Sam directly in the eyes. "Come on, babe. We've got this. You're going to be amazing."

"When you feel the need to push, remember, chin on your chest, Sam. Push down into your bottom." Jenny positioned herself at the end of the bed, thankfully blocking Lindsay's view. "Why don't you take the other side of your sister, Lindsay?"

Sam held out her hand, motioning for Lindsay to join her. Doing so, Lindsay could only watch the incredible love radiating from Luciana on the other side of Sam. Luciana's eyes never once left her sister. Her hand squeezing tight as Sam felt the wave of another contraction set to hit. Sam forced her chin down against her chest, holding her breath and pushing hard. When Sam finally came up for air, her face red with her hair stuck to her forehead, Lindsay brushed it away, gaining a weak, thankful smile from her sister.

"You've got this, Sam." Lindsay lowered her voice as she leaned down and pressed a kiss to her sister's temple. "And I'm so fucking proud of you."

"Linds..." Sam gasped for air, giving herself a moment of respite before they went again. "I'm so happy y-you're here w-with me."

"Wouldn't be anywhere else."

"C-Cheryl. She d-doesn't mind you being away tonight?" Sam felt another sudden urge to push. "O-oh!" Once again, her chin pushed into her chest, the sensation between her legs felt different to the last one. "W-what's happening? Is everything okay? Jenny?"

"Everything is fine, Sam." Jenny popped her head up, smiling. "Give me your hand..."

Sam obliged, reaching her hand forward and trusting Jenny with whatever the hell she was doing. Sam gasped when she felt a head of hair...between her legs. "Oh, God!"

"What?" Luciana panicked, her eyes flashing with concern as she switched from Sam to Jenny. "What is it?"

"Baby..." Sam found Luciana's eyes, tears in her own. "Place your hand over mine."

Luciana frowned, leaning down towards Sam's ear. "I'm not sure that's appropriate right now, Sam." With her voice low, Luciana pulled back to find a shocked look on Sam's face. "What?"

"Really?" Sam deadpanned.

"Well, I don't know." Luciana shrugged. "You've been kinda unpredictable lately."

"Give me your bloody hand." Sam released Lindsay from her grip, using her free hand to guide Luciana towards their baby's head. "Feel that?"

"O-oh! Is that what I think it is?" Luciana's eyes widened, an overwhelming sense of accomplishment roaring through her body. This moment, it was intense. Nothing had ever felt like this. Not even their wedding day. "Is that our baby?" Luciana's voice broke when she looked at Sam, her eyes glistening as she nodded yes.

"That's our baby."

"Ready to push again, Sam?" Jenny interrupted their moment. Sam could lie like this forever, but she wanted their baby in her arms. Not tucked away between her legs for the rest of time.

"I'm ready." Sam gripped the backs of her own thighs, desperately hoping this would be one of the last pushes. She felt as though things were moving along, and judging by the head poking out, they were.

Luciana watched on in awe. The woman she called her wife was one exceptional human being. Luciana was fully aware of how amazing Sam was, but every day she surprised her. "That's it, babe." Luciana cheered Sam on as she peeked at their baby once again. With shoulders now showing, Luciana's heart could barely contain her excitement. Her love for something she hadn't yet met. The absolute joy seeping from every pore. "Sam, you're doing amazing."

With one final push, Sam fell back on the bed, a sudden lightness to her body. Whatever was happening, had happened. She didn't feel the pressure between her legs anymore, the contractions had subsided dramatically, she felt free.

Lindsay sobbed in the corner, clearly shaken by what she had just witnessed. Sam wanted to console her, tell her everything was okay and the worst was over, but she couldn't. Her brain was shutting down—tiredness settling in.

"Congratulations, ladies." Sam didn't have the energy to lift her head, her entire body exhausted. "Luciana, if you'd like to take over here?"

Jenny handed Luciana scissors, the clamp already in place

around the baby's umbilical cord. Luciana swallowed hard, tears streaming down her face. "W-what do I do?"

"Cut between the clamp. Don't worry, you won't hurt *him*."

"H-him?" Luciana's heart burst from her chest, snipping the chord and freeing their son from Sam's body. In one swift movement, Jenny had slipped their baby under Sam's shirt, placing him against her chest. "Babe, it's a boy."

"Oh, God." Sam sobbed, her arms holding the chunky tiny human against her. Luciana was climbing into the bed beside her, weeping into the side of Sam's neck as she peppered kisses anywhere she possibly could.

"I'm so proud of you," Luciana whispered. "So proud of everything you are. So thankful for everything you have ever given me. I love you, Sam Foster."

"I love you, too." Sam's life had come full circle. Everything she'd been through was supposed to happen. It may have been messed up, unnecessary pain, but everything that was unfolding right now was supposed to be in her future. Sam felt it. She was connected to it. Life...it had truly fallen into place. Officially.

God, he's so beautiful. Luciana couldn't take her eyes off the miracle enveloped by her. His chubby hands, how he sucked his bottom lip into his mouth. This moment, she had no words. Nothing could begin to explain how she felt about the child in her arms. It was a love Luciana didn't think she was capable of. Of course, she was in love with her wife, but this? This was a different kind of love. A love that held no description. A love that shattered every illusion. A love that could destroy everything Luciana had ever believed. The world, tonight, was an entirely different place to what she had lived in before. The thought of their baby not being here, Luciana couldn't comprehend it. It was as though he had *always* been here. Safely in her arms. Loved and cared for.

Luciana glanced over at Sam who was sleeping soundly in the hospital bed of their private room. Her facial features appeared different. Relaxed. As though something had changed within her. Luciana felt exactly the same. They were no longer *just* Sam and Luciana. No, they were now mothers. Parents. With one hell of a reason to live. If someone had told Luciana some three years ago that she would have all of this, a wife and a child, she would have shown her ass out of the nearest window. This life wasn't ever supposed to happen to her. But was she appreciative? Damn right she was.

If Luciana closed her eyes, she could recall the moment they met. Sam's intoxicating but subtle scent. Her dull, lifeless eyes as Luciana sidled up to the bar in the tapas restaurant on the dock. The little black dress she wore that would have enticed Luciana even if she hadn't wanted it to. But, most of all, she would forever remember the respect Sam gave her. It wasn't common in her days of being an escort. One hint of her profession and the world looked down their nose at Luciana. Sam, she was different. Sam had an immediate respect in her eyes. One that Luciana would never forget. That respect was still visible to this day.

When all was said and done, they were made for each other.

"You know, I think I need to check that contract your mummy signed three years ago, buddy." Luciana's thumb gently caressed her son's cheek. He squirmed in her arms, pulling his little fists up against his chest. "She only wanted dinner and conversation. She somehow ended up with a wife and kid."

Luciana lifted her son, placing him against her chest as she rocked back in the chair she'd commandeered from their nurse a couple of hours ago.

Luciana giggled to herself. "Dinner and conversation. She saw me coming, son. There was no way it was going to end that way. I used my flirty eyes with her. I'll teach you. It'll get you all the ladies. Or the guys. Whichever you prefer."

Luciana pressed a kiss to her son's head, his mop of dark

brown hair potentially the reason for Sam's horrific heartburn throughout her pregnancy. At least, that's what Sam had declared once she'd taken a moment to relax after her labour. The internet had suggested it months ago, but Luciana explained that he would probably enter the world completely bald. No such luck. At least he would be prepared for the winter with so much hair.

"Do you think she'll want to go on a date with me when she's feeling better?" Luciana spoke to their son as though he was about to give her all of the answers to life's questions. "I mean, it'll only be dinner and conversation, but do you think she'll go for it?"

He squirmed again, his tiny eyes peeking open as a cry rumbled in his chest.

"No? Okay." Luciana stood up, rocking her son. "She's already got you around her little finger. Christ. Okay, so how about I woo her? She deserves to be wooed all day, every day. You think she'll go for that?"

"You're wooing me right now, beautiful."

Luciana's head shot up, finding Sam watching her. She had a beaming smile on her face, one that Luciana wanted to capture and keep forever. "Did I wake you?"

"Nope." Sam pushed herself up in the bed, sitting better as she adjusted her pillows. She groaned, wrinkling her nose as a throb set in between her legs. "Word of warning: never push out a nine-pound thirteen-ounce kid. It doesn't end well."

"You sore, babe?" Luciana closed the distance between them, the baby in her arms beginning to stir now that it was time to be fed.

"A little. I'm sure everything will be okay in a couple of days."

"What you did earlier was *very* impressive. I'm so proud of you."

"Couldn't have done it without you by my side." Sam scooted over in the bed, patting the space she'd created for Luciana. The vision she woke to had been a sight to behold, but now she wanted her wife and child beside her. "You two look so cute together."

"We were just hanging out until your boobs became available." Luciana shrugged, placing their son against Sam's chest. "I'm not impressed that I have to share them."

"Don't be so greedy."

"Babe?"

Sam noted how Luciana was chewing her bottom lip. "Yes?"

"They're not going to stay massive, are they?"

In times of pain and discomfort, Luciana would always put a smile on Sam's face. Regardless of the situation, she would always use humour as her way of coping. "You really are going to miss them, aren't you?"

"We got attached," Luciana said, feigning her disappointment as she offered Sam her puppy dog eyes. "We got along *really* well."

"You did. I can certainly vouch for that." Sam smirked, popping the buttons on her shirt to allow her son to feed. "I'm sure there are plenty of other things for you to play with."

Luciana groaned. Sam knew exactly what she was doing.

"I've been spoilt for choice since the moment I met you. I don't think I'm about to have to worry now…"

"I can't wait to get this one home with us." Sam sighed, her eyes studying the tiny face nuzzled up against her boob, his little fingers clawing at her skin. He loved his food; Sam was beginning to realise that.

"I was thinking while you were sleeping. Did you have any names in mind?"

"One or two but nothing that really grabs my attention."

Luciana got comfortable beside Sam, her arm slipping around Sam's back, her nails grazing Sam's scalp. "What do you think about…Luca?"

"Luca." Sam tested it on her palate. It sounded good. It sounded…perfect. "I…love it."

Luciana's lips curled upward. "Yeah? Really?"

"Really."

"You know, uh…I've been thinking." This news was going to

be huge, Luciana felt it deep in her belly. It would be surprising, but positive. Life couldn't be much better. "I'm leaving the brigade."

Sam's head shot up. "What?"

"It's time. And if that job is still available with you, I'd love to be considered."

"You're actually leaving? But, why?"

"I have a whole new load of priorities, Sam. You and Luca are my world. I don't want to ever risk my life again if it means I may never come home to you both. And maybe that's selfish and cowardly, but I don't care. If wanting to be with you and him until I'm old means I am...then I'm willing to be selfish. My family is what matters to me. Always."

"Wow."

"You're not mad?" Luciana asked.

Sam stared. Unable to take her eyes off her wife, her entire universe. This day had been something else, truly, but Luciana had just settled Sam's heart once and for all.

"Babe?"

Sam turned her head, capturing Luciana's lips desperately. "God, I could spend forever kissing you."

"So, the job?"

"I'll support you in whatever you decide. You've changed my entire life, Luciana."

Luciana frowned, pulling back. "Oh, because I thought I was only dinner and conversation."

Sam laughed deep from within her belly, Luca's body jiggling about as she did. "Dinner and conversation? With you? Not in a million years..."

SIGN UP TO WIN

Sign up to my mailing list to be the first to hear about new releases, and to be in with a chance of winning books!

www.melissaterezeauthor.com

FOREWORD

THANK YOU FOR PURCHASING THE CALL.

I HOPE YOU ENJOYED IT. PLEASE CONSIDER LEAVING A REVIEW ON YOUR PREFERRED SITE. AS AN INDEPENDENT AUTHOR, REVIEWS HELP TO PROMOTE OUR WORK. ONE LINE OR TWO REALLY DOES MAKE THE DIFFERENCE.

THANK YOU, TRULY.

LOVE,
MELISSA X

ABOUT THE AUTHOR

Oh, hi! It's nice to see you!

I'm Melissa Tereze, author of The Arrangement, Mrs Middleton, and other bestsellers. Born, raised, and living in Liverpool, UK, I spend my time writing angsty romance about complex, real-life, women who love women. My heart lies within the age-gap trope, but you'll also find a wide range of different characters and stories to sink your teeth into.

SOCIAL MEDIA

You can contact me through my social media or my website. I'm mostly active on Twitter.

Twitter: @MelissaTereze
Facebook: www.facebook.com/Author.MelissaTereze
Instagram: @melissatereze_author
Find out more at: www.melissaterezeauthor.com
Contact: info@melissaterezeauthor.com

ALSO BY MELISSA TEREZE

ANOTHER LOVE SERIES
The Arrangement (Book One)

THE ASHFORTH SERIES
Playing For Her Heart (Book One)
Holding Her Heart (Book Two)

OTHER NOVELS
Always Allie

Mrs Middleton

Breaking Routine

In Her Arms

Before You Go

Forever Yours

The Heat of Summer

Forget Me Not

More Than A Feeling

Where We Belong: Love Returns

Naked

CO-WRITES
Teach Me (With Jourdyn Kelly)

TITLES UNDER L.M CROFT (EROTICA)
Pieces of Me

Printed in Great Britain
by Amazon